**"Starboard shields to maximum.
Put us between the Romulan and the outpost.
Fire when ready."**

Picard heard an assent from the tactical station—even as Worf recognized the captain's presence. "Status, Number One."

Worf quickly yielded the center chair, still clearly furious. "A sneak attack, sir. A single warbird decloaked, firing on the array."

"And the outpost?"

From behind, Lieutenant Aneta Šmrhová, the chief of security, reported, "Commander La Forge's team has left the conning tower for a more secure area. Sixteen staffers are aboard the station. Structural integrity of crew areas holding."

Worf looked sharply at Picard, as if trying to read his superior's mind. "Captain, we cannot beam out the staff while shields are up. The best way to buy them time is to engage the Romulan."

"Agreed." Picard saw the warbird growing larger on-screen as *Enterprise* raced the length of the array. "Let's get their attention."

STAR TREK
THE NEXT GENERATION®

TAKEDOWN

JOHN JACKSON MILLER

Based on *Star Trek*® and
Star Trek: The Next Generation®
created by Gene Roddenberry
and
Star Trek: Deep Space Nine®
created by Rick Berman & Michael Piller

POCKET BOOKS
New York   London   Toronto   Sydney   New Delhi

Pocket Books
A Division of Simon & Schuster, Inc.
1230 Avenue of the Americas
New York, NY 10020

This book is a work of fiction. Any references to historical events, real people, or real places are used fictitiously. Other names, characters, places, and events are products of the author's imagination, and any resemblance to actual events or places or persons, living or dead, is entirely coincidental.

First Pocket Books paperback edition February 2015

POCKET and colophon are registered trademarks of Simon & Schuster, Inc.

For information about special discounts for bulk purchases, please contact Simon & Schuster Special Sales at 1-866-506-1949 or business@simonandschuster.com.

The Simon & Schuster Speakers Bureau can bring authors to your live event. For more information or to book an event, contact the Simon & Schuster Speakers Bureau at 1-866-248-3049 or visit our website at www.simonspeakers.com.

Cover design by Alan Dingman
Cover art by Mark Rademaker

Manufactured in the United States of America

10   9   8   7   6   5   4   3   2   1

ISBN 978-1-4767-8271-3
ISBN 978-1-4767-8272-0 (ebook)

To Maggie Thompson,
mentor and friend,
and to the memory of Don

HISTORIAN'S NOTE

The main events in this story take place in late November 2385, after Kellessar zh'Tarash of Andor takes the oath of office for President of the Federation (*Star Trek: The Fall—Peaceable Kingdoms*) and concurrent with the visit of the civilian science ship *Athene Donald* and the arrival of the People of the Open Sky to Deep Space 9 (*Star Trek: Deep Space Nine—The Missing*).

"Too much knowing causes misery."
—Lorenzo de' Medici

One

The one good thing about having a job that took you to hell and back was that you slept soundly. All your nightmares had already happened during the day.

William Riker had always slept well. But this morning, rising was the hard part—and he wasn't surprised in the least to discover he was already dressed. He'd slept in full uniform many times as an overworked ensign, never as an admiral. But this behavior made perfect sense: He'd been through the wringer in recent days. He was just glad he'd made it to the bed. Falling asleep in a turbolift wouldn't have done, at any rank.

He knew he'd earned being this tired. There had been another voyage to perdition—or worse—just behind him, but it made his head hurt to think much about it. It didn't matter. The best way to escape a bad day was to start the next.

Or to *try* to start it, at least. Riker's muscles objected as he attempted to sit up in bed, and he nearly fell back down. Standing was the next frontier, and that took longer to accomplish as well. Finally, he succeeded. Looking groggily around the VIP quarters aboard *Starship Titan,* he wondered for a moment where his wife was—before remembering the vessel's destination was Betazed, her homeworld. That was one of the last things he'd heard before going to sleep. Deanna had hoped to take their daughter to Betazed's capital city on a visit, if they had the time.

The time. He checked it as he shambled to the mirror. Sixteen hours, he'd slept. Riker shook his head. It was a good thing he wasn't on duty of any kind. But then, oversleeping was the bad dream of an ensign. Admirals' problems were a lot worse; he'd held the rank just long enough to learn that. And his body showed it. The face in the mirror was a fright. His dark, gently graying hair had gone this way and that during his repose, and a whole lot of new whiskers had appeared.

"Must have been some party," he mumbled. His condition owed to something else entirely, but it didn't matter. Drydock was about cleanup work, and that went for people just as well as their ships. He set to making himself presentable.

A short time later found Riker in the turbolift. He didn't fall asleep on this ride either—but he wouldn't have been able to snooze for long in any event. The doors weren't halfway open when a firm Vulcan voice declared, "Admiral on the bridge!"

"You make a fine wake-up alarm, Tuvok." Riker looked over to the tactical station, where the dark-skinned Vulcan didn't acknowledge the joke. Tuvok simply bowed his head slightly and turned back to his console.

Stepping onto the bridge, Riker looked up and saw through the forward viewport that *Titan* was indeed orbiting above Betazed, the vessel parked near a large mushroom-shaped space station. The ship had been ordered here for replacement of faulty parts for some subsystem or other; it wasn't Riker's job to know about it anymore. That responsibility lay with the woman who looked back at him from the captain's chair.

"Welcome, Admiral," Christine Vale said. "How are you?"

"Shipshape," Riker said, scratching his beard. "If the ship is a garbage scow that's seen better days."

"Forgivable, after what you've—" Apparently thinking better of her comment, Vale stopped in mid-sentence and gestured ahead instead. "I'm afraid you missed Counselor Troi by a few minutes. She said to let you sleep."

"She's nice like that."

Walking past the command chairs, Riker studied the scene outside more closely. He'd never heard of Betazed Station 4 before, much less visited. Its space-dock doors were open, waiting to accept the *Luna*-class vessel. Just beyond the station, he could see a shuttle heading for the blue-green planet below.

That's one of ours, he thought. But before he could ask about it, a chirp came from the communications officer's panel. "Shuttlecraft *Armstrong* hailing us."

Riker looked back to see Vale smiling at him. "Someone wants to say hello," the redheaded woman said. "On-screen."

Turning back forward, he saw the giant image of his little dark-haired daughter waving at him. *"Hailing frequencies open, Daddy."*

"Hello, Natasha." Riker put up his hand in a slight wave and smiled wanly. "You flying that alone?"

"She wants to," Deanna Troi said, appearing over the child's shoulder. *"She takes after her father."*

Riker nodded. *Titan*'s bridge wasn't really the place for a family call, and out of the corner of his eye, he could see members of the crew turning away to hide their amused expressions. Several seconds passed, silently, with neither of them talking: Deanna would have known he wouldn't want anyone else asking about his health, not here. She, at least, looked well rested—and as beautiful as the day he'd met her. "Why did you take a shuttle?"

"Admiral," Vale said, "we've taken the transporters offline in preparation for the new upgrade equipment we're getting from spacedock."

"Natasha thought it'd be more fun to fly over this way," Deanna said. *"She likes to look at the clouds as we—"*

Before Deanna could finish the sentence, an alarm screeched aboard *Titan*—and Riker heard an echo from *Armstrong*'s cabin, where a similar alert went off. "Warning," announced a computerized voice aboard *Titan*. *"Plasma storm approaching, high magnitude."*

"Here?" Vale seemed startled. "We weren't expecting anything like that."

"Origin unknown. Danger posed to orbiting vessels."

"How soon?"

Tuvok had the answer. "Four point seven seconds!"

"Shields up!"

Riker looked up to Deanna on the screen. *"Deanna, shields, now!"*

He grabbed for the railing at the rear of the bridge even as the world around him went sideways. *Titan* shook, apparently battered by a flood of plasma ejected from Betazed's sun. Yet his eyes never left the forward viewscreen. Lit by the unholy fury of whatever was outside the shuttle, Deanna clung desperately to Natasha. Riker could barely hear the child screaming over the din of impact.

Riker looked around, not understanding. Like many other populated areas, the Betazed system was monitored by satellites that transmitted information faster than light, via subspace. Even a freak plasma storm should have been preceded by some warning before a tsunami of fire and radiation struck. And yet, here it was, shaking *Titan* like a tree in a hurricane.

And *Armstrong* was bearing it far worse. "Counselor!" Vale yelled, clutching the armrests of her chair. "What's your condition?"

"Not good!" Internal lights strobing across her terrified face, Deanna punched at controls with one hand while hanging onto Natasha with her other arm. *"Shields failed. Losing structural integrity!"*

Forgetting who was in command, Riker barked, "Beam her out of there!"

"Engineering reports transporters will take three minutes to be placed back online," Vale said. "Helm, put *Titan* between the solar wind and *Armstrong*!"

"It'll take a moment, Captain," came a voice from behind her. "We're still oriented for spacedock approach."

Damned repair mission! With the ship turning into the storm, Riker lurched over to a control panel whose operator had fallen away. *Titan* rocked and quaked, fighting against the fiery tide. Riker found his bearings and checked the ships' relative positions, trying his best not to focus on Natasha's wail, now in the background but unmistakably there. "Any ideas?"

"I have one, Admiral," Tuvok said, his fingers a blur over the keypad. "I may be able to extend *Titan*'s shields to cover the shuttle."

"At this range?"

"It will require reshaping the shield on the side of *Titan* facing the shuttle into a hyperbolic paraboloid, to maximize its range and effectiveness."

"Do it!" Vale ordered.

"The spatial geometry needed is complex," Tuvok said, seemingly calculating even as he tried to make himself heard. "And *Titan* is in motion, further complicating—"

A deafening crack came from above—followed by plummeting metal beams as the supports holding part of the bridge's storm-weakened ceiling gave way. One girder swung down like a club, belting Tuvok from behind and slamming him into the console. He collapsed, bleeding and senseless.

"Tuvok!" Without regard for his own safety, Riker dove into the area near the collapse. Tuvok was alive but out cold.

Vale called out to him. "*Armstrong*'s hull is failing!"

Riker stepped over the fallen Vulcan to reach his console, hoping against hope that he only needed to push a button to enact Tuvok's stratagem. No such luck, he saw. "He never finished entering his equations!"

"*Will, do something!*" It was Deanna. He looked back at the huge display screen nearly in a panic. His wife and child were in mortal danger. He was powerless to help them—unless he could complete a mathematical sequence that it would take most people a lifetime to figure out. Still, he turned to the panel, looking at the maze of numbers and variables controlling the shields. There had to be something he could do, anything.

Another shock shook the ship. He heard Vale's voice. "Finish the sequence, Admiral!"

And now, Deanna. "*Do it, Will!*"

Riker focused on the figures on the screen—and suddenly saw clearly.

"I won't," he said, turning around to face the bridge crew. "It's not necessary."

Vale was flabbergasted. "What do you mean?"

Titan quaked again—but this time, Riker wasn't swayed. "I mean there is no plasma storm."

From his right, a plaintive call. *"Daddy!"*

"That's enough." Looking stern, he faced the terrified pair on the screen. "Whoever's doing this, you can stop now."

The bridge shook again, and then again, until all went silent. "As you wish," said a gravelly male voice behind him. Then the lights went out.

Two

When the lights came back up again, Riker was standing alone in an empty black room, glowing gridlines stretching across the space where *Titan*'s bridge had been.

Riker turned to see a holodeck entryway arch standing behind him, with a slender white-haired man dressed fully in black leaning against it. "How did you know," he asked slowly, "that this was a holographic simulation?"

The admiral crossed his arms. "Christine Vale's a kidder—but she respects decorum too much to make me take a personal call in front of her crew. You did that for my benefit, so I'd see my family was on the shuttle."

The new arrival nodded. The short, pointy-eared man looked ancient to Riker, his face pale and gaunt. Silver cane helping him to walk, he stepped toward Riker. "That could not have been your only clue," the man said. "Not with stakes like this."

"Deanna and Vale both know what kind of a mathematician I am. I'm no Tuvok."

A white eyebrow arched. "Hardly material evidence of deception."

"You also got the number of pips wrong on Vale's uniform. She's still a commander, running *Titan* while I'm on assignment for the Federation."

Black eyes looked up keenly at Riker. Then the trace of a smile crossed his face. "Always getting the ranks wrong. I forget how closely people pay attention. Your mind really went there?"

Riker stared down at the man hobbling past. "I've been through something like this before. I wake up in what I think are my quarters aboard ship—and then everything that follows is a lie."

He might have been having trouble recalling the past few days, but he remembered that experience well: years earlier, there had been a being of another species with tremendous powers, who had tried to make him think he was captain of the *Enterprise*. "Now why don't you cut out the nonsense and tell me who you are?"

"I'm more interested in who *you* are."

"Riker, William T., Admiral, Starfleet—"

"—on special assignment as diplomatic envoy for the United Federation of Planets," the old man finished.

"If you knew, then why'd you ask?" Riker studied the newcomer. "Never mind. And you are?"

"Simus."

"You're Vulcan."

"I could be Romulan," the old man said, looking back and making a show of pawing at his wrinkled forehead. "Of course, I don't have the characteristic cranial flaring over the bridge of the nose."

"But not all Romulans have it."

"You *are* the one for details. So yes, I could be Romulan."

"If you exist at all."

Simus seemed a little offended. "I'm not a simulacrum."

"Prove it—and let's both walk out of here." Riker was tired already when he woke up—and this game was wearing on him. He turned back to the archway. The doors closed before he could get there. He tried giving vocal commands, but nothing happened.

Simus shook his head. "I would like you to remain. Just for a while."

Seeing no way to open the doors, Riker looked back. "This doesn't look like a *Titan* holodeck," he said, surveying the size and shape of the room. "You've beamed me off the ship while I was asleep." Whoever had pulled off that trick knew what they were doing. *Titan* had gone into warp just before he went to bed. Had it arrived at Betazed, or dropped out somewhere short of it?

He didn't know—and the old man didn't say. Riker just knew that the way he felt, he didn't need another headache. "I'd appreciate it if you'd tell me what's going on."

Simus weighed his words carefully. "The people I represent brought you here, to me."

Riker couldn't help but grin at the evasive answer. This was how things were going to go with Simus, whoever he was. "Well, they've taken a Starfleet admiral captive. There are probably consequences for that, somewhere."

"The people I represent—"

"Those people again." Riker rolled his eyes.

"—believe it is important to see how you will respond to certain stimuli."

"Like endangering my wife and child? Whoever they are, they've got pretty poor taste."

"Nonetheless," Simus said, "it is imperative that we understand you better."

"What more do you need?" Riker waved around the big space that had been used to simulate *Titan's* interior. "You were able to depict all this. You must also have my service record. What part of William T. Riker could you possibly not know about at this stage?"

Simus placed both hands on the chrome knob of his cane and rocked for a moment, evidently thinking something over. Finally, he nodded. "All right. There is something I'd like to know more about." He drew back one of his sleeves and tapped on a small wrist control unit. "Watch."

"Another simulation?"

Simus said nothing. He walked away from Riker—and as he did, the scene around him shifted. It was another Federation starship bridge, but different from *Titan's*. The ship was *Saber*-class, Riker quickly surmised. It was likely a Starfleet Corps of Engineers vessel. Several crewmembers were at their posts; none of them paid him or Simus any mind. He didn't recognize any of them.

Riker was about to say something when, behind him, the turbolift doors opened. A stocky Tellarite woman in a Starfleet captain's uniform emerged. Clutching a padd in hand, she walked toward—and then *through*—Riker, rounding the command chairs to take her seat at the center.

"I'm obviously not an actor in this sketch," Riker said.

Leaning with both hands on the cane, Simus stared at the floor contemplatively. "You don't recognize the captain?"

"Should I?"

"Hmm."

The vessel's captain read from her padd and spoke to her crew happily and easily. "The new upgrades are working out better than we'd hoped. Helm, bring *Laplace* around for a look at the new transmitter units."

"Aye, Captain Kwelm."

Riker felt motion—or the simulation of it—and over his shoulder, he saw the space scene on the viewscreen changing. A sprawling space station composed of alternating gray hexagons with triangular assemblies nested between stretched off into space before them. A massive, towering metal prong tipped each triangular section.

"The Corvus Beacon," Simus said. "A deep-space transmitter, designed for contacting civilizations beyond the reach of starships."

"I'm familiar with the program," Riker said. His brow furrowed as he tried to remember the details. "It's near the edge of Federation space."

"Things that look to the beyond usually are," Simus replied.

Riker studied the station. He knew it was near the border with the Typhon Pact members. An alliance of convenience between the Romulans, Gorn, Tzenkethi, Breen, and other anti-UFP powers, the Typhon Pact had made life difficult for the Federation and its allies in recent times. He looked back to Simus with suspicion. "These people you represent—are they with the Typhon Pact? Is that your big secret?"

"You really should just watch—and listen." Simus

looked around. "Besides, none of these people seem worried to be out here, do they? The beacon is a low-value target."

Nearly a no-value target, Riker thought. He studied the captain again, wondering why he'd been asked to see this. There was something familiar about her, but much in his memory seemed to exist in a haze. Particularly the last few days . . .

"Proximity alert!" called the flight controller. "Ship incoming. She's dropped out of warp. Full impulse."

Riker looked to the captain. The Tellarite was clearly surprised. "Identify."

"*Vesta*-class. Registry NCC-82062," the conn said. Riker whispered the name even as the officer said it: "*Aventine*."

Turning, he saw the ship, still far off in the distance beyond the Corvus Beacon but approaching quickly. *Aventine* was Starfleet's test bed for many groundbreaking technologies; at warp, it was one of the fastest vessels around, outfitted with the revolutionary slipstream drive. And at impulse, it was almost as nimble as a ship half her size.

"We're being hailed, Captain Kwelm."

"On-screen."

A dark-haired woman in captain's uniform appeared on-screen. She had bands of freckles marking her as a Trill—and she also had a warning. "*This is Captain Ezri Dax of the Federation* Starship Aventine," she said. "*All personnel aboard the beacon need to abandon immediately!*"

Riker turned to see Kwelm's reaction. The Tellarite captain looked as one just hit in the face with a mallet. "What's going on?" she said. "Captain Dax, there have been no reports of any problems aboard the—"

Dax's piercing blue eyes implored her. *"Just do it!"* The Trill continued to talk, but a screech of static was all the *Laplace* crew heard.

Kwelm looked to her executive officer, a Bajoran male who shrugged. "In the absence of other information," he said, "we should do as she says."

Frowning, the captain turned and toggled a control on her armrest. "All crew aboard the Beacon, this is Captain Kwelm. Cease maintenance operations, gather your work materials, and make immediately for the shuttlebays."

On-screen, Dax's expression grew fraught. She couldn't be heard, but she called out again, imploring the same, Riker assumed: *Evacuate the Beacon.*

Riker watched as Kwelm stood and raised her hands. Many Tellarites liked to argue at the wrong times, and this seemed no exception. "Captain Dax, our people are in the middle of sensitive procedures on high-value systems. They can't simply drop everything without knowing what the reason—"

"Do what Captain Dax says!"

Riker's eyes widened at the sound of the new voice, crisp and free from static. He looked in astonishment at the giant viewscreen. There where Dax had been, was . . . *himself?*

"Laplace, this is Admiral Riker aboard Aventine!" the familiar face on the main viewscreen said. *The* background behind him wasn't the same setting that Dax was speaking from, but it was clearly a ship-to-ship transmission. *"This is a matter of Federation security. All personnel aboard the Corvus Beacon must beam back to* Laplace *immediately!"*

On the simulated bridge of *Laplace*, Riker saw

Kwelm's eyes bulge. "R-right away, sir," she said, plopping back down in her chair like an upbraided schoolchild. She tapped a button on her armrest. "Do it!"

Riker looked back up at his own face in bewilderment. Wraithlike, he approached the large viewscreen, spellbound. With the giant image of himself looming above, he turned back to study *Laplace*'s bridge. Seeing it from this angle, he nodded slightly.

A cloud began to lift. And to his right, he could see Simus watching him closely.

"*We've got everyone but the upgrade team,*" came a voice from the comm. It was *Laplace*'s transporter chief. "*They're still in the middle of the procedure, Captain. They don't want to lose their data.*"

"*Hang the data!*" the Riker aboard *Aventine* growled. "*We've told you, there's no time to explain. The threat's already here!*"

Kwelm gesticulated wildly. "But we don't understand! If you'd just—"

The on-screen admiral's eyebrows flared in a determined vee. "*Too late. You were warned.*"

The words were barely out of his mouth when the Riker on-screen disappeared—to be replaced by the view of *Aventine*, now mere kilometers away, spitting phaser fire at the Corvus Beacon. The first volley struck one of the large transmitter assemblies, blowing it to bits.

"Support team, drop everything!" Kwelm called out. "Beam out now!"

On the simulated bridge of *Laplace*, Riker didn't know where to look. Behind him, Kwelm and her crew were in a panic, rushing to ensure the return of her people—while on-screen the *Aventine* was firing one shot after another at the beacon's superstructure. The station was enormous, but flames had already erupted from two of the hexagonal power pods that served the array.

And off to the side was Simus, hands clasped over the knob of his cane, rocking back and forth as he watched it all. Riker couldn't read his expression.

"We've got everyone," someone called to the captain through the chaos.

"I am unable to raise Starfleet Command," another voice said. "There is a problem with the subspace network."

Nearly overwhelmed, Kwelm turned to face the big screen and toggled a control on her armrest. "Admiral Riker! You have to stop this. This is our life's work you're destroying! Please, just tell us—"

Riker had seen and heard enough. He turned to Simus. "Pause the simulation."

Simus put a hand to his pointed ear. "Pause what?"

Riker glared. *"Pause the recording!"*

Simus gestured—and the clamor immediately stopped. But unlike before, when *Titan*'s interior had vanished, the bridge of *Laplace* remained. Its occupant engineers and its frantic captain stood as frozen statues of fear. Riker stared blankly at them—and then looked up at the blazing wreckage on the screen.

Finally, he said something. "This isn't another simulation. This happened."

Simus hobbled toward Riker. "Yes, it did. This is a ship's log from approximately two weeks ago."

Feeling his exhaustion returning, Riker looked down at the deck. "Why are you showing this to me?"

"The people I represent were curious to see your response."

"What is there to say?" Riker looked up, tired blue eyes filled with dread at his own words. "I was aboard *Aventine*. And we attacked the Corvus Beacon. *And that's not all . . .*"

STAGE ONE:

MELTDOWN

---

*"A false report, if believed during three days,
may be of great service to a government."*
—Catherine de' Medici

Three

It troubled Will Riker that with all the advances made in the field of biology, no one had yet invented a pill that replaced the need for exercise. There ought to be something possible, he thought as he worked out on the rowing machine. Perhaps you could pack the effects of running a mile into a hypospray. Or maybe nanites in the bloodstream could do your kayaking for you. By not having invented anything, Starfleet Medical was really falling down on the job.

In years past, Riker hadn't minded physical training at all: it was one of the service requirements, of course, but it was also a way to escape the routine of shipboard life. And holodecks like *Titan*'s were excellent at generating interesting programs, masking exercise within sports or other activities. But that was before he became an admiral. Now, with all kinds of other matters demanding his time, he looked resentfully at the ritual of working out and the time it stole from his day.

He continued to go to the *Titan* holodeck to work out; putting the equipment in his office would ensure he never exercised at all. But no longer did he bother with generating holographic mountains to climb or rivers to swim. Now it was about getting it over with, as quickly as possible. He wondered sometimes why it was worth the bother. Part of the idea behind advancement was to not have to be the one running around, tussling with hostiles.

But he also knew that diplomatic work wasn't necessarily a life sentence: he might find himself on the front lines again, somehow. The greatest mind in the universe would be of no use if it couldn't interact with the world around it. Exercise was the rent the body charged for granting the mind space. He'd pay it.

And then there was the other reason he stayed in shape. She was standing in the open door of the holodeck, watching him sweat.

"You look tired," Deanna Troi said as he stopped rowing.

"Thanks." He disentangled himself from the machine. "Program off," he said, and the thing disappeared.

Only a towel remained in the room beside him. Deanna walked in, picked it up, and put it over her husband's perspiration-soaked head. "We're almost to the Paulson Nebula," she said, rubbing.

"Tidings of joy."

"It's a diplomatic mission. Do you want me along on this one?"

Riker smirked from beneath the towel. "I can't keep dragging you along every time the Federation sends me to sit at a negotiating table for days at a time. That's marital cruel and unusual punishment."

"I don't mind," she said.

"They should have made *you* the admiral, then." Riker stood up and wiped the sweat from his face with the towel.

Troi studied him pensively. "You're still regretting the promotion."

Riker took a deep breath. "No, it's not like that." He didn't cling as desperately to the captain's chair as some did; his mentor, Jean-Luc Picard, would only leave the bridge of the *Enterprise* feet-first. Something about asking for a demotion didn't set well with Riker. And Starfleet had been accommodating. Admiral Akaar had understood his desire to be in motion and had made sure the Federation's missions involved going places to do things.

But the things weren't all equally interesting, nor were the countless reports he was expected to file. It seemed every official in the Federation wanted a personal update about something or other. He gave a weary smile to his wife. "I'm just about ready for some real R-and-R, that's all."

"You'll have to settle for a shower."

He grasped for her. "That would be relaxing."

She pulled away, chuckling. "You're doing our mission briefing in half an hour, remember?"

Riker's shoulders sagged. "Oh, yeah."

He trudged out of the room after her, thinking that just once, it would be nice if someone would let him forget something.

The United Federation of Planets and the signatories of the Khitomer Accords were not at war with the Typhon Pact. That was the official line, and it was also the case in fact—*mostly*. What had been observed in practice was something else.

The Typhon Pact was a loose agglomeration of powers seeking to counterbalance against the Federation and its fellow signatories of the Khitomer Accords, which included the Ferengi Alliance, the Klingon Empire, and the Cardassian Union. The Pact's members included the predictably problematic Romulans and Gorn, as well as groups whose aims were frequently unfathomable, such as the Tzenkethi, Tholians, Kinshaya, and Breen. No wider war appeared to threaten, but that didn't stop the Pact members from causing troubles on their own, any one of which might lead to an all out conflict. Riker's main assignment had been making sure that didn't happen.

There was no way to restrain the ambitions of the Typhon forces—nor, really, to prevent those on his own side from acting precipitously. Riker and *Titan* had been involved in a couple of dust-ups with the Breen a few months earlier: both were efforts to prevent the Breen from taking control of neutral systems without the consent of their residents. At Garadius IV, shots had been fired, and *Titan* had disabled several Breen ships, forcing them out of the system—but that episode hadn't escalated into a wider conflict. The Breen were out for themselves, and their ostensible allies weren't about to be pulled into a galactic war over a gambit gone wrong.

In the absence of better angels landing on the shoulders of all the galaxy's decision-makers and line officers, Riker was nearly convinced that what needed to happen was some sort of unspoken agreement about how territorial ambitions were to be managed. The Federation did not endorse the concept of carving up space into exclusive expansion zones: local races deserved the chance to decide their fates for themselves. The Prime Directive stated that self-determination was an inherent right. Riker agreed with the principle, but obviously, centuries of history had showed reality worked differently. By simply agreeing to Neutral Zones with the Klingons and the Romulans, for example, the Federation had, in essence, made a decision not to embrace some of those who might have wanted to join it. Their planets were just in the wrong place.

It was not a perfect galaxy—and until it was, people like Riker would have to sit at tables and talk. And talk, and talk. And now that the Federation was sending him to what promised to be the biggest talkfest of all, he did the only natural thing he could. He gave a briefing.

"Four commanders and an admiral," Riker said, seeing the *Titan* officers already seated at the table as he entered the observation lounge. "Sounds like it ought to be a poker hand."

Tuvok said nothing, but there was light laughter from Christine Vale, Troi, and *Titan*'s chief engineer, Xin Ra-Havreii. The top-heaviness of *Titan*'s senior staff had long been a thing of some amusement to Riker: at the moment, they had everything *but* a captain. "Lieutenant Commander Keru sends his apologies," Vale said as he took his seat at the opposite end of the table. "His security team has threat profiles to go over."

"I'm afraid we're just wasting his time," Riker said, "but then, we're all in that boat." He placed his padd on the table. "You all got the mission specs?"

Vale nodded. "Someone on the Typhon Pact side called for a general meeting—with one representative each from four powers." She looked at Riker. "One, and only one—for however long it takes."

He nodded. "No rest for the weary."

"Seems odd to have a peace conference when there's no war," Vale said.

Tuvok templed his fingers. "There are many points of conflict where discussion would be useful. The question is, which ones do they wish to discuss?"

Riker rolled his eyes. "I haven't got the slightest idea. The invitation was short, specific—and relayed by the station we're heading toward. It was undoubtedly from the Romulans, as near as our analysts can tell. And our Khitomer partners also received the same invites."

Troi read the names. "Romulan Star Empire, Tzenkethi Coalition, Gorn Hegemony, Tholian Assembly, Klingon Empire, Cardassian Union, Ferengi Alliance, and the United Federation of Planets." Four from each side. "And no notion as to topic?"

"They could want to hold a group therapy session, for all I know," Riker said, smiling at her. "Maybe we should have sent you instead, after all."

The counselor smiled primly. "I have a low tolerance for futility."

Riker took a deep breath. Her assessment was almost certainly right, of course, but he probably shouldn't make too much light of the mission. "The Federation isn't about to ignore a possible olive branch—especially not when it involves the Gorn."

Vale nodded. "You still think there's a chance to lure the Gorn out of the Typhon Pact?"

"Nobody over there wants to be a junior member of anything," Riker said. "That's the flaw in the whole concept. The Gorn are pretty sure they're the lowest on the ladder—and the Tholians are still catching heat for the whole Andorian affair. Maybe a little face time will crack the ice a bit more. Who knows?" He looked to the white-haired engineer. "You've had a look at this meeting place?"

"I have indeed," Ra-Havreii said. "We got a recon of the site from another Starfleet vessel going past." He touched a control, and a holographic image appeared, floating above the table. "What's the name your invitation gave it? The Far Embassy."

The space station was shaped like a tall drum; one end featured an octagonal cap that branched outward into eight docking portals. The other end terminated in what appeared to be an enormous deflector dish of some kind. "Whose station is it?" Riker asked.

"Admiral, I couldn't begin to tell you," Ra-Havreii said. "Or I *could* begin, but I'd never get finished."

Riker rolled his eyes. *Titan's* Efrosian chief engineer had both a temper and a tendency to explain far too much. At least Ra-Havreii was becoming more aware of the latter. "Give it to me in two sentences, please."

Ra-Havreii scratched his long moustache. "It's as if somebody went to a salvage yard and built a station out of spare parts. *Everybody's* spare parts."

"Salvage?" Riker squinted at the visual of the Far Embassy. "The thing looks brand new."

"And it may be. Its various docking ports precisely match the specifications used by several of the attending powers." The engineer flipped through the various views. Riker recognized portals of Starfleet design—if a few years out of date—as well as tractor-beam-assisted docking interfaces used in Klingon, Cardassian, and Romulan facilities, among others.

"Awfully kind of them." Vale rested her chin against her fist as she studied the display. "Whoever it was over there that built it, they've gone to a lot of trouble to be accommodating."

Ra-Havreii shook his head. "But not *completely*

accommodating. Our scouts detected a transporter inhibitor field in operation. I suspect the docking ports simply ensure arrivals are first directed to guest quarters environmentally designed for them."

Riker frowned. "The Typhon Pact isn't known for its hospitality." He thought again. "Well, not *most* of the Pact. The Romulans will do what they need to do to make an impression—usually a false one."

Troi looked to her husband with concern. "The whole thing could be a trap. The Breen were trying to kidnap you back on Garadius—for no other reason than to capture a Starfleet admiral."

Tuvok shared her concern. "The Breen are not among the invitees."

"I'm perfectly ready for shenanigans," Riker said, "and from what I understand, our partners among the Klingons, Cardassians, and Ferengi will be on the lookout, too. Transport inhibitors aside, Christine's already said Ranul Keru is planning sixteen ways to get me out of this place should trouble arise. And as far as the Breen being absent goes, would you really want the Breen anyplace you expected to sit down and talk for hours on end?"

More laughter. The Breen spoke in purposefully untranslatable squawks and had seldom been much of a presence at the negotiating table.

"I see both the threats, and the opportunity," Tuvok said. "It is right to attend."

"The Federation Council agrees," Riker said. "And if it doesn't amount to anything, we're back to the regularly scheduled exploration mission. Out to the Genovous Pulsar, I believe it was." He thumped the table surface once. "That's everything. Dismissed."

Everyone began to rise. Troi looked to him. "You really should rest a little before you go."

He nodded. "And maybe I should eat. No idea what kind of cuisine they'll be serving over—"

A high beep sounded. *"Admiral, we have arrived at the nebula. Station is on our scanners. Other vessels are already here."*

Vale's eyes narrowed. She spoke to the air. "Affiliation?"

"Klingon, Ferengi, Cardassian, and Tzenkethi. One vessel each," Ensign Lavena reported. *"They are sending shuttles to dock with the station. We haven't seen the Gorn vessel, but its shuttle is here."*

"The Romulans and Tholians have not yet arrived," Tuvok said.

"Fashionably late." Riker smiled wanly. "Well, everyone's playing by the rules so far." He shot his wife an expression he knew she was familiar with: *Here goes nothing.*

Four

Wearing his finest senatorial robe, Bretorius made his dignified walk onto the bridge of the diplomatic vessel. It was a small space, dimly lit; the eyes of the crew were on their work, not him. That was as it should be. Diligence came before fealty.

But now, the balding Romulan thought as he approached the seat beside his young and beautiful aide, it was time that they heard from their important passenger. He had always thrilled to that as a cadet in the Imperial Fleet. It made people feel valued, like an important part of things, when those in power deigned to speak with them.

He reached the command well and turned. Facing the others, he raised his hands. "Crew of the *R.I.S. Accipiter*," he declared, "you are present for a most important occasion. The Khitomer powers have seen our superiority and sued for peace with the Typhon Pact. And so, I, Senator Bretorius, have been chosen to attend the summit. Now, the differences between our peoples are many, and the odds against resolution are great—"

"This is a complete waste of time—which is why he was selected for it," muttered his dark-haired aide.

"Nerla," he quietly chided, nervous eyes to the side. "Not so loud."

Nerla grumbled something unintelligible. The senator continued. "The messages we and our allies received from the various powers came as a surprise. We must be on the lookout for deception." He put his hand to his chest solemnly. "And since only one representative from each great power is permitted, the praetor felt that *I* would be the one most likely to be able to see through any ruse."

"Or the one least likely to be missed if they blow the whole place up," Nerla said.

Bretorius looked back at his dark-eyed assistant and hissed in anger. "I am a senator of the Romulan Star Empire, and I am owed respect!"

"And my family scrapes the scum off of mollusk collector drones for a living," Nerla said, leaning back in her chair. "And I have a better sense of how to do your job than you do!"

Looking back and seeing none of the bridge crew was really listening anyway, Bretorius gave up and sat down beside Nerla. Lowering his voice, he appealed to her. "Nerla, this is a big assignment—I need to make a good impression. I know I've had some difficulties, but things are about to improve, I assure you—"

"That's what you told me back on Beraldak Bay when you offered me the job—back when I was waiting your table. And may I say: it has been no seaside holiday!" Crossing her arms, the young woman looked around the glum shuttle. "Here I am, thinking I'm signing on for the big time as your attaché. Power meetings, the high life. Yet out of a hundred politicos that vacation there, I pick the one senator who's never been invited to as much as a senatorial luncheon!"

Defensive, Bretorius put up his hand. "I told you, I had some problems with the cook staff a few years ago. But that's all forgotten. I simply have to grease the right palms to get my dining privileges back, and then we can—"

"Another promise. What about that *house* you promised me? The one down on the beach?"

"The vacation home? My wife's brother is staying there. Just for a while."

"The while that never ends. And what about those luxury apartments we were supposed to have across from the capital? Are your sisters-in-law still using them for their revels?" She pointed her finger at him. "I'll tell you, Senator, if you renege on one more thing, the Tal Shiar won't be able to hide you from me."

At the mention of the dreaded Romulan intelligence agency, Bretorius turned away to face the viewport and clasped his hands together in thought. Nerla was right, as always. About his prospects, yes, but also about the mission. The Empire could have sent anyone to this so-called Summit of Eight: they'd sent Bretorius precisely because he *wasn't* anyone.

A good politician always knew which way the winds were blowing: a better politician made the weather himself. Bretorius had been caught in the doldrums for years, and he was completely out of breath trying to make something happen. Something good, anyway.

Other senators paid biographers to write glowing accounts of their careers. Bretorius had hired three so far, each of which had given up after a few months, claiming nothing could be done to make the former warbird commander's life appealing. Bretorius suspected two of the writers would have quit sooner if they weren't having affairs with his wife.

The early chapters were never the problem. He had come from a line of honored warriors, several of whom had served in the senate. It was only natural to expect that Bretorius, too, would amount to something. His mother had pushed him into an arranged marriage and the Imperial Fleet on consecutive days, figuring that even a mediocre individual with his family name could advance.

Unfortunately, Bretorius had found mediocrity too high a bar. He had advanced in the fleet the old-fashioned way: he'd stuck around so long they had to give him a command, or muster him out. He'd commanded a vessel that had managed to miss every major engagement the Romulan Star Empire had participated in during his tenure. The critical battle of the Dominion War was waged without Bretorius's ship, when his entire crew came down with food poisoning after an ill-advised prebattle celebration. And during the time that Shinzon was courting allies in the Imperial Fleet for his eventual coup, Bretorius was never contacted once. It wasn't that Bretorius wanted to overthrow the government, but it would've been nice to have been asked. What did it take to be invited into a secret cabal?

He had always been at the wrong place at the wrong time—but he'd never cost the Empire enough at any one moment to make anyone care, and so Bretorius had always slipped past. He was the man with that famous name, a placeholder for a family that had known greater glory. His appointment to senator, six years earlier, was the essence of a compromise: battling factions reconstituting the Romulan senate had arrived at a deadlock and needed a compromise candidate no one would object to.

He'd thought that an opportunity at the time, figuring people on all sides would be trying to court his favor. His instincts were wrong again. Every time Bretorius took a half-step in any faction's direction—*even to cast a vote*—he instantly lost whatever committee post he had. He wasn't supposed to figure in the electoral math. It was hard to have visions of becoming praetor or proconsul when one was the junior senator on the committee for public works maintenance.

Even his hopes of financial gain had been thwarted. Where the other officials were on the receiving end of bribes aplenty, Bretorius had never been very good at asking for them. He'd always ended up paying somehow. And while he'd been pushed to marry for money, it wasn't long before he discovered his wife's fortune was more of a phantom than his was. Yet instead of doing him the favor of divorce, she had heaped one indignity after another upon him, carrying on with whichever artist or musician was in fashion. Bretorius figured he had personally funded half the unfinished sculptures in the capital city of Ki Baratan.

And the less he thought about his sponging in-laws, the better.

He looked back at Nerla. She was half his age and had twice the sense of anyone in his wife's family. She could be a powerful spouse, a cunning partner in politics. It was partially why he had offered her a job. But she hadn't shown an interest in him as a mentor or anything else in a long time, and now she was leaning against her armrest, idly counting the malfunctioning lights on the control panels of the battered *Lanora*-class vessel. His stomach began to hurt, and he struggled to find something to say. He had to do something to improve his station—both in the political world and with Nerla.

Why was she being so openly derisive? Why now?

Without looking back at him, she somehow felt his stare. "What?" she asked, exasperated.

"You know something, don't you?" He looked around the room, making sure no one else was listening. "The Proconsul's going to have me replaced when I return."

"You're the last to know, as always," Nerla said. "Your seat's a valuable commodity to all the factions. Just not with you in it. Not anymore."

Bretorius shook his head. "I have to do something. Something that would prove my worth to them."

Nerla looked back at him, incredulous. "Bret—you can't really think that, can you?" She counted off his flaws on her fingertips. "You're the least assertive, least imaginative, most predictable person ever to set foot in the senate chamber. They are not expecting you to come back with a full surrender from the Federation, with Klingons carrying your luggage. They're sending you on a fool's errand for a week while they change the name on your office door."

Bretorius frowned. "There's still time. I can change that."

She stared at him. "Oh yeah? *Show me.*" Then she turned away.

Bretorius watched her for a moment—and then turned back to face the window. There, outside the viewport, was the strange drumlike station named in the invitation as the Far Embassy. Far from Romulus, certainly. There were Federation elements to the design—or were they Ferengi? He'd never been any good at recognizing that sort of thing.

He just knew that that place held his last chance. And if it was in there, he was going to grab it. He would show Nerla—and everyone else.

Five

The thing about peace negotiations, Riker thought, *is that they can be held just about anywhere.* He had attended several held in great capitals and lavish retreats; those had always seemed discordant to him, given how removed they were from the pain and squalor of the battlefield. Truce sessions held directly on the plain of battle lacked for amenities and promises of personal safety, but they felt a lot more honest.

The Summit of Eight, meanwhile, had looked for a moment as if it might be the first interstellar peace meeting held inside a piece of luggage. That was how cramped he'd felt in the airlock after exiting his shuttle. While the Federation portal was designed specifically for a bipedal humanoid as Ra-Havreii's reconnaissance imagery suggested, it was sized to admit exactly one inside.

And once the door had shut behind him, he'd realized the pressurized compartment wasn't actually an airlock, but a turbolift car of sorts. He'd felt motion, jerky at first but soon smoothing out—a pneumatic tube to . . . *somewhere*. *Titan*'s sensors had been unable to penetrate the interior of the station, and seeing the Far Embassy up close hadn't even given Ra-Havreii and his specialists many clues as to which faction had built the place. There was evidently a betting pool in engineering as to the answer: Tzenkethi manufacture was the favorite at three to one.

Emerging from the cramped compartment, Riker didn't know if he'd be able to make any bettors happy. The wide domed atrium was completely featureless save for seven other portals lining its circumference. Ambience-free, but at least the air was cool and circulating.

Riker tapped his combadge. "I'm inside," he said. Vale acknowledged. That was exactly all he was allowed to transmit under the protocols he'd received. There wasn't much else to say, anyway. He couldn't tell where the light in the place was coming from, but there was plenty of it. Enough that he could see several other arrivals milling around.

A golden-skinned Tzenkethi stood against the wall at the far opposite site, her wide oval eyes darting from doorway to doorway. A reptilian Gorn was stalking about, apparently trying to take the lay of the land: since there was nothing at all to see here, Riker hadn't the slightest idea what the green-skinned female was looking for. He looked up uncomfortably. *This had better not be a damned gladiatorial arena*, he thought.

And off to the left in a gaggle, Riker recognized the other leaders of the Khitomer signatory powers from his Federation briefing. There was Charlak, the Klingon general: she had been recently demoted by the Defense Forces for having broken the nose of a member of the Council who had denied her a promotion.

No peacemaker, she—and the giant woman looked none too pleased to be here. Riker decided to give her a wide berth.

She was ranting about something to Igel, a DaiMon of the Ferengi Alliance. According to Riker's notes, the Ferengi was so thoroughly old-school that he was still obsessed with his finances. He had reportedly sold the dilithium crystals out of his own starship once to cover a margin call on the Ferengi Futures Exchange. Never mind that he had left his crew stranded for three weeks: Igel had priorities.

Finally, there was Gul Rodrek, who may well have been the oldest Cardassian he'd ever seen. Rodrek had some experience with diplomacy that Riker was aware of: during the discussion of the Federation-Cardassian treaty of 2370, he had demonstrated that his people were not to be trifled with by staging and winning drinking contests—some unopposed.

How Rodrek kept his job under Castellan Garak was a mystery; it frankly didn't matter to Riker. The leaders of the Federation's allies were certainly showing their faith in the proceedings by the people they'd sent.

"Ah, the United Federation of Planets," Charlak snarled. "How kind to grace us with your presence."

Riker shrugged and stepped forward. There wasn't much chance of blending into the woodwork when there wasn't any woodwork—and if he couldn't talk to the Federation's ostensible friends, he wasn't going to get far with its adversaries.

He bowed, and Charlak responded with a Klingon salute. "It's three against two," she said. "Should we begin the beatings now?"

"I don't know what protocols say about beatings,"

Riker said, smiling. He was glad that the invitation hadn't included the Kinshaya, a people who virulently hated the Klingons.

The Ferengi forced a hand into his. "You are William T. Riker, of *Enterprise*?" Igel asked.

"Once upon a time."

"I've heard of you. Very glad to make your acquaintance." Igel shook Riker's hand vigorously and smiled with all his many teeth. He eyed Riker's collar. "You are now an admiral?"

"Just recently."

"Fine, fine," Igel said, still not releasing Riker's hand. He pulled the human closer and put his other hand around his shoulder. "I imagine they pay admirals pretty well," Igel whispered. "Tell me, are you in the market for a new luxury home? Because I have some property in development that may just interest you."

Riker didn't know what to say—and couldn't for the life of him imagine why the Ferengi was whispering. The Klingon was hardly a buyer—and a quick glance at Gul Rodrek told him the Cardassian was fully fortified before he set foot aboard the Far Embassy. "I'll think about it," Riker said, pulling himself away.

"Don't miss this chance," Igel said. "Starships are fun to fly around in, but they're no place to entertain."

"I'll say," Rodrek said, pulling a flask from his vest. "This is the worst party I've ever been to."

Riker wasn't about to argue. Nor did he intend to stand in the way when the Klingon woman took up the old Cardassian on his offer of libations. The admiral looked around awkwardly for a moment. The Tzenkethi and Gorn representatives had no evident desire to talk, and he wasn't about to engage the Cardassian if he could help it. What was the idea behind this place—simply putting representatives in the same room until they drove each other mad?

Igel was approaching Riker with another sales pitch when a door opened off to the right. Riker's face brightened. *Thank God, it's the Romulan!*

He chuckled to himself as he walked across the atrium, having realized that they were strange words for a Starfleet officer. But it didn't matter. He could count on the Romulans to be serious—usually, *too* serious—about whatever was going on. With the Romulan representative on the scene, odds were they'd get to the point of this thing quickly, provided it had a point.

"Admiral William T. Riker of Starfleet, representing the Federation." He offered his hand.

The Romulan didn't take it, drawing his hands back into the sleeves of his robe. "I am Senator Bretorius." He looked around, sniffed at the air, and wandered past, as if Riker wasn't there.

Bretorius. Starfleet Intelligence had missed on that one. Riker had been given a list of likely envoys; Bretorius's name was at the very bottom. They had turned up precious little about his career. He was a near-total blank. Normally for a Romulan, that would make him a likely member of the Tal Shiar. However, they had sent him in a smaller vessel, not a warbird. That didn't say much for the senator's status.

I'm losing respect for myself for just being here, Riker thought. This was not a club he wanted to belong to. But at least he didn't need to take his selection for the mission personally: *Titan* happened to have been nearby the nebula when the call came. *Lucky me.*

Riker took a deep breath and approached Bretorius

again. "Well, you called this meeting, Senator. What's the program?"

Bretorius seemed as if he were about to take a step backward. His eyebrow arched. "Your attempt to confuse me will not succeed."

"Good to know."

"You know very well that the Federation called for this meeting."

"That's news to me. We got *your* invitation."

Bretorius's eyes narrowed. "It may well be, Admiral Riker, that your government does not tell you everything."

Riker thought about asking further, only to stop when he decided Bretorius was more likely describing his own situation. Few knew what went on inside the impenetrable black box that was the Romulan political system. The praetor might well have sent this underling without telling him who had called for the meeting.

"It would be wise not to waste my time," Bretorius said, putting his hand to his chest. "I am a significant person with important responsibilities."

"Noted." *Whatever gets you through the day*, Riker thought. However Romulan senators got their jobs, it wasn't for their personalities. He looked around the room, slightly amused. "The Cardassian said this is the worst party ever," Riker said. "Nobody wants to dance."

"I will not join any conversations until our last ally arrives."

"Fair enough."

Seeing that the Tzenkethi and Gorn representatives were keeping their distance, Riker found his mind wandering to his dinner plans back aboard the *Titan*. Deanna had promised to arrange for something special whenever he returned, assuming—correctly, it seemed—there would be nothing for him at the summit. He now figured he'd be getting back to it sooner than he'd expected. It looked as if his crash-course preparations for the meeting would be for nothing. Food and then bed—and one of the less gripping episodes in the history of galactic diplomacy would come to a close.

Across the room, he saw a door open. A six-legged crablike form, nearly two meters tall, skittered from it. As the new arrival turned, Riker could see a torso above the legs, topped by an opaque helmet. The dark sphere changed color, as if lit by an inner fire—and a second later, Riker could see the glowing, blazing hot skull carapace of a Tholian inside. The suit was necessary, as Tholians required high temperatures and gases poisonous to the humanoids in the room.

The door closed behind the Tholian. Now they were eight—and as if in response, the room began rotating. Riker knew because he felt it, and also because Gul Rodrek fell to the deck, losing his flask. As the Cardassian rose, cursing, Riker saw a hole open in the exact center of the floor of the enormous room. Twisting open like an iris counter to the floor's rotation, the gap was soon filled by something rising from beneath the deck. It was a second platform, on which sat a large octagonal table surrounded by eight chairs custom-shaped for the visitors' physiologies.

"Finally," the Klingon woman said as the new platform locked into place, becoming a raised dais. She helped the Cardassian up the step and into his seat.

Riker saw that she had purloined his flask in the process.

Bretorius looked mildly at Riker as the other Typhon representatives headed for their respective seats. "After you, Federation."

"Thank you," Riker said. He looked back at the Ferengi, who was still trying—and failing—to get a message out via his communicator. "DaiMon?"

"This is a wholly unprofitable use of our time," Igel said. "I'm losing a slip of latinum a minute being here."

"Who knows," Riker replied. "We sit at the table long enough, maybe something will come of it." *Probably boredom*, he did not say. But he would do his best for the Federation—and his best to stifle his yawns. That dinner couldn't come soon enough.

Six

Deanna Troi was changing from her uniform to her evening clothes when she heard the outer door to the admiral's chambers opening. "Natasha, is that you?"

Hearing no answer, she quickly finished dressing. Natasha was staying over with friends tonight; it had seemed like a good idea, given the uncertainty over the timing of her husband's return from the Far Embassy. Had Natasha forgotten something? It was hard to believe: she'd packed every toy in sight.

Troi walked into the antechamber—and was both startled and delighted to see Will Riker back at his desk in the sitting room.

"You're back early," she said, smiling. "No peace for the galaxy?"

Riker looked up at her from behind a terminal and rolled his eyes. "I've been to livelier funerals."

"No one wanted to talk?"

"There was a Ferengi who wanted to sell us some seashore property—probably on a desert planet, I'd have to check. That was about it."

She approached the desk, disappointed for him. "I'm sorry, Will. I guess they weren't serious after all." Deanna walked to the quarters' replicator. "Can I order you dinner?"

"I don't know that I'm hungry," Riker said, eyes scanning the screen in front of him.

She chuckled. "They had a buffet?"

"No." Riker shook his head. "I'm just not hungry." He looked up at her. "Stress, I guess. But you should go ahead and eat. I need to file my report."

She walked back to where he was sitting and slipped behind the desk, embracing him from behind. "If it really was a waste of time," she said in a soft voice, "maybe you could leave the report until tomorrow."

"No, I should turn it in now. No peace for the galaxy—and no rest for the weary." He gave her arm a patient pat that seemed to suggest he wanted to be left alone.

Troi pulled her arms back. Her husband was focused on his work, yes, but he didn't really seem that tired to her. "I thought you'd be exhausted," Troi said. "You were already worn out before you went over there."

"I do what I have to do," he said. He looked back at her and flashed a smile. "You should have dinner."

She stepped away and walked toward their living room, pausing just for a moment to look back and marvel at his diligence. Starfleet was definitely getting a bargain in William T. Riker.

ROMULAN FRIGATE *ACCIPITER*
DEPARTING THE FAR EMBASSY

Nerla hadn't greeted Bretorius when he returned to *Accipiter*, and for a change, it hadn't mattered to the senator at all. He had things to do—and he had been doing them, bustling from one console on the bridge to another, frequently brushing aside whatever Romulan officer was stationed there.

"Not good," Bretorius said, poring over an operations terminal. "Not good at all."

The captain, a one-armed man older than Bretorius's mother, looked at him with aggravation. "What is it, Senator?"

"This vessel is unequal to our needs."

"Needs? What needs? I was instructed to deliver you to the conference and then to return."

"The vessel's top speed," Bretorius said, gesturing to the panel before him. "This won't do at all."

"I don't know what you're going on about. If there were a hurry to get you back, they'd have sent another ship!"

Bretorius looked up at the captain, accusatory. "And these armaments. You call this a warship of the Grand Fleet?"

"I call this a ship with a number of systems not worth repairing—which is why it gets such choice assignments." Disgusted with the senator's meddling, the captain looked over to Nerla. "Can you do something here?"

Nerla set down the padd she was using and sighed. "What is it now, Bret?" She rose to face him. "Did meeting a real, live Klingon send you into a fit of terror?"

Bretorius ignored her. There was nothing to tell about the summit meeting, of course: they'd all sat at the table for a few minutes before it became a race to see who would get up and leave first. He had other concerns now. And scanning a grid depicting vessels within range of the sector, he saw something that might help with them. "Ah," he said. "The *D'varian*."

"It was your old command," Nerla said. "So?"

"She's not far from here," he said. *D'varian* was a *D'deridex*-class warbird—and while there were stronger and faster vessels in the fleet, it certainly trumped *Accipiter* on all scores. And it had other assets that might come in handy. "Call her commander."

The captain looked at Nerla, who made little effort to hide her "just humor him" expression. Grumbling, the senior officer complied.

A few moments later, a subspace connection had been achieved. A brown-haired Romulan captain with a scar over one eye appeared on-screen. *"This is Commander Yalok of* D'varian.*"*

Bretorius recognized the man who had succeeded him aboard his former warship. "You know who this is, Yalok. I'm on an urgent mission for the Empire—and I need your ship to meet me." He typed something at the tactical console. "I'm sending coordinates of a location partway between us. Make all speed for it, right away."

Yalok looked amused. *"We're on an important mission ourselves, Bret—excuse me,* Senator *Bretorius—patrolling the frontier. I'm sure you can do what you need to do in whatever you're aboard now."*

"You didn't hear me, Yalok. I require *D'varian*. You will make all speed this instant to rendezvous with *Accipiter*. I will transfer my flag then."

"Your flag?" Yalok made no effort to stifle his guffaw. *"I don't know if you're homesick for the fleet or not, but you ought to at least remember the rules. You're a civilian now, and you don't have any right to—"*

"You are relieved," Bretorius barked. He had never liked Yalok anyway. "I hereby commandeer *D'varian* under Article Twelve of the Imperial Senate Emergency Reestablishment Act. *D'varian* subcommander!"

The woman to Yalok's side, as surprised as her captain was, looked up. *"Yes?"*

"You are now acting commander," the senator said. "You will deliver *D'varian* to me immediately—and you will place Commander Yalok in custody until I arrive and give further orders. Is that understood?"

The subcommander looked nervously at her superior aboard ship before saluting. *"Yes, Senator!"*

"Now stop talking and move. *Accipiter* out."

Nerla looked at him in amazement. "Where did *that* come from?"

Bretorius's attention was back on the star map. "Where did what come from?"

"That sudden burst of—of *whatever*," Nerla said. "Did the Tzenkethi give you a pep talk?"

Bretorius's lip curled slightly. "Nerla, you have always underestimated me."

"And what's this Article Twelve?" She shook her head, bewildered. "Where did you come up with that?"

"It was in the senatorial orientation files. 'Where matters of transport are concerned, the Imperial Fleet may not obstruct a Senate-level agent on special diplomatic assignment for the praetor,'" he cited from memory. "The rule is little used in recent years, but it happens to still be in effect."

"How did you remember it?"

Bretorius looked up for a moment. "It just came back to me."

Nerla smirked. "Whatever you want, Bret. It gets us home faster, I guess."

She kept talking after that, but the senator had already returned to poring over the starmap. It was a nice feeling, him being the one to ignore her for a change.

TITAN
FAR EMBASSY

Yawning, Deanna Troi emerged from the bedroom she shared with Will. Stretching, she saw the meal she had brought him sitting untouched—and the man himself still behind his terminal.

She was incredulous. "Don't tell me you worked through the night? I thought there was nothing to say about the summit."

"Well, the higher-ups don't see it that way." Riker looked up—and scratched his cheek where his beard had attempted to colonize the rest of his face overnight. "In fact," he added, "they want me back at Command right away."

Troi rolled her eyes. "You can't catch a break."

He rose and took her hands. "You needn't worry about me. *Titan* will be rendezvousing with *Aventine*. They'll take me to Earth."

"*Aventine*? They're in the area?"

"For a ship that fast, everything's in the area. I've just ordered *Aventine* diverted." He looked at her, his eyes asking forgiveness. "I won't be long. Give my regards to the Genovous Pulsar."

Realizing what he was suggesting, Troi sighed. "Federation widow again." She embraced him. "You'd better catch a shave first."

"And a shower," he said.

She whispered in his ear. "I could join you."

Riker smiled. "I *know* I don't have time for that."

She pulled away from him and laughed. "Now I *know* you're taking this promotion too seriously. Are you looking to become president of the Federation or something?"

Riker chuckled. "Of course not," he said. But she noticed that it took him a moment to think about it.

Seven

The dark-haired woman identified herself as she approached the security officer outside the brig. It was obvious who she was—every being on *Aventine* knew the captain. But stopping at the checkpoint was regulation, and it was good for Ezri Dax to show that she could do things by the book. Everyone on board was certainly aware of the times when she'd thrown the book away.

The security officer allowed her to pass. The brig aboard the *Vesta*-class starship wasn't large, and often it wasn't occupied at all, but it still had to be crewed. *Regulations, again.* Dax walked to where Ensign Wilson Englehorn, a bearded young human, met her with a smile. "Captain."

Dax said. "What have we got?"

Englehorn chuckled. "Just one customer today." He checked to see that his phaser was in its holster— that was regulation too—although nothing about his manner suggested that they were heading to see a dangerous criminal.

Dax approached the cell. Through its protective

force field, she saw a human form on the top rack inside, huddled and facing the wall. The figure let out a low moan when Englehorn cleared his throat. "Leave me alone, Wilson," said a high-pitched voice. "I had enough of your sarcasm."

"How about some of mine?" Dax said, leaning against the cell's door frame. She knew who it was now.

Hearing the captain's voice, the startled prisoner sat up abruptly, clocking his spiky white-haired head against the bulkhead above. Dazed and bewildered, the young human shook off the shock—and Dax saw Nevin Riordan gawking at her. She smiled primly and gave a gentle nod. Realizing he needed to come to attention, the twenty-something ensign moved quickly to shuffle off the bunk. Hitting the deck, Riordan quickly composed himself and stood ramrod straight.

"Captain," Riordan said, uniform unfastened.

Dax stared at him. Blue eyes glanced down at his feet.

"Sir?" Riordan asked, defensively. Then he looked down and realized his bedsheet still had hold of his right ankle, forming a cloth umbilical connecting him to the rack. For several moments, the slender man stood, evidently weighing whether or not to do something about it. Finally, Riordan knelt, working to free his foot.

Englehorn crossed his arms. "Typical."

Dax waited with bemused patience. Riordan had been an ensign more than five years, unable to advance in part because of his mouth. The computer specialist had a habit of contradicting his superiors, even his captain on occasion.

"What brings you here, Ensign?" she asked as he returned to attention. "I'm doubting it's the accommodations."

"Stupidity," Englehorn said.

Sullen, Riordan snapped at the security officer. "Shut it."

"Ensign," Dax said, the slight raise in the petite woman's voice enough to command the prisoner's attention. "Lieutenant Englehorn's a superior officer. Is that mouth what you're in for?"

"Sorry, sir," Riordan said, only slightly chastened. "Familiarity breeds contempt."

Englehorn explained, "Nevin and I bunked together at the Academy, Captain. It was an experience. I guess we're roommates again, sort of."

"With a force field between," Dax said. "What did you do, Ensign?" She nodded to the padd sitting on the guard's station. "I could always look it up . . ."

"No, no," Riordan said, raising his hands and looking away. "Captain, it's really not important why—"

The lieutenant spoke up. "He programmed all the food replicators on deck seven to replace tomato paste with hot sauce."

"Ah, a classic," Dax said. She rolled her eyes. "What are you, twelve?"

Riordan continued to wave his hands defensively. "It was just a harmless joke."

"It would've been," Englehorn said, "had it not been for Ensign Altoss and her habanero pepper allergy. She only got out of sickbay today."

Dax eyed Riordan, her mien serious. "Stupidity's one thing, but an attack on the digestive tract of a fellow officer is a major offense." Then her expression softened. So it was the food that had brought him here, after all.

Forgetting any need to stand at attention, Riordan started wandering the little cell, speaking to the overhead. "It started out small . . . a game of one-upmanship between engineering and security."

"A game?" she asked.

"Yes, sir."

She looked at the big security officer. "You return fire?"

Englehorn's shoulders drooped a little. "It's all in fun—usually."

"But it's hardly fair when they've got the brig and the power to arrest," Riordan said.

Englehorn looked back in at the cell. "Hey, how fair was you programming the ship's computer to wake me in the middle of the night with a rendition of Mahler's fourth symphony?"

"It was the fifth, you lunkhead."

"Silence!" Dax raised her voice. She shook her head. *Aventine* had been idle for several days, running checks on the slipstream drive. Was that why this stunt had gotten out of control?

Some people needed more to do, she thought. Well, she could provide that.

"This is your lucky day, Ensign," she said. "We're heading to pick up Admiral Riker from *Titan*—and I want *Aventine* completely shipshape. You're going to make sure that every running light on the ship's hull is working properly."

Riordan blinked. "Me? I'm a computer technician, not a maintenance guy."

"It's a computer issue. When we tangled with that Andorian ship, the *Tuonetar*, we must have taken a hit to one of the subsystems somewhere. Now when we activate the starboard running lights, a handful of the portside lights flicker for a few milliseconds."

"And vice versa?"

"No," Dax said, dragging out the syllable as if there were some great mystery to it. "That's what's strange. I'll need you to take every light offline at the local EPS to see what's going on."

Riordan's eyes narrowed as he considered the task. "There've got to be dozens of nodes to check." Then, thinking of something else, he shivered visibly. "I'm not going to have to walk outside on the hull, am I, Captain?"

Recognizing sheer terror when she saw it, Dax quickly spoke up. "Do the ones you can get to from inside. We'll have the rest checked out in spacedock."

Riordan sagged. "Crawling around in all those Jefferies tubes . . ."

"You seem to have plenty of energy." She gestured for Englehorn to release his prisoner. "It's got to be more interesting than being in here, right?"

Englehorn deactivated the force field. "Our cells are roomier than some of those conduits." He patted his broad chest. "Which is why I'm in security and not engineering."

"Reason one of a series," Riordan said, glaring at the guard. Again, too late, he appeared to realize he was mouthing off to a superior officer before the captain. "I guess I'd better get started."

"Dismissed," Dax said. She shook her head as the ensign walked swiftly out of the brig.

Englehorn smirked as Riordan vanished. "There isn't anything wrong with the running lights, is there, Captain?"

"He'll think twice before going to such extremes."

She looked around at the empty cells. "My job here is done."

The towering man nodded. "Captain, permission to speak freely. You're a good egg."

"I'm not sure how to take that," she said.

"You've been coming down here every day for two weeks. This is a brig—it's not like making the rounds visiting the folks in sickbay."

"Seven hundred forty-seven people on my ship," she said, turning toward the exit. Dax patted the frame of the brig door as she walked out. "I'll see you tomorrow—if you've got any more takers."

Outside, Dax stood waiting before the turbolift and looked back at the entrance to the brig. Englehorn was right. She'd been visiting the brig more often lately—and increasingly, she'd been finding ways to commute whatever sentences had been imposed. She didn't need a visit with Susan Hyatt, the ship's chief counselor, to know why. It hadn't been that long ago that she'd been held in a penitentiary on Jaros II, after she'd defied orders and interfered on behalf of the Andorian people—and her friend and former lover, Julian Bashir, who was trying to save them from a medical crisis that threatened the entire species.

The orders Dax had defied were extralegal, the result of a scandal in Federation administration that had since been uprooted, and she'd been given her command back. But while she and those who served under her had received commendations for their actions, Dax still didn't feel wholly vindicated.

It wasn't that the imprisonment was that bad. It was less than a moment in the existence of Dax, the centuries-old symbiont living inside the Trill named

Ezri: compared with some of that being's past experiences while inhabiting previous Trill hosts, her time in prison was a holiday. No, the problem was that defying orders, even for a good cause, had a way of marking an officer within Starfleet as a certain type.

A century ago, James T. Kirk had set the standard for defiance, stealing—and then losing—*Starship Enterprise* in order to help a friend. Today, he was regarded as one of Starfleet's greatest heroes. But Kirk had always drawn upon a seemingly immeasurable reserve of luck, and it wasn't right to expect other mere mortals to match his results. Just because one person could fly close to the sun and emerge safely on the other side, that didn't mean Starfleet wanted all its other captains defying orders.

So she'd caught a chilly vibe from several fellow captains since leaving incarceration. Oh, nobody had been openly rude to her—she wouldn't expect that in Starfleet, where keeping decorum ranked just beneath exploration as its reason for existing. But it was that exact code that Dax had offended by going off on her own, and now whenever she was in the presence of other captains, they invariably spoke more about their own advancement prospects, not acknowledging that she might not have any. Ezri Tigan had been a counselor; Ezri Dax was excellent at hearing what people weren't saying. As far as they were concerned, commendations might be all that she'd ever be in line for.

That was fine if you were Jean-Luc Picard, another occasional rebel who sought no further promotion in the service. He existed to captain *Enterprise*. But the symbiont that lived inside Ezri had lived all sorts of different lives through its hosts. And she and it had decided—for they thought with the same mind—that *this* life would be the one devoted to seeing just how far a Dax could go within Starfleet. It was deflating to think this could be it.

Their mission to fetch Admiral Riker was a simple shuttle detail. But maybe Riker's visit was a good omen. He'd been present during at least one of the occasions when Picard had found it necessary to step beyond Starfleet's strict orders, saving the Earth from being destroyed by the Borg, and it hadn't harmed his career in the least. True, Riker hadn't been in command, as Dax was during her "incident." The *Enterprise*-E's feat was Kirk-level astonishing. And fair or not, saving the Andorians wasn't quite saving the Earth and everyone on it. But maybe he might have a word of advice for someone whose career had stalled.

She wondered for a moment if the turbolift car had stalled, too, when she realized she'd never summoned it. *Distracted again.* When she did call, it arrived instantly. Stepping inside, she hadn't asked for a destination yet when her communicator badge chirped. She toggled it. "Dax."

"Captain, we've reached the rendezvous point." It was Sam Bowers, her first officer. *"Titan is preparing to beam Admiral Riker to us."*

"How many staff?"

"Just him."

That bodes well, she thought. A lot of admirals tasked with diplomatic duty loved traveling with entourages, assistants that couldn't help but get underfoot. Riker was evidently not of that sort. "Meet me in the transporter room, Commander."

She was about to click her badge when Bowers spoke again. *"Stand by, Captain."* A moment later, he continued, sounding puzzled. *"Admiral Riker has requested that he be beamed directly to holodeck one."*

Ezri blinked, baffled as well. "Do it." She clicked her badge twice and ordered the turbolift onward. *Riker might be a nice guy,* she thought, *but he's still an admiral, and admirals are a strange breed.*

Eight

Commander Sam Bowers met Dax in the hallway. "Riker's already on the holodeck," the brown-skinned man said. He shook his shaved head, knowingly. "This is going to be another one of *those* trips, isn't it?"

"Another one of what trips?" She walked fast to keep up with the taller officer's pace.

"You know. Another flight of the *U.S.S. Peculiar*."

Dax stifled a laugh. *Aventine* was built as a proof-of-concept experimental vehicle, and its capabilities had made it the perfect choice for many challenging missions. But its speed had also resulted in it being called upon to ferry admirals and Federation mucky-mucks—and even the odd banjo-playing professor. Without fail, every one had left the vessel as a figure of shipboard legend—and not in a good way.

The Federation administrator who made them turn around and go back to a starbase because he had forgotten to feed his fish. The Bolian envoy who was convinced that warp travel using the slipstream drive was somehow feeding negative emotional energy into his quarters, causing him and his spouses to argue more. The very senior admiral who had eschewed using an antigravity chair, insisting instead that the transporters beam him from room to room. These episodes had made the crew wary of high-ranking passengers.

This time, Dax was sure, the concern wasn't necessary. "We know Riker well enough to say you're all wet," she said, rounding a corner with Bowers. "He's perfectly normal."

"Oh, I know. For exec officers like me, he's the gold standard. And we both saw him in action as a captain—he's a tower of power." Bowers chuckled, gesturing to his insignia. "But that extra little rectangle around the pips has a way of making folks . . . entertaining."

Approaching the double doors of holodeck one, they quickly composed themselves. As if on cue, the doors opened, and Admiral Riker stepped out to greet them. His hair was a little grayer since she'd seen him last, and he hadn't shaved. Dax figured he'd had to leave in a hurry.

But his expression was warm. "Captain Dax." He offered his hand, surprising Dax a little.

She shook it. "Welcome to *Aventine*, Admiral."

"Commander Bowers."

"Glad to have you aboard, sir," Bowers said, shaking the admiral's hand vigorously. Dax had always sensed a little hero worship of Riker on her first officer's part after Bowers had met him during the Borg Invasion. Bowers would soon see that Admiral Riker was just the same as Captain Riker had been.

Riker studied them both. "I appreciate the help you were able to provide us at Zellman's Find. Starfleet needed *Titan* elsewhere."

"Glad to lend a hand," Dax said. "Although it sounds as if all the action went with you that time. I'm just glad we were in position to be of service—and to help you now."

They stood for a moment, just long enough for Dax to feel uncomfortable. Unable to keep from remarking on it any longer, she looked over Riker's shoulder. "Did you have luggage? It's not every day we beam our guests to a holodeck."

Riker looked at her for a second—and then laughed. "I guess not. Here, come in."

They stepped through the portal and beheld what appeared to be a tastefully appointed apartment—a sitting room with a small kitchen to one side and a doorway leading to a bedroom. The main area had a large desk with a computer terminal and an antique faux-leather chair behind it. Plants and Betazoid art objects sat on shelves near the walls, and a case for a trumpet and a music stand could be seen off in a corner.

Dax looked around the room—and then back out through the holodeck arch, just to remind herself that she was not in *Aventine*'s VIP quarters.

Riker seemed amused at his guests' expressions. "It's my living quarters and personal office from *Titan*." He walked the carpeted floor, playing the role of a happy host showing off.

Bowers gave Dax a knowing look. *Perfectly normal?*

Dax did a double-take. "I'm sorry, Admiral—I don't quite understand. We have office space and quarters here on *Aventine*."

"And I'm sure they're wonderful—just like all the other guest quarters I've seen in Starfleet." He rolled his eyes. "Well, some of them aren't so wonderful. But this is all about efficiency. I don't have to spend any time here remembering where things go—and I'm able to have a workstation like I'm accustomed to." He gestured to the chair. "One thing you learn as you get older: the secret to a happy work life is finding a desk chair you can live with. And as an admiral, you spend a lot of time on your keister."

Dax looked around and laughed. "I suppose the only thing that's missing is your wife and child?"

Riker chuckled. "Deanna has a definite aversion to being depicted in other people's holographic illusions."

Dax walked farther inside and touched the back of one of the chairs across from the desk. It was an interesting idea, for sure. "If you've got your own program, why not? Only your wardrobe would need to be real."

Riker snapped his fingers, remembering. "Well, there is something else." He pointed to the terminal on the desk. "I'll need this patched into *Aventine*'s main computer core so I can do my work—and I'll also need a secure communications link routed here. I need to consult with Starfleet right away."

"Right away, Admiral." Dax touched her badge and issued the order to Mikaela Leishman, her chief engineer. If the lieutenant found the requests unusual, she didn't say so. Short moments later, they heard a ping from Riker's terminal. He walked to it and sat down.

The admiral looked impressed. "I'm up and running."

Dax was pleased. "You won't have access to the ship's tactical and propulsion systems from here."

"Naturally." Riker nodded, looking up and around. "The checks in your holodeck systems probably came from the task force I was part of years ago. We didn't want any more fictional Victorian villains running away with the show." He patted the terminal and rose. "Good work, all of you."

"This is pretty nice," Bowers said, still marveling at the room. "Is it accurate?"

"Huh?" Riker looked around. "It's close enough, I guess. I don't think I got Deanna's *objets d'art* just right."

"You'd better delete the program when you go," Dax said. "I'm not sure I want our crewmembers staging any holodeck fantasies in admirals' chambers."

"You mean they don't already?" Riker flashed a winning smile. They laughed. He nodded to the arch. "Now, if you'll excuse me, I need to check in like I said."

Dax and Bowers nodded, turned, and left. The interlocking doors closed behind them.

"Well, there goes a holodeck," Bowers said, walking up the hall.

"I think we can forego some rest and relaxation," Dax said, "to give the admiral a place to work."

Bowers grinned. "Put another way, you're willing to go without, if it means not having an admiral—even a perfectly normal one—hanging over your shoulder, watching every move you make."

"Sam, I've told you, Will Riker will be fine. He's a straight shooter. He's not one of the eccentrics."

Bowers slapped the side of the wall. "I knew there was something I was going to ask about. Did you let that little guy out of the brig?"

Dax blinked. "Ensign Riordan?"

"I saw him on my way over here. He's loose."

"Yeah, I gave him a detail so he could work it off."

Bowers clicked his tongue. "I throw the kid in the brig, you let him out. We're going to get a reputation as a bunch of softies, Captain."

"These people are just bored," she said. "I don't want people's records being ruined." She didn't want to say that there might be more to her leniency, and to his credit, if Bowers suspected otherwise, he didn't say anything.

"Well, I don't know that chauffeuring Admiral Riker is going to create a lot of extra work," he said, grinning. "That's a man who knows how to pack."

Her badge chirped. It was Riker. *"New orders, Captain."*

"Already?" Dax looked behind her. They had just left him five minutes earlier. "What's the—"

"Cancel the trip to Earth. Hold station here until I send new coordinates."

Dax's eyes widened. "Where, sir?"

"I don't know yet. I'll be in secure conference for the next hour—I'll send the destination down when I have it."

"Hold station." She looked at Bowers, whose face showed concern. She spoke to the air. "Is there a problem, Admiral?"

He didn't mince words. *"Yes, there's a problem. I want to meet with senior staff as soon as I'm able to. I'll explain everything then."*

Dax was quick to answer. "Aye, aye, sir."

"Sorry for the change in plans. Riker out."

The Trill captain double-clicked her badge. "Now what?"

Bowers looked at her, flummoxed. "Things go from happy to hectic in a heartbeat, don't they?"

Dax nodded. That, she would agree with him on.

ROMULAN WARBIRD *D'VARIAN*
EN ROUTE TO ROMULAN SPACE

Bretorius had lived many years on *D'deridex*-class warbirds, and in all that time, he had never really figured out his way around. Seen from the outside, the ship had two winglike sections connected at the tips, mounted behind a large talon-shaped command section—the warbird's beak. But that was the vessel's only nod to symmetry; the interior was something else entirely. It was almost as if the structural engineers had tried to capture the byzantine nature of the Romulan society in how they arranged things. Just like life on Romulus, success aboard ship favored those who had been around, who knew where things were, who could think in more than two dimensions. The new recruit got lost because the new recruit was supposed to get lost.

Even as commander of *D'varian*, Bretorius had never found his way to the Ter'ak Pen—the colloquial name for the most secure holding facility onboard. Bretorius's *D'varian* had never captured an important enemy needing its sophisticated interrogation devices; it had never held any prisoner requiring its heavy-duty disruptor-proof walls to hold. But he had unerringly made his way there to confront Commander Yalok.

The conversation had not gone well. When Yalok refused to even speak to the senator—much less yield to his authority—Bretorius had ordered the guards to take their former captain to one of the interrogation rooms. There, an increasingly unnerved Nerla had watched in astonishment as Bretorius had applied some of the chamber's more punitive devices in an attempt to gain Yalok's cooperation. It had not come, and Bretorius had stopped, deciding to leave Yalok with his one good eye. But the episode made an impression on the guards—and on his aide.

Nerla had earlier seen him dress down another officer when he shamed Subcommander Quarlis for asking too many questions. Nerla had never known Bretorius to even recognize when someone else was his inferior, much less to use his power effectively. Now, having just seen him commandeer the office of the Tal Shiar officer in the Ter'ak Pen, she couldn't stop staring.

Seated across from her at a desk in the dimly lit room, Bretorius didn't look up from the computer interface. "You have something you wish to say, Nerla. Say it."

"Where have you been hiding this version of yourself?" Out of the corner of his eye, he could see her searching his face, apparently looking for anything she recognized. "The Bretorius I know is passive, ineffectual—and on his last chance."

"Don't you think being on one's last chance could be a motivator?"

"For some people. Not for you." She frowned. "You would be even less likely to succeed. You can't handle pressure."

Bretorius looked at her—and pushed away from the desk. "So the only possible explanation, then, is that you were incorrect about me before now."

"I don't know what you mean."

He clasped his hands together thoughtfully. "Consider the tumult and distress in the Empire in the aftermath of Shinzon's coup. The Imperial Romulan State severs from the Empire, later to be reabsorbed. Chaos is all around. Somewhere in there, a man, Bretorius, is given a role in the Senate because he is considered a zero, harmless to any one side." The room's sole light glinted in his eye. "But there is a difference between being a zero—and being an *unknown quantity*."

She stared at him before blurting, "Come on! Do you really expect me to believe you've been feigning mediocrity all this time, just to . . ." She trailed off. "To do what? You're not exactly at the seat of power, ready to make your move."

"Don't assume all power is in the capital—or even on Romulus," he said.

That made her stop to think. Bretorius rose and began surveying the room, and the rooms it was connected to.

"Wait," she finally said. "You learned something? Back at the Far Embassy, at that meeting?" He looked back at her to see her eyes narrowing with suspicion. "Did you cut a deal to sell out the Empire, somehow?"

"Not at all, Nerla. You could say I simply understand a lot more." He patted the wall and looked up to the ceiling, considering where he was in relation to other rooms. "I understand our adversaries' strengths and weaknesses. I understand where the pressure points are that will cause the Federation's alliance with the other Khitomer signatories to collapse. Having the pressure come from the Empire will elevate us beyond our Typhon allies."

"And who's going to apply this pressure? You?" She gawked at him, still incredulous.

But he could tell his words had moved her, if only a millimeter. And perhaps a millimeter would be enough. He didn't need much, after all. Bretorius turned and stepped to the desk where he'd been working. He passed her a padd. "I will require the following from the ship's crew. I could arrange for these things myself—but it will go faster with your help."

Her eyes scanned the list. "This is pretty technical. Do you even know what these things are?"

Bretorius returned a canny smile. "What do you think?"

"I don't know. I think you've gone mad."

He chuckled and began nudging her to the exit. "Nerla, you have two choices, I should say. You could report me to the first officer—or free the captain—and together, inform the praetor. And the reward for selling out a known incompetent?" He shook his head. "I can't imagine it would be much. You'd be back waiting tables on the bay in a week—or scraping mollusk collectors with those parents of yours."

She looked at him skeptically. "Or on the other hand?"

"On the other hand, you could, just this once, humor a man you previously found to be feebleminded and ineffectual. A very small wager, unmissed if it is lost." He pulled her closer, surprising her. He whispered into her ear. "But if you win, the gain could be incalculable. I promised you that you would gain stature in my employ. I will make good on that, beyond your wildest imaginings."

Her eyes lingered on the padd, seeming to struggle with the decision.

"You'd better be right about this," she finally said. "I'll take it to the subcommander. What if she says no?"

Bretorius nodded toward the back hallway, leading to the interrogation chamber where they'd left the ship's commander. "Tell Quarlis that if she doesn't meet my needs, you'll take the list to Commander Yalok—offering to free him if she fails to fulfill the request."

"And then do it?"

"You won't have to. Quarlis is this moment sitting on the bridge in terror, wondering if the Imperial Fleet will reinstate Yalok on our return. And that will make her help you."

Nerla nodded, again impressed by his tactics. She stood in the hall, looking back at him. "And what will await *us* on our return?" she wondered aloud.

"Parades."

He watched as she left.

In fact, Bretorius knew they weren't returning any time soon. But Nerla didn't need to know that, and she wouldn't have understood anyway. He had work to do.

Nine

"**Y**ou're going to want to sit down for this," Riker said, striding purposefully into the observation room aboard *Aventine*. "Thank you for your prompt attendance."

Captain Dax exhaled as the others took their seats. She had just barely made it, herself. Riker was ready before she'd expected. She had been on the bridge getting *Aventine* under way to the location the admiral had ordered: the ship had been at warp for several minutes, racing toward some featureless point in deep space. She was pleased to see that her senior officers had arrived early. Bowers was flanked on one side of the long black polished table by Chief Engineer Leishman and Lieutenant Commander Gruhn Helkara, the saggy-faced Zakdorn senior science officer. Lonnoc Kedair, the green-scaled Takaran security chief, sat across from Bowers, along with Counselor Hyatt and chief operations officer Oliana Mirren. There wasn't a seat to spare. An admiral's briefing brought everyone out.

Dax sat down at the end of the table, expecting Riker to take the open chair at the far side. Instead, he remained standing.

"Some of you may know I was at a summit meeting recently with representatives of several Typhon Pact powers," he said, his tone grave.

Dax did know that, but not much else. Starfleet had made *Aventine* aware of the situation in case an incident there made a rescue—or reinforcements— necessary. But when Vale had passed along Riker's request for *Aventine*, she'd suggested the whole thing was a yawner. "Not much happened there, right?"

"I wish," Riker said. "I wasn't able to speak of it until now, but I was informed there of a new threat— one that Starfleet Command has just instructed us to deal with."

Dax straightened in her chair. "*Aventine* is ready, Admiral."

Riker walked to the room-length ports and looked out, his back to Dax and her officers. "What you're about to hear is so secret I can't show you the specifications for it. This is hot—red hot." He turned, backlit by the stars streaking by. "It's called Takedown. It is a program that, when received as a transmission via subspace, has the capacity to hijack the systems of any receiving station, like the computer worms of old."

All eyes were on Riker as he paced the length of the room. "Nothing can detect its presence in a system and nothing can stop it." He paused, his brow furrowing. "And it's in the hands of the Holy Order of the Kinshaya."

Riker's words prompted startled reactions in the lounge—and a whistle from Bowers. This was trouble.

The Order, Dax knew, was a theocratic society in the Beta Quadrant whose territory bordered the Klingon Empire. The Kinshaya considered the Klingons to be unholy creatures, only worthy of destruction; the Klingons had responded to that predictably. The Kinshaya belonged to the Typhon Pact, but their tendency toward rogue actions had made them a liability.

"This may sound," Riker said, "as though the Kinshaya plan on a mass conversion, pun intended, of our subspace communication systems. Well, that's exactly what it sounds like to me and Command. The Kinshaya could send all of us back to the age of radio waves—or could hold the Federation hostage until they got what they wanted."

"Were the Kinshaya at the summit?" Dax asked.

"No."

She thought for a moment. "Why would the other Typhon powers inform the Federation of a Kinshaya project?"

"Goodwill?" Riker grinned darkly. "Honestly, I don't know. We know the other members of the Pact were none too happy when the Kinshaya tried to conquer Krios and H'atoria from the Klingons. Maybe they think this program is so dangerous that if it gets loose, it could blow back on them. The Order could use it on them, too."

Bowers rolled his eyes. "All-day religious propaganda jamming the unsanctified. Something to be avoided."

Security Chief Kedair clasped her hands together. "This thing, Takedown—it sounds like a virtual version of the Borg, assimilating everything in its path. How could there be security holes like that in our systems?"

"I don't think there can be," Leishman said. "This doesn't sound possible." She looked to the admiral. "Has Command sent us any specs on Takedown?"

Riker shook his head as he walked to his seat. "Sharing the data just multiplies the odds someone will use it one day." He put a padd on the table and sat down. "Starfleet Command believes that the flaws in our systems can be fixed, but they don't know the time frame. It won't be overnight, I can tell you that. And if the Kinshaya discover that we know about it, they'll act immediately."

"A weapon unfired is no weapon at all," Dax said. Curzon had been fond of saying that. "But what are the chances the Kinshaya would use the program on us? It's the Klingons they hate."

"The way Takedown works, it doesn't matter," Riker said. "Anyone the Klingons contacted would find their systems infected. They'd spread it just by calling for help. Someone would get the message, and then we'd all have it. Until we have a chance to fix the flaw, we'll have to enact countermeasures."

"Countermeasures, sir?" Dax asked.

Riker picked up the padd before him and activated it. "I've just sent you all mission parameters for what we're calling Operation Shutdown. *Aventine* is going to sortie across the border into Kinshaya space and destroy a long-range transmission array. We believe to a high degree of certainty that's where the Takedown program was designed and where it will be originating from." He paused as the others checked their padds for the information. "*Aventine* will destroy the station's abilities to transmit and immediately depart."

Dax studied the mission specs. Their orders were plainly spelled out—and at the end there was that magic imprimatur: *Fleet Admiral Leonard James Akaar, Commanding Officer, Starfleet Command.* It wasn't a name she saw on many orders, not ones that were issued to *Aventine* alone. But she could understand why this came directly from the top—as did Bowers, who spoke up as he read: "Admiral, this is a kind of mission that could start a war."

"Or it could stop one." Riker looked around. "The

histories of many worlds are replete with preventative military operations. When they go well, they solve a lot of problems before they start. As for the rest—well, I know the risks. It's why I recommended *Aventine* for this mission. It has—*you have*—the best chance of success."

"Thank you, Admiral," Dax said. She pursed her lips and focused on the mission details on her screen. It would be challenging. Crossing an interstellar border was tricky in any situation; she little wondered why he and Command had selected *Aventine* for the mission. With its slipstream drive, it stood the best chance of getting in and getting out before too much went wrong.

But some of her officers were less eager. "It sounds—" Kedair started, before lowering her voice. "I'm sorry, Admiral, but it sounds like a trap. The Typhon powers, goading us into attacking one of their members?" She crossed her arms. "It could be an attempt to capture *Aventine*, to get hold of her slipstream drive technology."

"And I would accept that if Command hadn't already confirmed that Takedown exists," Riker said. "The Kinshaya are too unreliable to hang a strategy like that on. I don't think, 'Let's you and him fight' is the play over there. There's too much danger of everyone being drawn in."

Leishman looked troubled as she paged through the notes on her padd. "We really should try to get hold of this research somehow. If we could get aboard the station, we could see how the Kinshaya were able to come up with something like—"

Riker spoke sharply. "Do you want to learn how fire was discovered, Lieutenant Leishman, or do you want to put one out?"

A little startled, the engineer sat back in her chair. "The latter, sir."

"We're going to take the match out of the arsonist's hands, and we're going to get out fast. Is that understood?"

Dax let Leishman say it for her. "Loud and clear, Admiral."

"One more thing," Riker said, standing. "In order for this to work, we need to observe comm silence. We cannot send nor receive for the duration of the mission. The Kinshaya could use Takedown on *Aventine*." He looked from face to face. "Am I understood on this? Anything could open up *Aventine* to infiltration."

"Understood, Admiral." Dax knew her crew: they could fly across half the galaxy by dead reckoning if she asked them to. And the fewer words exchanged with the Kinshaya, the better. Where they were concerned, terms like *short fuse* and *tinderbox* came to mind. No wonder Riker had chosen the fire metaphor.

"Dismissed," Riker said.

Dax stood and looked around at her officers. *Opportunity knocks,* she thought. It was time to get to work.

Ten

Aventine tore out of warp like a thing afire. This would be that most difficult of operations, Dax thought: the blind raid. Riker had knowledge of the Kinshaya station's location—and its ominous name, the Annunciator. But that was all. Starfleet's encounters with the race were so few in number that they barely mattered as help in preparing; all that *Aventine* had to go on were combat profiles provided by the Klingons.

And those were of definite concern. The Romulans, Tzenkethi, and Breen had provided weapons and shielding technology to the Kinshaya in the early days of the Pact's formation, before they knew just how capricious the Holy Order would be with their use. Dax had ordered shields to be raised immediately upon the disengagement of the slipstream drive, expecting that the Annunciator would be heavily armed.

What she wasn't expecting was what she saw now—or, rather, what she didn't see as *Aventine* raced toward the Kinshaya facility. "No defenders? Can that be right?"

Kedair spoke up from the tactical station. "Nothing. Scanning station now for defensive capabilities."

The Kinshaya had located their station in the neighborhood of a lonely brown dwarf star; the system had only one world, several hundred million kilometers from the Annunciator. Many kinds of arrays, Dax knew, were better placed in distant, untraveled reaches—free from interference generated by populated areas and clear of occluding nebulae. That didn't explain why the Kinshaya would leave such an important target unguarded.

Riker offered a theory. "They're trying to make it look like they're doing peaceful work—not attracting any attention."

That made sense to Dax. But then again, Kinshaya space wasn't exactly a big tourist destination, unless you were planning on making a pilgrimage to join the true believers. Who, exactly, was likely to stumble across this place?

The captain focused on the station quickly growing on the viewscreen. It resembled a jet-black sunflower, with massive gridlike petals connecting to a central spherical hub. She also recognized several more primitive broadcasting devices. "Lieutenant Mirren, are you hearing anything?"

At the ops station, Oliana Mirren brushed back dark hair to listen closely to the small analog radio receiver Leishman had fabricated for her. The engineer had come up with the idea of using a small unit not attached to *Aventine*'s systems so that a single crew member could safely listen in on what the station was putting out; after some thought, Riker had agreed it would not compromise their systems. A little twentieth-century Earth technology might aid in their reconnaissance. Mirren tuned the unit. "There are channels broadcasting locally in multiple languages." Arriving at a broadcast she understood, she brightened. "I have something. It sounds like prayer. Or possibly a sermon."

"Let's hear it."

Mirren began speaking slowly. "*'Aya, and though the devils do tempt with ways of wickedness, the right-minded shall ever prevail—*"

Dax shook her head. "That doesn't exactly sound like a general alarm being sounded."

"It's the station's cover," Riker said. "A place that uses multiple broadcasting methods, subspace and local, to proselytize. Perfect for spreading mischief."

That also made sense to Dax. And the fact that many of the channels would likely have no listeners at all was very Kinshaya.

Helkara spoke up from the science station. "Admiral, if it's a basic audio broadcast, we could put it on the ship's systems and analyze it."

Riker glanced over at the Zakdorn. "If they had activated Takedown, Commander, you wouldn't be able to tell right away. It might not register. But later on you'd know it for sure. No, it's safe for Lieutenant Mirren's ear, and that only. Even putting the audio out onto the bridge still gets it into *Aventine*'s systems."

Mirren was still listening, though she was evidently struggling to make sense of it. "I think we've caught them on a worship day."

Riker grinned darkly. "They're all worship days here. They've given us the opening. Let's take it."

The distance between *Aventine* and the Annunciator halved, and then halved again. "Ready phasers," Dax said. "Give me life-sign readings of every targeted structure. If anyone is aboard, bypass it." It wasn't something Riker had told her to do, and Dax now looked back at the admiral, searching to see if her order had evoked some kind of reaction. "Admiral?"

He didn't hesitate before answering. "Of course. We only want to prevent Takedown from being broadcast."

"The transceiver panels are not crewed," Helkara said, his voice betraying the excitement of the moment. "Precision fire to sever them should spare the inhabited areas."

"We're in range," Kedair announced.

"Forward phasers, target panels only," Dax ordered, just to be absolutely sure. "Fire!"

Orange rays lanced out from *Aventine*, striking the black blossom and shearing off two of the colossal panels. *Aventine* veered right, with the port phaser banks continuing the fire. Dax watched closely as the starship completed half a circuit. It was almost surgical, what they were doing—and not entirely unlike a child pulling petals off a flower.

Or was it the wings off an insect? The thought entered Dax's mind for a moment, and she shivered a little. The Kinshaya weren't fighting back—

"Incoming fire!" Kedair called out. Disruptors on the Annunciator's rearward side opened up on *Aventine* as they passed, just missing.

"Continue firing," Dax said. The design of the station was such that its weaponry had a narrow field of fire—and she took advantage of that, keeping *Aventine* in its many blind spots.

Riker, standing to her right, watched with great interest. On the flight controller's station, he pointed. "I think we've got company!"

"Good eye, sir," Bowers called out. "Kedair, what have you got?"

Aventine had already moved to where the vessels Riker had seen were out of sight, but her sensors had more information. "I mark three—no, four attack vessels of the kind the Klingons told us about, all coming from the planet in the system."

Dax keenly studied the Annunciator—now mostly an orb with sparking spikes sticking out of it—floating amid a sea of debris. "Give me a damage assessment on the target."

"The transmitter is done for," Helkara said. "I estimate ninety percent of the structure disabled."

"Kinshaya combat vessels have charged weapons and are closing," Kedair said.

Dax wanted a better look. "Long-range view, on-screen."

The image changed to a rear view, and she spotted several black, spherical spacecraft—identical except for unique designs etched into their hulls, which served to identify their captains. Or at least that was what the Klingon intel reports had said. Whoever was aboard them, they were all in a race to catch up with *Aventine*.

It was a race none of them could ever win. "We've done our job," Riker said.

Dax was glad to hear it. "Lieutenant Tharp, take us out of here."

She felt a surge of acceleration that she did not try to fight, allowing it to push her back in her chair. The tension of the moment was finally subsiding. Bowers, who had been worried since the staff meeting, seemed much relieved—and from his admiring glance, quite impressed with his hero Riker's plan. He gave her a thumbs-up gesture, out of sight of the admiral.

And looking up to Riker, she saw an approving look on the admiral's face. *He said it,* Dax thought, her heart warmed. *We've done our job.*

"Set heading for Staging Area Two," she ordered. It was a location Riker had chosen beforehand, back in neutral space. There, they could reactivate only his connection to Command—the most secure link they could manage—to send word of their efforts.

"Heading set, Captain."

"Slipstream drive, engage." Dax let out a breath as she heard the system powering up. "I'm glad that's over."

Then she looked across and saw Riker's smile fading. He seemed to be considering something else. As much as she hated to break the jubilant mood on the bridge, she chanced a question: "It *is* over, isn't it?"

"I wish I could tell you that," the admiral said. Then he turned and left the bridge.

D'VARIAN
NEAR JOURET

Bretorius had always admired Nerla's hearty complexion; it came from growing up on the shores of Beraldak Bay, Romulus's vacation paradise. But the woman who returned to his commandeered office had no color to her face at all.

"It is Praetor Kamemor," she said, the padd in her hands nearly about to drop. "She wants to speak . . . *with you.*"

The senator reacted with mild amusement. "Calm down, Nerla. You handle important political calls for me every day. Why should this unnerve you?"

Nerla's eyes locked on him. "Half your 'important calls' are from retirees looking for a state pension—

and the other half are from your creditors. Not from the praetor of the Empire—wanting to know why you haven't returned!"

Bretorius waved his hand dismissively and activated the terminal on the desk. Nerla had the link set up. He smiled at her primly. "Would you like to stay around for this? I'm sure the praetor would like to say hello."

Nerla answered by darting out the door.

The senator touched the screen. The image was shaky, but he recognized the silhouette of Gell Kamemor. "Praetor," he said, not bothering to bow his head.

"Bretorius!" Kamemor's voice came through loud and clear—and her anger was unmistakable. *"What are you doing? I was told you transferred to* D'varian *to return here—and now I hear you've unseated her captain and ordered the ship to hold position in Federation space!"*

Bretorius wasn't surprised she knew. There wasn't any chance of Subcommander Quarlis not sending that piece of information to Romulus. But Bretorius also knew that the praetor would seek answers from him first, rather than admit to a junior officer in the fleet that she had lost control of someone. "What I have done is for the good of the Empire," he said.

"Don't tell me you want your old command back so bad that you—"

"You will hear me," Bretorius said, blithely interrupting a woman he had not dared to speak a word to in his entire service in the Romulan Senate. "At the Summit of Eight, I learned that Commander Yalok was a spy for the Federation."

"What?" Kamemor's features faded in and out. *"You can't be serious. Yalok is a twenty-year veteran and loyal! And even if he were a spy, this is a matter for the Tal Shiar! Not some fool—"*

"There could be no delay in bringing him to justice," Bretorius said. "Order demanded it."

"Order? Order demands that you return with him now!" The screen went blank for a moment, before the Praetor's image reappeared, still railing at him.

"That won't be possible, I'm afraid. There are things to do."

"Won't be—?" The normally dignified leader of the Romulan Star Empire looked ready to explode. *"I don't need this distraction right now. We've just suffered a mad act, an attack on our communications systems. By of all things, a* Ferengi—"

The transmission ended. Bretorius checked: it was indeed a failure of one of the connections upstream, between *D'varian* and Romulus. That was fine. The praetor had told him several things he needed to know.

He reached for the padd he had been working with and stepped out into the hall. Nerla was there, supervising the three workers Quarlis had sent down to turn the Ter'ak Pen's offices into something he could use. She looked back at him nervously—and followed him as he walked around the prison deck, checking the workers' modifications.

"So are you sacked?" she asked him, her voice dry. "Are you—are *we*—under arrest?"

"Clearly not. But I can understand your confusion."

"I'm asking about the praetor. Can you at least be serious?"

He smiled. "Very well. If that idiot Quarlis called for the staff meeting I asked for, you'll see how serious a man I can be . . ."

Eleven

> Captain's log. We have arrived at Epsilon Outpost 11,
> a communications array in the Beta Quadrant. Years
> ago, this facility was constructed as part of a chain of
> stations keeping watch on the Klingon Empire; now, it
> serves as the home for the Brightman-Laird Subspace
> Telescope, listening across vast reaches of space to
> find new civilizations, ready to begin an exchange . . .

Jean-Luc Picard deactivated the recording and sat
back in his desk chair, frustrated already with the
entry. It was difficult to make what *Enterprise* was
doing now sound interesting.

At the end of the tumult that followed the death of
Federation President Bacco, Picard had been assured
that the *Enterprise* would be spared any further role
in interstellar politics—returning to the mission it
was designed for: deep-space exploration. *Enterprise*
had indeed been dispatched toward an unexplored
region. But extended expeditions depended on a
long lifeline for support, and they had realized the
transceiver at Brightman-Laird wasn't properly cali-
brated. It wasn't near the place they were exploring,

but rather one end of a long chain. A very important end, as it happened.

So back again we go, Picard thought, standing up. He wondered how far Ferdinand Magellan would have gotten if he'd needed to return to Seville every time some little thing went wrong.

But at least the setback seemed temporary. Commander Geordi La Forge was across at the outpost, bringing the systems in line with what was needed. Soon, they would be off again, with little recollection of this side time. He'd let his wife, Beverly Crusher, know he was back, but there was no chance of visiting her this time. She was running the medical facilities at Deep Space 9, on the complete other side of the Federation. They had decided it was better for her not to say hello to René, their young son. It would be better to wait for a real reunion.

Picard left his quarters and made for the nearby turbolift. He knew he could count on La Forge not to drag out whatever needed to be done at the outpost. Voltaire was right: *Le mieux est l'ennemi du bien.* The best was the enemy of the good. They didn't need perfection, they simply needed to make sure the facility could help them communicate as they found their way across the—

A tremor shook *Enterprise.* Crimson lighting in the hallway activated, as well as the Red Alert siren. Keeping his footing, Picard slapped his communicator badge. "Bridge, Picard. What's going on, Number One?"

The Klingon first officer's voice was full of urgency. *"Captain, we are under attack!"*

"Attack? By whom?"

"The Romulans."

Picard goggled—but he didn't ask any more. "On

my way." Worf would be busy, taking the steps the captain knew he would to protect both *Enterprise* and the outpost. The turbolift doors opened and he rushed inside. "Bridge!"

The ride was fast, as always, but it felt interminable. All he could think was, "Here we go again." When would they escape this cycle of crisis after crisis? It wasn't just a selfish desire to get back out exploring. Didn't everyone deserve peace, at last?

The turbolift doors opened and he stepped onto the bridge. *Enterprise*'s command crew was in full battle mode. On-screen, he could see the vast, gray metal expanse of Outpost 11 and its communication arrays branching outward, part of it in flames. A Romulan *D'deridex*-class warbird soared past, launching photon torpedoes at it—even as its disruptors fired in *Enterprise*'s direction.

He hurried to the command well on the bridge, where Worf was giving out orders to counterattack. His eyes glistened with rage, but he controlled it. "Starboard shields to maximum. Put us between the Romulan and the outpost. Fire when ready."

Picard heard an assent from the tactical station—even as Worf recognized the captain's presence. "Status, Number One."

Worf quickly yielded the center chair, still clearly furious. "A sneak attack, sir. A single warbird decloaked, firing on the array."

"And the outpost?"

From behind, Lieutenant Aneta Šmrhová, the chief of security, reported, "Commander La Forge's team has left the conning tower for a more secure area. Sixteen staffers are aboard the station. Structural integrity of crew areas holding."

Worf looked sharply at Picard, as if trying to read his superior's mind. "Captain, we cannot beam out the staff while shields are up. The best way to buy them time is to engage the Romulan."

"Agreed." Picard saw the warbird growing larger on-screen as *Enterprise* raced the length of the array. "Let's get their attention."

WARBIRD *D'VARIAN*

On the warbird's bridge, Senator Bretorius watched with delight as another of Epsilon Outpost 11's long masts shattered to pieces under *D'varian*'s attack.

"Withdraw and begin another run," he said, pounding his fist on the top of the commander's chair.

"Do as he says," Subcommander Quarlis muttered, not looking back at him. Her eyes were focused on the destruction outside.

Nerla sat off to the left, hands clasped together, her gaze darting between the viewscreen and the senator. He could see the fear and worry in her face every time she looked at him; he could only let her see his confidence.

The vessel's crew had finally gotten him what he needed down in the Tal Shiar agent's office without complaint, but putting them on their present course had taken something more. He had met with the senior staff, delivering the message he had "received" from Praetor Kamemor—modified to support his order for a strike against Outpost 11.

And this was the right place for a strike. Outpost 11 was just across the Romulan Neutral Zone in a small wedge of Federation space along that body's once-fortified border with the Klingons. The Empire had seen a potential threat coming from this region for years. Quarlis had quickly commenced the attack at his command—after he had implied that Commander Yalok would be sure to do it in her stead, if she wavered.

Now, they were doing his bidding. Destroying—and exercising mercy. "No needless deaths, if possible. We want the survivors to remember this lesson."

Some members of the bridge crew naturally objected; all knew what kind of a provocation they were involved with. Starfleet would respond, whether lives were taken or not. But Bretorius had brought just enough of the right people to his side to give his commands credence. All Romulans operated in a realm where information was strictly compartmentalized; few knew the reasons behind every mission. Bretorius used that to his advantage. If he could talk a Tal Shiar agent into giving him his office, he could convince anyone of anything.

A barrage from behind struck *D'varian*'s shields, shaking all on the bridge. "We're being hailed by the commander of the Federation starship," came a voice from the side. "It's the *Enterprise*."

Bretorius took a breath at hearing the name—and then smiled. Everyone had heard of *Enterprise* and her captain. It would be interesting to take the human's measure. "Put Captain Picard on-screen."

A bald human in Starfleet uniform appeared. "*Commander, Romulan vessel: cease fire at once. This is an unarmed facility.*"

Subcommander Quarlis, already agitated at the sound of Picard's name, shuffled uncomfortably in her chair at the human's voice. But she played her part. "This outpost is not peaceful. It is directing signals into Romulan space, supporting your spies in the Empire!"

"Untrue," Picard said. *"Scan the array's output. The signals are bound for space far beyond your territory."*

Before anyone could check, Bretorius spoke up. "An amusing ploy, Captain. Of course, you could transmit such signals as a cover. When, in fact, this facility is meant to speak to your agents on Romulus. You seek to undermine and destroy!"

"That is not our way—"

"Oh, really?" Bretorius pointed out the Klingon first officer on the image before him—and the Cardassian crewman, visible at a station just behind Picard. "You have allied your so-called peaceful Federation with gangster states. You have taken their warriors onto your ships. You intend nothing less than to carve up our Empire. You will give the scraps to your allies, and you will claim the heart, Romulus, for yourselves. That I will not allow!"

Before Picard could respond, Bretorius ordered the communication cut.

He looked to the sides to see the officers—and Nerla—stirred by his words. "Intensify firing," he said. "Focus on the remaining intact segments of the outpost's array. Hit them with everything."

"What about *Enterprise*?" Quarlis asked, her voice quavering a little.

He looked forward and smiled. "I already know what they'll do."

ENTERPRISE

"Outpost is showing structural failure in several locations," announced Ravel Dygan at ops. The Cardassian male looked concerned.

Picard glared at the viewscreen, still puzzled and

irritated at being summarily dismissed by the Romulan who had spoken to him. He glanced at Worf. "Options?"

"The outpost is likely out of commission. We must protect the lives of those who remain."

Picard looked on the Klingon with admiration. He had come such a long way from the angry young man Picard had known years earlier. "Cease fire." The captain called back to the human woman at flight control. "Mister Faur, cancel pursuit. Full stop."

"Full stop, Captain."

"Minimize our profile facing the warbird. When we pass out of range, drop shields."

The process took less than thirty seconds. It was fortunate that only a skeleton away team had been aboard and that the station was mostly automated since the days of its construction more than a century before.

A call came up from the transporter room. *"We have the maintenance team, Captain."*

"Resume pursuit!"

It was too late. The warbird, having done its damage, sped away and faded from sight, its cloaking device activated.

Picard sat back in his seat and took a breath. The main superstructure of the array was intact, but multiple sections had calved off like metal icebergs in space, and sections still glowed intensely, fires clearly burning in the outpost's interior.

La Forge called up from the transporter room. *"We got everyone out, Captain."*

Picard nodded. "Are you all right, Mister La Forge?"

"I'm a little confused. What did we do to them?"

Picard stared at the wreck, bewildered. *What, indeed?*

Twelve

The fusion of symbionts with the bipedal natives of Trill resulted in beings with one mind and one will. But life with two cerebral nuclei with their own brainwave patterns was something one needed to prepare for—and Ezri's Joining with Dax had been unplanned, necessary to save the latter. In the days immediately after, her own doubts about "living up to Dax" had led to many a sleepless night.

She was having another one now, worrying over *Aventine*'s guest. Walking quickly through the halls with Kedair, she was dreading another meeting.

The black-haired Takaran tried to cheer the captain. "Admiral Riker will be fine. We did a great job at the Annunciator. It's all over."

"I'm not so sure it is." Dax had reason for her doubts. After-action reports normally took place in an observation lounge, where all concerned reported. But Admiral Riker had scheduled the post-Kinshaya action briefing for stellar cartography. That suggested to Dax that what lay ahead of them was more important than what they had just done.

Riker was already inside, standing amidst the stars of the galaxy. They were holographically projected around the catwalk and balcony he was on. Bowers stood beside him. The admiral was looking up and around, Dax saw, his face lit by stars and with fascination. Meanwhile, Bowers looked at the deck, as worried as she'd seen him.

"What's the story, Sam?" Dax asked.

He looked up. He hadn't slept much either. "I was just about to tell you about it when I ran into the admiral. It's about the admiral's report back to Starfleet."

Dax's heart jumped. "Did . . . they have a problem with it?"

"They never got it," Riker said, not looking back at them. "The subspace message never got through."

Bowers nodded. "From our location, there are three different subspace repeater stations we normally would relay messages through." He turned and pointed to some blinking images above his head. "Two of ours, and one run by a nonmember world in Federation space. They're all offline."

Kedair bristled as she looked up. "Even Outpost 11?"

"Nothing."

"There's only one rational explanation," Riker said, turning to face them.

Dax felt a headache coming on. This was the sick feeling that Bowers had already gotten. They'd failed, had been too late in disabling the Annunciator. "The Kinshaya have already used Takedown. That's why they weren't on their guard."

"That's not it." The admiral shook his head. "It's what I was afraid of. *Someone else* used Takedown."

"Who?"

"I think I know." Riker touched a control at the railing, and a nearby sector of space enlarged. "The Annunciator was one of two places we suspected might unleash Takedown. Admiral Akaar told me that a nearer vessel would deal with the other one, but now we have to assume that mission failed. There's no doubt that the other target was trickier." He turned and pointed. "The other transceiver is operated by the Breen."

The Breen? Dax's eyes focused on the location Riker was pointing to. There was no image of any station, just the golden twin-crescent symbol of the Breen Confederacy floating in air. The Breen were a multi-species coalition operating in the Alpha Quadrant—obfuscation was their stock in trade. Breen encased their bodies in armor and used vocal encoders to hide what race they belonged to; an egalitarian gesture that also meant no outsiders could see with whom they were dealing. The Breen had been on the other side in the Dominion War and were one of the charter members of the Typhon Pact. They were a strange and difficult people.

She wasn't expecting to find a Breen installation in this neck of the interstellar woods, however. "What's a Breen station doing in the Romulan Neutral Zone? They're a long way from home."

"That's the reason for it," Riker said. "It's a repeater station, capable of communicating across long distances with their Typhon Pact allies. That ought to be enough reason to blow it away."

Dax and her crewmates looked at each other, startled by his last statement. "Excuse me, Admiral," Bowers said. "*Blow it away?*"

Seemingly realizing that he'd put things too forcefully, Riker turned to face them and backtracked.

"If we were at war, I mean. But we have cause—and orders—to put it out of commission today. You were asking earlier how the Kinshaya got hold of the Takedown program. I can tell you now that it was the Breen that developed it for them."

Dax inhaled. It made sense. The Breen always spoke in their encrypted speech using their vocoders; they weren't much interested in communicating with anyone else the normal way. If they wanted to damage all outsiders—including their ostensible Typhon allies, who, Admiral Riker reported, had just met at the Summit of Eight without them—this would be a way to do it. "It's not too far from here."

"Four hours and seven minutes at warp nine point eight," Riker said.

Dax looked up at the display. Distance was calculated next to the station, but not travel time. She grinned. "You just did the math?"

"I've been thinking about this a lot." Riker passed her a padd. "We are now acting under contingency orders signed by Admiral Akaar. The other ship clearly failed. We have to take the Breen station offline."

Kedair's violet eyes were filled with puzzlement. "But the damage from Takedown has already started."

"As long as they can propagate it, we're charged with stopping them. We will disable the station and return to what I've labeled as Staging Area Three." He spoke in low, serious tones. "And we can make no mistake now. We can't just run silent. We have to run deaf—not even ancient radio sets. If Takedown is being transmitted by the Breen via subspace, *Aventine* is at risk—and anyone *Aventine* communicates with. Is that understood? This ship's electronic systems are the target. You have to shield it as if it's just another crewmember." He paused. "No, more important than any other crewmember."

Kedair nodded. "I've already been working with Lieutenant Leishman to harden our systems—and plug any leaks."

"*Aventine* will be an island unto itself," Dax assured him. But she shared Bowers's concern. "Has Starfleet thought through the ramifications, here? Nobody takes the Kinshaya seriously. But I know the Breen, Admiral. Attacking them like this could quickly spin out of control."

"It's already spinning," Riker said. "There's been a strike at our communications systems."

"But that's not attacking a manned station," Dax countered.

"Isn't it?" The Admiral looked directly into her eyes. "This kind of thing isn't new, Captain. Cutting telegraph lines was a common tactic in the nineteenth century on Earth. In those days it was the prelude to an attack—but now we understand it as an attack all on its own. It doesn't matter whether Breen fleets start moving on us the next day. It's begun. They don't have to kill our people to damage us."

Kedair nodded in agreement. "And if we attack, the political situation wouldn't necessarily metastasize. The Breen attacked *Titan* at Garadius, and it didn't spin out of control then."

Bowers was still troubled. "It's different when your house gets hit. We were lucky the Kinshaya outpost was so easy. These things have a way of going wrong. We could try as hard as possible to be surgical—and still accidentally kill Breen."

Riker raised his hands to end the debate. "People, caution is healthy—to a point. These are very big fleets operating out there, sometimes bumping each other and crashing. And if there's one thing I've learned from being on the diplomatic side, it's that not every incident is the start of something else. My experience tells me this operation is both necessary—and unlikely to snowball."

He gestured back to the holographic display. "I think this is simple. I think the Garadius incident caused the Breen to lose standing with the rest of the Typhon Pact. The Breen decided to let everyone have it, signing on junior partners in the Kinshaya. Maybe the Holy Order was supposed to be their patsy in this—I don't know. But the Summit of Eight was called by the Typhon Pact so we would take care of it." He deactivated the holographic display, the false night being replaced by warm lighting. "And take care of it, we will."

"Yes, sir," Dax quickly said. Under normal lighting, she could see dark circles under Riker's eyes. He seemed to have all the energy in the world, but even admirals were mere mortals. "Sir, have you gotten any sleep? Your orderly said you sent him away from the holodeck—I mean, from your office."

Riker walked past the officers toward the exit. "I can make my own bed, Captain. And if I need anything, the holodeck will provide."

"I'm sure, Admiral. I'm just concerned."

"Noted and appreciated." He looked back from the doorway. "Give the Breen your attention. I don't need it."

After seeing the doors close behind Riker, Bowers turned to Dax and Kedair and threw up his hands. "I don't know what you two thought, but that man was five steps ahead of us during that whole conversation."

"That's why he got the call," Kedair said.

Bowers shook his head, looking searchingly at Dax. "You think Starfleet is playing this right?"

Dax shrugged. "Above my pay grade, Sam. Let's get ready."

Thirteen

Picard had no problem walking around the fallen girders. For all the ordnance expended by the Romulan warbird—the ship had been identified as *D'varian*—astonishingly little damage had been done to the living area aboard Outpost 11. But almost all of the external systems were down, and EPS feedback had fried many of the computers.

Worf had joined him in his tour of the damage. The Klingon's mood had not improved since the Romulan warbird went to warp—and seeing the condition of the outpost's command center hadn't helped. "This area was barely touched. We should have given chase."

Picard nodded. He certainly would have liked to, but there was no way of knowing what sections of the station would be spared, and securing its personnel came first. That, and sending a warning to Starfleet— which they had done.

Or rather, they had *tried* to do it. La Forge was working on that problem.

The captain walked around the command center,

glancing both inside—and out, looking through the large ports toward the metal morass floating outside. "Number One, does anything about what the Romulans did strike you as odd?"

"Everything about the Romulans strikes me as odd."

"I mean the nature of the damage, here."

Worf looked around the command center. "They took pains to preserve the inhabited areas of the station. You think they intend to return and put it into operation for their own use?"

"It's a possibility," Picard said, although even as he said it, he couldn't imagine what value the place held in its current condition. "I don't think a dozen Geordis could get this place running within a year."

"And you only have one," La Forge said, eyes glistening slightly blue as he appeared in a darkened doorway. He didn't need a light with his synthetic ocular implants, but the repair workers behind him had them. "From the diagnostics we can still check from here, one of the inward-pointing arrays seems salvageable. But the Brightman-Laird equipment is done for."

Picard shook his head, disappointed. "It's complete madness. There wasn't a single offensive thing about the work this station was doing."

"'A mad Romulan' is redundant," Worf said.

"Let's hope they don't try to repeat this somewhere else." The captain looked to La Forge. "We still haven't received any confirmation of our alert."

La Forge shook his head. "No, sir." *Enterprise* hadn't been able to raise Command on any of the regular channels, although they had connected with a number of vessels that promised to relay the alert. It was a peculiar state of affairs and suggested that other stations just like Outpost 11 had been interdicted.

But that seemed impossible. "Could something be interfering with the functioning of the other stations?" Picard asked.

"Like a Romulan photon torpedo?" Worf asked, not joking.

"Let's hope not," the captain replied. "But I had more in mind something technical—like a cyber attack on the stations themselves."

La Forge thought for a moment. "It's possible, I suppose. The Federation has a lot of protections against that, but not all the stations are ones we built." The engineer found a working display console and pointed to locations on the starmap. "This region is already poorly served. This was always such a chancy place to build, being situated between us, the Klingons, and the Romulans. Apart from the defensive installations, like this one used to be, there's not much out here. And we know what happened to the starbases out here."

Picard well remembered. Starbases 157, 234, and 343 had been destroyed in the Borg Invasion. *Enterprise* had listened to the hopeless distress call from one of them.

Picard gestured to the hallway La Forge had emerged from. "You said one of the arrays might function. Is there any way to get us a direct link to Admiral Akaar? We're in a position to do something to stop the *D'varian*." He saw Worf's eyebrow rise approvingly at that sentence. "But we still require orders. We can't just send a message—we have to have feedback."

La Forge pointed to a small dot on the starmap. "If I can get the array working, I think I can bounce a signal off the Ferengi station."

"They have one out here?"

"Their merchant fleets were eating up local comm capability, so the Federation permitted them to build in our space."

"Industrious."

"I'll have to be, too, to make this work. I need to get some power back online out there."

"We'll hold the fort," Picard said, watching the engineer returning into the darkness.

Actually, the captain knew, there wasn't a reason to stay. They'd seen everything—and every moment his first officer remained only seemed to annoy the Klingon more.

"Speak your mind, Worf."

"I do not believe this was an isolated incident—and I don't think our communication problems are unrelated. There is a plan here, coordination." His eyes glinted. *"And that makes it Romulan."*

AVENTINE

The Dax symbiont had been in many different kinds of space combat before—including frequent raids while joined to Jadzia, aboard the *Defiant* during the Dominion War. Jadzia Dax had seen that many space battles were little more than three-dimensional chess games, a pastime starship captains favored for obvious reasons.

Yet Ezri Dax had never seen a game that had ended so soon after the first move—especially not when the competitors were so mismatched.

It was a rout. A rout, by a single ship, against three Breen battle cruisers. *Titan* had successfully fought off a single cruiser and three landing vehicles months earlier at Garadius IV, but that force had nothing like the firepower of the force *Aventine* had faced. And it had ended in less than ten minutes.

Nobody knew with a degree of certainty what the Breen called anything. The station had been known, in *Aventine*'s planning sessions, by the tactical nomenclature Breen Array Alpha, a term whose acronym had resulted in a number of sheep jokes. No one had expected the Breen to act that way when the wolf was in the fold, however, and they hadn't. The cruisers had been alerted to something; Dax had assumed it was the raid on the Kinshaya. Dax remembered wondering, on seeing the vessels guarding the station, how *Aventine* could ever execute its plan.

Then Riker had stepped in.

As with the attack on the Annunciator, Riker had positioned himself just off to the right of the command chairs on the bridge, standing without apparent fear of being toppled by any impact. He had been mostly silent, but on seeing the Breen defenders, he had spoken up. Dax and Bowers had divided their responsibilities on the mission so she could focus on attacking the array while Bowers coordinated *Aventine*'s defense against the Breen. Her first officer had yielded when he heard Admiral Riker begin to issue orders.

Riker had called the shots, directing which of *Aventine*'s defensive batteries fired at which Breen ship. At the same time, he had called out to Dax angles of approach that would best suit both the ship's defense and her own task. Freed of the need to dictate navigation, Dax was fully able to act as bombardier, directing photon torpedoes against the station's dark metal spars festooned with sending and receiving apparatus.

Left with nothing to do, Bowers had sat, dazzled. She knew he regarded Riker as one of the best officers

ever to sit second chair. Now he had a literal ringside
seat. Kedair had offered, with the most polite irritation
in her voice, to step aside and let Riker take the tactical
station—but he had simply held his position, calmly
calling out one instruction after another.

It was the sort of thing every captain feared admirals would do on their bridges; the sort of thing Dax
imagined that Riker himself would have been annoyed
by. Yet it was hard for anyone to get too upset when
the man was constantly right in his calls. *Aventine*
had screamed away from the Breen array without a
scratch—and left behind a disabled station and three
cruisers with neatly severed warp nacelles.

And then Riker had simply nodded, offered his
thanks to the crew, and walked off the bridge into the
turbolift. Dax knew she wasn't alone in wondering for
a moment whether applause was appropriate.

Now, in her quarters for what they were calling late
supper, Dax sat with Bowers and Kedair, marveling
over it all again.

"That was the most amazing display I've ever seen,"
Bowers said. "Riker was computing angles of attack
in his head—without a computer, just the viewscreen.
That was all dead reckoning." He shook his head as he
stirred his stew. "Astounding."

"I'll tell you what's astounding," Kedair said, pushing away an empty bowl. "They've put together the
battle damage assessment. I don't think the Breen suffered a single casualty. Not on the station, not on the
ships. Captain, every shot he called, every torpedo you
placed, was targeted perfectly to disable."

"I was only able to do my part because you all kept the
Breen from shooting at us." Dax raised her mug in a toast.
"That's the way to run hostilities. Nobody gets hurt."

Bowers didn't lift his glass. Staring into his bowl, he stirred it idly. "We're still running silent?"

"Until further orders." Dax studied him. "What's up, Sam?"

"I tell you, I'm torn. Riker is magical—but I live by the book. And we are off into some things that aren't even in the appendices."

Kedair nodded. "I wasn't going to say anything, but yeah, this is new territory. We're turning into a one-ship wrecking crew. And all while we can't call home. I know it needs to be done—but it's definitely different."

Dax took a deep breath. She'd had the same reservations—but there simply hadn't been time to voice them. There had been too much to do, too few moments to reflect. She studied Bowers. "Sam, what are you worried about? Really?"

Aventine's first officer looked around—a needless act in Dax's quarters—before pushing aside his unfinished bowl and leaning across the table. "I'm worried," he said in low tones, "about being in a Maxwell incident."

"Oh," Dax said, nodding with understanding. Starfleet officers didn't talk much about Benjamin Maxwell, the battle-damaged captain aboard *Phoenix* who had tried to start a war with the Cardassians. Some instructors at Starfleet Academy might tell the story as a cautionary tale, but others avoided it. Either they felt the stain on the service it represented was too great, or they feared giving new recruits any ideas. Whatever it was, the name Maxwell was never invoked lightly.

"Look, you know I think Riker is a fine officer," he said. "You remember the day I met him—there on

Enterprise during the Borg Invasion, when he'd been forced to leave his away team, including his wife and Commander Vale, behind. And he was going ahead with everything, doing his duty. I admire the hell out of that. And what we've been doing doesn't fit the pattern of someone spreading wanton destruction around."

"It sure doesn't," Kedair said, a little offended. "We wouldn't have done it otherwise."

"Precisely," Bowers said. "We've been given the exact information we need to get us to go along with this."

"Then what's the problem?" Kedair asked.

Dax caught his drift. "Exactly that. We've been given the exact information we need to get us to go along with this—and that's the problem. You're worried that Riker is playing us, Sam? Sending us off on something unauthorized?"

Bowers blinked, his face fraught with guilt over having even suggested the notion. "Don't listen to me. I'm just tired."

"No, let's just think it through," Dax said. After the business with Federation President Ishan, a little paranoia was occasionally helpful. "We know the orders were good. Akaar's imprint was on the documents I read. And I can't imagine how he'd know about the Breen array without some input from Starfleet Intelligence. That thing wasn't on any chart we've ever seen."

"I know." Bowers pushed his chair away from the table and sat back in it, hand covering his chin as he thought. "Is it odd that the second staging area we went to—the one we retreated to after the raid into Kinshaya space—was ideally positioned as a jumping-off point for going after the Breen?"

"No. Admiral Riker knew the Breen might be next. That's just good planning."

"Good planning, yeah." He looked to Kedair. "Where'd he take us to? Where are we now?"

The Takaran looked out the ports at the motionless stars. "Just outside the Romulan Neutral Zone, in Federation space. Nearest thing's a Ferengi commercial station, a million kilometers away. It's light years to anything remotely hostile."

"Not exactly poised on the enemy's doorstep," Dax said. "Admiral Riker was given a covert mission, and he's handled it like any of us would." *Better*, she thought. She started to rise. "What this crew needs is some rest. We're fighting this thing we can't see, this Takedown—and we're jumping at shadows."

Bowers nodded. "I think that's the problem. The enemy has no face. I never like that."

Dax was gathering her dishes when her combadge chirruped. "Dax."

"Captain, we have a problem," Riker said. *"Meet me in the observation lounge with your senior officers."*

"Understood." Dax gave the others a tired look. "I'm thinking of throwing this damn combadge away."

Fourteen

*T*akedown, Dax now thought, could well refer to a Typhon Pact plan to cause *Aventine*'s senior officers to collapse from exhaustion.

Sitting at the table in the observation lounge, she could already tell what her officers were thinking. *We've been here before.* Another secret mission from the admiral, another raid that had to be thrown together while they were under way. Which unlucky Typhon power would the spinning *dabo* wheel stop on this time? The Romulans? The Gorn?

The truth was something else.

"You want us to attack a Ferengi comm station?" Dax asked, flummoxed. "The Ferengi are signatories of the Khitomer Accords."

"Yes," Riker said. He pointed out the port to the cylindrical station, which somewhat recalled Ferengi ears with its two enormous transceiver arrays suspended on exterior vanes. Riker had asked Dax to move *Aventine* within visual distance of Ferengi Station 71 before the meeting.

But she didn't know he had intended this. "They're

allies, Admiral. It's why we allowed them to build this station in Federation space. It's why they haven't reacted to our approach." That wasn't entirely true, she knew; readings showed that the Ferengi who were staffing the station had been hailing them for some time. But *Aventine* only knew of the attempt to communicate, studiously avoiding receiving anything passively, per orders. And now her orders were to disable this station, too. "What's the rationale?"

Riker looked tired of explaining—and tired in general. "I don't know if we were too late with the Breen or the Kinshaya, or if Takedown was separately introduced to the Ferengi station's systems. But it has been infected—and I have just been ordered to cut the place off before more damage is done."

Bowers looked baffled. "How did they tell you? We've broken all contact with Command. Even your secure link."

"I've received a coded message from Starfleet Intelligence. That's all I can say."

Dax and Bowers looked at each other. *Did admirals have some secret communications system they all used?*

Mikaela Leishman seemed unconvinced. "Begging the admiral's pardon—but I don't see how that's possible. We've plugged up every system that could transmit or receive. How did you talk to Starfleet, sir?"

Steely eyes fixed on the engineer. "You don't need to know," Riker said, sternly.

Dax was bewildered. "No, sir, we do. Admiral, if you've got some kind of backchannel method you think is secure against Takedown, we've got some questions we need answered."

He shook his head. "Because of the dire circumstances, SI had to contact me. Top-secret protocol. We have our orders. This is wasting time."

Dax and Bowers looked at each other. She read her first officer's mood—and it matched hers. "Sir, I'm not going to just open fire. We're here. They're friendly. We could send over a team to—"

"That's absolutely the wrong thing. Just contacting them—whether it's by subspace or any part of the EM spectrum—puts *Aventine*'s systems at risk."

"Then we fly a shuttle over and knock on the airlock door," Bowers said. "Weren't the Ferengi among the powers invited to the summit you were at? Aren't they already aware of Takedown?"

"There's a difference between being aware of it and grasping the seriousness of the threat," Riker said. "The Federation's experts were able to quickly confirm that the program was what we were told it was. I'm not as confident in the ability of the scientists on Ferenginar to do the same study as fast as we did." He flexed his fingers. "And then I'm sure Starfleet Command wouldn't want to spread the word that Takedown worked. I've told you how dangerous the knowledge of its mere existence is."

Dax was thoroughly confused. "But if the Ferengi already know about it, we wouldn't be compromising anything by talking to them about it. Would we?"

Now other voices spoke up—and over each other. Riker slapped his hand on the table, bringing an immediate stop to it. "Further discussion is not helpful. Communication disruption and hijacking—those tactics were once preparatory to invasion. Now they *are* the invasion. Time is short. We can't control this forest fire without setting some burn zones of our own."

But they're not our zones to burn. Dax felt the room closing in. The table went silent, as all eyes went from the admiral to the captain. There was only one way out, she knew. She looked out the port to the Ferengi station, swallowed hard, and said what she had to say.

"Admiral, I deem that *Aventine* is out of contact with Starfleet Command in a circumstance in which she cannot act without clarified instructions. We—"

"You *have* those instructions, Captain. I got them—"

"—we will not execute this one order, judging it to be a violation of Article I of the Khitomer Accords. I deem our duty to keep to the article's terms supersedes the admiral's authority." Her heart thumping, she looked at him. "With apologies, sir."

Riker said nothing, dark eyebrows turned downward as he stared at her.

Well, there goes another career, Dax. Maybe next life.

Finally, he nodded. "It's your ship. May I ask what you plan to do?"

She took a deep breath and straightened in her chair. "We're going to make for Starbase 23, continuing to operate under silent running. Once there, if their systems are secured against Takedown, I'll consult with Admiral Akaar directly." She looked at her officers. The confusion in their faces from earlier was gone, replaced by resolve. "I'm sorry, Admiral, this concerns the safety of the Federation and our allies, I have to get guidance on this."

"That's it, then." He looked down at his padd— and Dax again noticed how physically drained Riker seemed. "You know, Ezri, I'm out on the same limb with the rest of you. You're asking me to violate *my* orders—and potentially allow the Ferengi station to continue infecting other systems."

Then we go over and get them to turn their array off,

she wanted to say. But that battle had been fought. Instead, she looked down at the table. "I understand your situation, Admiral. Do what you feel is right, as far as disciplinary measures. But I can't attack an ally, even to protect them from something. We've been lucky with our first two engagements that nobody got hurt."

"Was it luck, or skill?" Riker asked, rising.

"You can't always count on either working when you need them," she said.

He walked to the door. "I'm going to my office. I'll be in touch."

The door shut behind him. A gloom hung over the room, and for more than a minute, nobody said anything.

"Well, here we are again," Bowers said in low tones, almost as if he were worried the admiral could hear through the wall. "And once more, our last position was exactly where we needed to be for where we had to go next."

"I know." Dax didn't need more convincing. "Doctor Tarses?"

Simon Tarses had been sitting at the end of the table, not taking part in the briefing. If Riker had noticed the ship's chief medical officer in attendance, he had said nothing. But Dax wanted to know what Tarses thought, and he was senior staff.

"The admiral shows outward signs of physical exhaustion," the doctor said. One quarter Romulan, the slender man templed his fingers before his chin as he spoke. "He doesn't look as though he's eaten in a while, and he's taken no food from the replicators. But I sense a mind that is sharp. Extremely sharp, despite the circumstances and pressure."

Dax looked to Hyatt, the counselor. "I concur," Hyatt said. "He's perfectly rational, as far as I can tell—and he seems to believe he's doing the right thing."

"That's the problem." Bowers, who had been staring numbly at the table, looked up. "They always think they're doing the right thing."

Her engineer had always been skeptical of Takedown—and Dax found Leishman solidly in the "something's wrong" camp. "With our hands over our ears, we can only tell what the Ferengi station's doing by looking at the secondary evidence. Energy output signatures, and so on. I don't see a single thing showing that there's *any* abnormal activity over there."

Dax believed her. But it was important to press the matter. "Is there any way the admiral could see something that you can't? Could he have some resource that we don't?"

Leishman thought for a moment. "I've gotten reports that he's been requisitioning equipment from engineering since he boarded. Small pieces, a really odd list."

"And nobody asked why?"

"He's an admiral. None of it could be used to build a handheld Takedown detector, if that's what you mean. Or any secret method for calling Starfleet Command. I don't know what he's basing his claims about the Ferengi station on, but it's not data."

Quiet fell over the room. Kedair looked to the captain. "What do we do?"

"I said what we would do."

"I mean," the security chief said, "about Riker."

Everyone at the table tensed when the Takaran asked that, but Dax waved it off. "There's nothing *to* do. As long as he doesn't try to take command, he can stay in his holo-office as long as he—"

She froze. "What is it?" Kedair asked.

Dax's eyes locked on the Ferengi station outside the port. It and the shuttle docked with it appeared to drift across her field of view. She knew something else was happening. "We're moving."

Bowers nodded. "We're at impulse."

"Bridge," Dax demanded, "why are we moving?"

"Captain," Lieutenant Tharp sounded alarmed. *"I was about to contact you!"*

"Why are we moving?"

"My sensors say we're not. But we're moving. I can't explain it—and we can't shut the engines down."

Everyone at the table stood at once. Kedair's eyes widened. "It's Takedown. *Aventine* is infected!"

Fifteen

"I have it, Captain," La Forge reported as he stood in the doorway of *Enterprise*'s ready room, looking out onto the bridge. The incredibly talented engineer had passed up on advancement so he could continue to serve under and learn from Picard. And he'd just spent hours working with his staff to set up the most basic of things: a simple person-to-person communication.

Hours of painstaking work had been required to coax Outpost 11's lone salvageable long-range transceiver into service. La Forge gestured behind him to the computer on the ready room desk. "I don't know how long the connection will last, but I've got Starfleet Command."

Picard stood from his command chair and gestured for Worf to follow him. Then he saw Dygan at ops. "Please join us," he said. "You were on duty during the battle. Your observations would be helpful."

The Cardassian looked a little surprised to be invited. "Aye, Captain."

Picard knew Dygan had recently gone through a rough patch on a difficult covert assignment.

The young Cardassian's skills had helped resolve a matter of the highest importance, but Picard well knew that undercover work could take a toll. It was important to help officers adjust to regular duties. He led the two into the ready room and took a seat at his desk.

"This might be the most complicated connection I've ever had to route," La Forge said as the others stood opposite their captain. "I heard from a Ferengi station that a lot of their links upstream to the Ferengi Alliance and Sector 001 aren't functioning." The engineer finished adjusting the computer on the desk. "I could only give you basic encryption. I think we may even be bouncing off an Orion casino or two."

"Well done, Geordi," Picard said. "Send our action report again."

After a moment, La Forge indicated it had been sent.

The screen crackled, and the imposing form of Admiral Leonard James Akaar appeared. The grim-looking Capellan brightened marginally when he recognized who he was looking at. *"Ah, Picard. They finally got you."*

"They actually missed," Picard said, "but they weren't shooting at us."

"Missed? Picard, we've been trying to reach you since Outpost 11 went offline."

Picard looked dour. "The station has been disabled, but there were no casualties. I've just sent you my report."

Akaar appeared flustered. *"The accounts are coming in from everywhere, Jean-Luc. Starfleet communications have been hit in surprise raids conducted by multiple parties."*

"It is war," Worf said.

"Not yet," Akaar cautioned. *"We're getting nothing but denials and confusion from the other powers—on the backchannels that still work. There's been no declaration of intent or claim of responsibility from anyone."*

"There's no doubt about responsibility here, Admiral," Picard said. "The attacker was definitely Romulan."

The news seemed to sadden Akaar, but not surprise him. *"Who was it?"*

Picard nodded to Worf, who spoke up. *"D'varian,* a *D'deridex*-class—under command of a Senator Bretorius."

"I've never heard of him," Akaar said. *"There have been confirmed sneak attacks by Gorn and Tzenkethi vessels, which would seem to support the notion of a Typhon Pact action. Our Khitomer Accord allies report similar provocations, coming additionally from Romulan and Tholian attackers."*

"The targets?"

Akaar looked down, clearly skimming over a series of reports. *"All communications systems, so far as we can tell. It's what's made it so damned hard to get confirmation."* Akaar looked up, gravely. *"We have an unconfirmed report that one of our arrays was attacked by the* Cardassians.*"*

Dygan, an officer holding the rank of glinn in the Cardassian military, looked up in surprise. Catching the captain's eye, he said, "Sir, that is simply not possible."

Akaar continued his litany of madness. *"And Starfleet Intelligence tells me that a Cardassian station was targeted by the Klingons."*

Worf shook his head in disbelief.

Akaar's eyes narrowed as he leaned in. *"And don't even ask me to make sense of what's coming in from our diplomatic channels. It borders on mass hysteria."*

Picard looked around the room, astonished—and saw the same reflected in the faces of the other listeners. "It sounds as if galactic order is in a state of . . ." He grasped for a term. *"Meltdown* is the only word."

"Meltdown . . ." Akaar rubbed his forehead. *"However, the governments involved haven't responded the way they would if this were an intentional move to war. I believe they are all in the same situation as the Federation."*

They could be overwhelmed, too, Picard thought. The very systems tasked with sharing information were under attack. Still, he couldn't imagine that nothing else was known. "How many vessels from each power are involved in the attacks?"

"Unknown."

"Sir," Worf asked, "have we captured anyone?"

"No," Akaar said. *"However, all of the attacks are carried out with precision and guile."*

"As with Epsilon 11," Picard said.

Akaar cleared his throat. *"SI proposed that this is a cabal of rogue officers who are acting without orders and with the assistance of loyal crews."*

Picard nodded. "With all the politicking that goes on in the Romulan fleet, I agree. Romulan diplomats would be reluctant to acknowledge if that was the case."

"One moment, Enterprise." Akaar turned to someone off-screen.

"That explains the Romulans," Dygan said. "What about everyone else?"

"Forces from opposing sides have acted in collusion before," Worf replied. They all knew about the events in the run-up to the signing of the Khitomer Accords of 2285. A cabal—including Klingons, Romulans, and some Starfleet officers—had attempted to prevent the signing of the treaty between the Federation and the Klingon Empire. "It is a dishonorable way to achieve a goal."

Picard clasped his hands together and considered personalities and motives. *What could possibly be the goal of those involved?*

As he wondered, the image of Akaar flickered. La Forge quickly attempted to make adjustments. "We're losing the signal," the engineer said.

Akaar reactivated the audio. *"We're sending you the locations that have been targeted and what we have on Bretorius."*

Picard looked to Dygan while Akaar was once more called away. "Would you coordinate our investigation?"

Dygan blinked. "Certainly, sir, but Lieutenant Šmrhová is security chief—"

"She will be one of many involved. But this mystery touches on several different spheres. I'd like a non-Federation perspective."

Dygan nodded. "I'll do my best, sir."

Picard was pleased with the young man's response.

Akaar seemed to freeze for a moment, and Picard wondered if the connection had failed. But then he realized the Capellan was receiving new information from someone they couldn't see.

"Enterprise, there is more," Akaar said in low, even

tones. *"I have just been informed that a Ferengi station in your sector is currently under attack."*

Picard asked, "By the *D'varian*?"

"I wish it were." For a few long moments, it appeared that Akaar didn't know what to say. *"The* Aventine *has gone rogue. And Admiral Riker is aboard."*

Sixteen

"**W**hat the hell just happened here?" Dax wanted to know as she stared at the main viewscreen. The scraps of what had once been the Ferengi station floated in deep space before *Aventine*, even as the shuttle that had been attached to it jumped to warp.

"I did nothing," Flight Controller Tharp said. "I swear, Captain, *Aventine* did not move on the station, and we *definitely* did not fire!"

"We definitely *did*," Dax said, trying to remain calm. She had felt *Aventine* shudder slightly as she and the others stepped onto the bridge. She'd watched in horror as a photon torpedo was fired at a transceiver panel, which sheared off its vane. She had just ordered *Aventine*'s bridge controls locked out on her personal voice command when another photon torpedo rocketed from *Aventine*. No portion of the target was spared this time: the gleaming missile struck Ferengi Station 71 dead center, blowing it to bits.

It was the assassination of Klingon Chancellor Gorkon all over again—and she and *Aventine* were in the unenviable roles of Kirk and *Enterprise*. Alive during that scandal, Dax remembered the horrifying news stories. She knew there were no secret conspirators hiding among her crew, harboring a grudge against the Ferengi. *What the hell is going on?*

Helkara spoke from the science station. "Everyone got out on the shuttle." The Zakdorn scratched his fleshy cheek-wattles as he studied his display. "But one thing doesn't make sense."

"Just one thing?" Bowers asked.

"Someone on *Aventine* checked to see if all of the Ferengi had evacuated."

Leishman, nearly out of breath from her constant conversation with her engineering team belowdecks, hustled to Helkara's side. "You didn't run that check?"

"No one did." He pointed at the science station.

Dax looked around the bridge. At the tactical station, Kedair shrugged. She had already found the same thing—and her security forces aboard *Aventine* had reported seeing nothing unusual anywhere. Bowers, as unwilling to take a seat as Dax was, gave her a plaintive expression that said what she was thinking. *What now?*

Dax knew that Admiral Riker had been listening in remotely from his makeshift office since the first weapon was launched. He'd said nothing, letting them work the problem. *Aventine* should be heading to Starbase 23; instead they had destroyed an ally's station. Dax wondered if Command would believe her—or if her passenger could help in any way. Their last conversation had ended so badly, but there wasn't much choice. He was the superior officer on board. Bowers leaned in and whispered, "We have to ask."

She knew. "Bridge to Admiral Riker."

"Riker."

"Have you ever seen a starship act on its own, Admiral?"

"Not without an explanation. You and I know what that explanation is, Captain."

Dax held up a hand to forestall Leishman, who was certain that there was no hostile programming inhabiting any of *Aventine*'s systems.

"Chief?" Dax asked.

"There were seven separate commands," said the engineer, checking the station Helkara had vacated. "We went to impulse and executed an aspect change. A targeting resolution and one torpedo fired. Then a life-sign check of the shuttle, another resolution, and another torpedo. Seven commands, not ordered from any bridge station, nor anywhere else, that my people have been able to find." She stepped into the command well. "Frankly, I would start looking for other explanations."

"What's left?" Dax asked. "Nanites? The paranormal?"

"May I?" Riker asked over the intercom, sounding polite.

Dax looked to the ceiling. "Certainly, Admiral."

"I think the only thing to do is to find the nearest Corps of Engineers ship and rendezvous with them. Have them find out what's wrong with Aventine.*"*

Leishman gave a start. "Admiral, our team knows this ship better than anyone."

"There could be . . . other benefits to having another ship around."

He means a ship to evacuate to, Dax thought. The very idea gnawed at her gut. But it might be necessary. "Admiral, is it safe to get near another vessel, if our systems are infected?"

"Captain, you decide what procedure you think is

best. If you want to power down completely and lifeboat across, that's acceptable."

Dax looked at her first officer, who like her, had noticed the resignation in Riker's voice. "Admiral," she said, "what you're proposing would end our mission."

"It would." He sounded defeated. *"This sequence of events has gotten out of hand. If we are infected, as I think we may be, then we need to be out of the game."* He paused. *"Aventine is your ship, Captain Dax. You decide what's best for her and your crew."*

"Where's the nearest S.C.E. vessel?"

They heard a weary chuckle from the speakers. *"I'm in a holodeck, dressing for bed. I'm actually going to get some sleep."*

The communication ended.

Dax felt as though a weight had been lifted. No captain liked to go toe-to-toe with a superior officer—and certainly not a respected admiral. "Okay, let's do this." She looked back to Mirren at ops. "We've been out of touch for a while. Any S.C.E. vessels stationed near where we are now?"

She looked. "*Laplace* at the Corvus Beacon. If they're still there."

"They are," Leishman said, her arms crossed. She was still steaming from the twin ideas that something was wrong with *Aventine* and that her people couldn't fix it. "*Laplace* is on a long-term refit of the beacon. Captain, do you really think we need to go there?"

Bowers shook his head. "I'm not sure we should."

Dax looked to him. "Sam?"

Looking around the bridge, he leaned in closer to her. Speaking softly, he struggled to put his reservations into words. "The thing Admiral Riker was trying to get us to do, against our will, happened. He just shrugs and goes to sleep." He shook his head. "This isn't right."

"What are you saying, Sam?" she asked, matching his tone. "Are you saying you believe that he took control of our propulsion and weapons systems?"

"He didn't seem at all alarmed by the fact that we just lost control of *Aventine*. And he's not unhappy with the results. The Corvus Beacon is another communications installation. Do we really want to go there?"

"It's a deep-space listening post. It's not part of the wider comm network—and it's down." Dax pointed out, "If Takedown *does* exist, it's not going to do a hell of a lot to it."

"Great," Bowers grumbled. "Something the admiral *doesn't* want to blow up."

"Sam!" Dax whispered.

He put his hands before him apologetically.

This was more than they could handle, Dax realized. Whether or not rogue code had invaded her vessel, paranoia certainly had. There was only one thing to do.

"The Corvus Beacon, Warp Factor 8."

Seventeen

Aventine had attacked a Ferengi outpost. It had taken every bit of strength Picard possessed not to rush across the light-years to the Ferengi station to get answers the second Akaar had announced the news. But *Enterprise* could not risk its tenuous link with Starfleet Command—not getting every last bit of vital data Akaar was sending.

Just moments after *Enterprise* received the data, the screen had gone black. Picard was left wondering if another vital station had been destroyed. The last scan the Ferengi station sent—relayed to Starfleet Head-quarters—was an image of the ship that was about to destroy it. Racing for their lives, the Ferengi aboard the shuttle had retained the presence of mind to turn their sensors on the attacker.

Picard had seen a *Vesta*-class ship, clearly visible through the debris of a photon torpedo strike on the station. Only half of the vessel's hull lights were on, but the "NCC-82602" was unmistakable. It had been confirmed by further visual analysis that it was *Aventine*.

The Ferengi's frantic last communication had revealed that all had escaped the station and that *Aventine* was making no move to pursue. When a quick check confirmed that the Ferengi station had a warp-capable shuttle, Picard decided against a rescue mission. There wasn't any sense in appearing someplace one of the attackers had already visited, and there was no suggestion in Akaar's report that other ambushing vessels had stuck around their targets. Picard also already knew from their time at Outpost 11 that no invasion force had come to take possession of the place. A target, once struck, was left behind.

Enterprise's play had to be appearing at a station before it was attacked. And that meant analyzing the events of the last few days in detail, poring over the data Akaar had provided.

Picard and his officers had gotten to it immediately. Worf and La Forge were among Riker's closest friends. Worf had been married to Jadzia Dax. The proud Cardassian, Ravel Dygan, still stung from the suggestion that his people had attacked the Federation without provocation. It simply wasn't possible that Riker and *Aventine*'s crew could be part of some wide-ranging cabal of rogue officers.

They had to catch someone in the act.

Whether it was Will Riker or not.

Stellar cartography was too restrictive for the analysis: they were interested in where attacks had taken place, and Picard knew they also needed to look for other patterns, such as who had attacked what and in what order. As instructed, Dygan took the lead sifting through the information, putting his unique perspective of covert intelligence operations to work. He had established an investigation center on holodeck three, where several of *Enterprise*'s security, intelligence, and communication experts studied every minute detail in Akaar's report. Dygan attacked the job with vigor: Picard knew the exchange officer had been struggling trying to live with his actions on an earlier assignment, and nothing communicated the Federation's friendship with Cardassia like putting one of their own in charge of *Enterprise*'s investigation.

Picard felt as if he had looked at all possibilities after an hour in Dygan's "evidence room." Less than eight hours had elapsed since the jarring news, and holodeck three buzzed with activity. The room was divided into specialized areas. One was devoted to the attacking ships that had been identified. Only *D'varian*, *Aventine*, and the *G.C.S. Glavakh*, a Gorn *MA12*-class cruiser, had been visually confirmed as being involved in attacks. Another focused on the information available on the other assailants involved. Officers labored in each of the areas, trying to narrow down who else might be involved.

Picard stopped by the team focused on the Romulan warbird. Senator Bretorius of *D'varian* had once been the captain of that vessel: according to Starfleet Intelligence, he had served with no distinction other than his rank. His senate career appeared to have gone the same way. They had no idea why he was aboard *D'varian*, or why he would be in command of a warbird. But then, they didn't know why Riker would be aboard *Aventine*, either. He'd reportedly transferred off *Titan*, now out of reach at the Genovous Pulsar, after some Federation assignment Akaar was reluctant to discuss over their secure channel. There hadn't been time to learn more about it before the connection had failed.

Less was known about Vekt, identified as the female Gorn who commanded the *Glavakh*. She had distinguished herself enough that Starfleet had at least heard of her, but nothing they knew was fresher than a decade old. *Not the best and the brightest,* Picard thought.

Dygan knew he was risking backlash by setting up research nodes into Will Riker and Ezri Dax, but it had to be done. Riker was one of Starfleet's shining stars, though his career was not without blots. Dax had found herself in command of a starship, much like Picard, elevated by a battlefield promotion. The captain knew from experience she could be bullheaded and willing to break the rules to do what she thought was right. She had been removed from command, though she had later been fully exonerated. However, Dax had had many hosts, some of whom had lived shadier lives. The Dax section of the evidence room was larger than Riker's; Picard was glad that Worf, who had been married to Jadzia and remained friends with Ezri, had thus far avoided that section.

Picard rubbed his face in exhaustion and cast his eyes again across one of the several table displays that had been holographically prepared to help cross-reference information. So much information. It seemed to swim before his eyes. But Riker might be in trouble—and so might everyone else. They had to go on.

"It doesn't make sense," Picard said as Dygan joined him at the display. "It's hard to draw a line from one event to another, saying this attack provoked that one. They seem to have started at the same time."

The Cardassian nodded. "But at least for now, it's only the initiators causing the incidents. That won't be the case for long. There will be counterattacks."

Perhaps that was the plan, Picard thought.

He heard Worf, calling out from the section he'd been working on with La Forge. "Captain, a moment."

Picard and Dygan walked to the other side of a display table where La Forge stared intently at a holographic projection showing the locations of attacked stations.

"We have been looking at the positions of the targets," Worf said, "but maybe it's better to focus on the nature of the targets. What do they all have in common?"

"They are all subspace communications facilities," Dygan said. "Listening posts, comm boosters, and early warning sensors. I believe the intention is to leave the affected powers deaf and blind to future attacks."

Picard nodded. "And to sow confusion." The captain looked at the engineer. "What is it, Mr. La Forge?" He knew when Geordi had an idea he was working on.

La Forge frowned. "Captain, some of the targets are only connected tangentially with communications. They're not logistical. They're purely scientific in purpose. They're pointed *outward*."

"But they *could* be used for logistical purposes. Brightman-Laird was going to assist us. Disabling it certainly harmed our mission," Picard said.

The engineer countered, "That's just it, Captain. Since we were going to be the first to explore the region Brightman-Laird was focused on, nobody should have known the array *had* a role in helping us."

Worf's eyes narrowed. "Riker would have known."

"Yes—but that's not what I was going for," La Forge explained. "It means that whoever is doing this isn't discriminating between different kinds of communications systems. They're going after all of them—including ones where the communicating is all one-way."

Dygan scratched his chin. "It isn't a selective strike at the senses."

"I think I see what you're getting at, Mister La Forge." Picard studied the projection. "Computer, add an overlay to this map depicting all deep-space listening posts of a scientific nature."

A beep followed, and an instant later several holographic stations appeared, glowing golden.

"What is the largest intact one in the region closest to where *Aventine* was last reported?"

Another beep—and they saw it, shining brighter than the other virtual stations.

"That's it," Picard said, turning. "We're going there. Number One, with me."

"Aye, Captain," Worf said, brightening.

Picard walked livelier, too. He didn't know whom, if anyone, they would encounter—but having a destination felt marvelous.

Eighteen

"It's the end of—of whatever this is," Nerla said in the Tal Shiar agent's former office. She had lost her once-radiant glow, having nearly surrendered to nervous exhaustion—and to the flask in her hand, which she'd found in the agent's desk. She'd taken to carrying it around. "They're not going to go any further with you, Bret. Subcommander Quarlis is terrified."

"So what else is new?" asked Bretorius as he checked the crystal-clear cables running from the back of the computer. They snaked underneath Nerla's chair and out the door.

She took a drink of whatever was in the container. "It was one thing when you ordered them to take out the Federation and Klingon spy stations. They were sure you were acting on secret orders you'd received from Romulus. And they were all—" She corrected herself. "And *we* were all amazed at the tactics you prescribed against the Klingons. If you'd been that kind of leader as a captain, you'd have gone further."

"Continue."

She stared at the flask. "Once the communications

links back home started dropping out, Quarlis started to balk. Her senior staff—they're all on edge. And your new orders to strike a Gorn array aren't going anywhere. They doubt your authority. And maybe your sanity."

Romulans. Bretorius sighed. Aboard a Federation or Klingon starship, a leader might get his way—crushing doubts with persuasion and violence, respectively. Not the case in the Imperial Fleet, where suspicion was part of the normal diet. "You have explained to them that I have information the Gorn are about to betray us all? That their station in the Neutral Zone will be used to coordinate an attack on us by the Khitomer allies?"

"I've explained it. They're going home—and the praetor is going to purge us both." She took another healthy swig and wiped her face. "Will they just kill us, or will we go to a labor camp?"

"Neither," Bretorius said, finishing his work and rising. "Come."

Reluctantly, Nerla pulled herself out of her seat and followed him. In the hallway, he grabbed her arm to prevent her from tripping over the cabling, which stretched off into the cellblock. Between that and the replicators, he had all he needed to control his own destiny. "Are you ready for me to play my trump?"

"Your what?"

"It relates to an ancient Earth game of skill and chance."

She leered at him drunkenly. "Since when do you know anything about ancient anything?"

He chuckled. "You will learn to respect me, Nerla, and probably sooner than you imagine. But to get to that moment, I need you to do something. Go to the entrance of the brig and seal the door."

She chortled. "With us inside? That'll save time."

"I want you to activate the force field. You will not want for food or a place to stay while here with me. And you can sleep in any cell you want, except for Commander Yalok's." He pointed back in the direction of the Tal Shiar agent's office. "I'll call for you if I need anything."

"Lovely," she said, casting the now empty flask to the deck. "All right, Senator. I guess if I'm turning myself in, I'd rather be in here and the torturers out there." She ambled off.

AVENTINE
CORVUS BEACON

"Let's get ready to power down the ship now," Dax ordered. "The full smash, as soon as we leave warp."

Belowdecks, Leishman would be doing as they'd discussed. *Aventine* would leave warp—and as soon as they saw whether *Laplace* was there, she would take the slipstream drive offline and begin shutting down the impulse engines. Only life support would be left on.

Ezri Dax looked around to her alpha-shift bridge crew, ready to handle anything. "Do not hail the Beacon. We're going to shuttle over and explain in person." It had been decided that was preferable to using the transporters, on the remote chance some of the code associated with Takedown could ride along. It seemed incredibly unlikely—but given how they still knew nothing about the thing, it wasn't worth it.

"This is it," Bowers said, grasping his armrests as he saw the countdown to the destination ticking down. "You've been fun, *Aventine*. Hope they can fix you up."

At the tactical station, Kedair looked around. "Where's the admiral?"

Dax thought it was just as well he was where he was. "We're coming up on it. Stand by!"

The mainviewer showed the warp effect ending. Their destination was unmistakably ahead. The Corvus Beacon was far larger than any they'd visited on their campaign of destruction. It was just as well Riker had never ordered them to a place like this, an expansive field of alternating metal polygons, stretching off into the distance; it would have taken a good while to put it out of commission. Thankfully, it was already out of commission. And just as they had hoped, a *Saber*-class engineering vessel was in orbit.

"That's *Laplace*," she said. "Full stop. Leishman, go!"

"Going."

Dax looked at Bowers, a little nervous. The nightmare she'd had the night before was banal and predictable: the ship had not stopped on her command.

"We're not stopping," Bowers said.

"Impulse drive remains active," the Bolian flight controller said, nearly shouting. "Controls non-responsive."

"Ah, hell," Bowers said.

Dax agreed. "Engineering, what have you got?"

"Security force fields have activated, sealing the area. Aventine thinks we've had a hull breach in engineering. We can't shut her down!"

"Ah, hell," Dax repeated. *Laplace* and the beacon were growing on the viewscreen. There was only one thing to do—if the ship would let them. "Open a channel to *Laplace*!"

"If we open a channel to them," Helkara said, looking over his shoulder, "we could be putting them at risk for infection if Takedown is in our systems."

"It's a chance we have to take. They've almost certainly got repair crews working on the beacon. Hail them!"

A moment later, *Laplace*'s Tellarite captain appeared on the viewscreen, seated beside her Bajoran first officer. Dax started speaking immediately. "This is Captain Ezri Dax of the Federation *Starship Aventine*. All personnel aboard the beacon need to abandon immediately!"

Laplace's captain appeared stunned. *"What's going on?"* Kwelm asked. *"Captain Dax, there have been no reports of any problems aboard the—"*

"Just do it!" There was no time to explain about Takedown, or anything else. "We've lost control of our weapons!"

"Captain, we are no longer transmitting," Mirren said. "We stopped before your last sentence."

Dax looked back in aggravation. "But we can still see and hear them."

"And they can see us—I think. But our audio is not reaching them. All our other messaging systems have just shut down."

What now? Dax wondered in consternation. *Write a note?*

She'd assumed *Laplace*'s crew would react to her initial warning, at least. She hadn't expected they would comply with no questions asked—but neither had she imagined they would stop and hold a staff meeting to consider it. The Trill listened to the audio feed with impatience as the officers on *Laplace* discussed the problem. And while Dax was relieved finally to hear Captain Kwelm give an evacuation order, her jaw dropped when she heard it was to be an orderly exit— aboard a *shuttlecraft*. "There's no time for all that!" she called. But no one on *Laplace* could hear her.

Kwelm started to question Dax. The Trill stopped listening and looked around at her crew. They were all working diligently, trying to wrest control back of

Aventine. But they weren't getting anywhere. Dax was ready to begin beaming people off the array herself, if *Aventine*'s transporters would—

"Do what Captain Dax says!" called a voice over the communications system.

Dax looked up, astonished.

"Laplace, this is Admiral Riker aboard Aventine! *This is a matter of Federation security. All personnel aboard the Corvus Beacon must beam back to* Laplace *immediately!"*

Dax's brow furrowed. "He's able to talk?"

Lieutenant Mirren called from the ops station. "Admiral Riker has executed a priority override of *Aventine*'s communications system."

"How—?"

It took several moments for Dax to process that information. In that time, she could still see and hear events on *Laplace* on the viewscreen. The Tellarite captain was squirming, struggling to get her engineering team off the Corvus Beacon. But they weren't going fast enough. Not for the force now controlling her ship.

Riker raised his voice. *"Hang the data! We've told you, there's no time to explain. The threat's already here!"*

Dax saw the Tellarite captain on-screen flailing, trying to buy time—even as she heard the low hum of *Aventine* stopping. *"But we don't understand,"* Kwelm pleaded. *"If you'd just—"*

"Too late," Riker's voice said. *"You were warned."*

Kedair called out, frantic. "Captain, our shields are being raised!"

In a flash brighter than the phaser fire now erupting from *Aventine*'s forward banks, Dax realized that Riker was right. The threat *was* already here.

And it wore an admiral's insignia.

Nineteen

It had happened. It *was* happening. *Aventine,* under the command of Rear Admiral William Thomas Riker, was destroying the Corvus Beacon, one incalculably expensive module at a time.

And here—wherever *here* was—William Riker was watching it happen, as seen from the simulated bridge of *Laplace.* The old man who'd called himself Simus had started the holographic re-creation again, but had set it to play out slowly, so Riker could see every volley striking the station. And every pained, panicked expression that appeared on the faces of *Laplace*'s crew of engineers.

"Moment by moment?" Riker said, incredulous. "Pretty sadistic, showing it to me this way."

"Sadistic?" Simus repeated. He mused for a moment. "Admiral, how would you describe the actual acts we're witnessing? Acts that *you* committed?"

"You have no right to know what I feel," Riker said, defiant. "Not when you haven't told me who you represent—or where we are."

"I told you, the people I—"

"This is no Starfleet board of inquiry, though I certainly deserve one. I know what those are like," Riker said.

Simus nodded. "It is not."

"Now, we're getting somewhere. What is it, then?" He counted on his fingers. "I first attacked the Kinshaya and the Breen—I know you aren't speaking for them. And you don't have the ears for a Ferengi."

Simus said nothing.

"So what are you, then? A freelance judge, an inquisitor? What's the point showing me this?" Riker's ire rose.

But if Simus noticed, he didn't respond. Instead, the old man hobbled past the holographic Tellarite captain. Her Bajoran executive officer had just risen from his seat to study the tactical display at this point in the slow-motion playback of history. Simus took the opportunity to plop down in the officer's chair. "I thought he would never get up," Simus said, setting aside his cane. "All this standing around is tiresome."

Riker wanted to be angry—but it was hard to remain so as the elder man made himself at home in the artificial surroundings. Whoever he was, Simus had a placid nature that seemed to dispel strong emotions. "You're pretty relaxed, to be lounging around in the middle of an interstellar incident."

"And you were fairly relaxed in causing one," Simus said. He gestured to the screen. "I have a question. You tried to give the crew of *Laplace* time to evacuate their people—even though it delayed you from your objective. Why did you do that?"

Riker stared as if he'd just been asked why he had two feet. "There were innocent people on the station."

"You also saw that *Aventine* ran a scan for life signs on the Ferengi array, making sure it was evacuated before destroying it. The reason for this?"

"I told you," Riker said, losing patience. "I had to."

"Ah," Simus said. "Just like you had to attack the beacon, and the others?"

The admiral frowned and looked away. "That's different."

"How so?"

Riker fixed his eyes on the darkest corner of the room. He felt as if it were coming toward him, ready to swallow him up. He exhaled and reached for his forehead.

"Headache?" Simus asked.

"Yes."

He turned back to see the old man peering at him, his head tilted sideways. "Earlier, you didn't recognize *Laplace* and the beacon," Simus said. "It wasn't until you saw yourself that you knew them. Isn't that right?"

Riker cast half a glance up at the main viewscreen, which was more than enough. "I've just been so tired—like I'm all used up." He looked warily back at Simus, his suspicion suddenly renewed. "Was I drugged? Is that why I feel this way—why the memories are coming back so slowly?"

"Yes and no."

"You're a big help," Riker said. "Is there someone here who can give me some answers?"

A trace of a grin came across Simus's face. "I've heard *that* somewhere before."

"What? Where?"

"Here," Simus said, touching a control on his wrist—and an instant later, the figures in the room began moving again at normal speed. The holographic crew dashed around *Laplace*'s bridge as *Aventine* resumed its pummeling of the Corvus Beacon, having switched to photon torpedoes.

Laplace was no match for *Aventine*, and while Riker

could imagine a number of tactics that the engineering ship might use to mitigate the damage, it would mean the destruction of the ship and death for the crew.

Simus saw *Laplace*'s first officer returning to his appointed chair. "I suppose I'd better get up," the old man said, reluctantly rising. The Bajoran sat in the seat Simus vacated and began punching buttons on the armrest.

"We can't establish communications with Starfleet over this," the Bajoran said. "Something's wrong with the subspace network."

Another *Aventine* torpedo hit the beacon, and then a proximity alarm sounded. "Arrival from warp," *Laplace*'s tactical officer yelled. "A hundred thousand kilometers and coming this way fast!"

"Who?" Pushed to the edge of her wits, Captain Kwelm looked about in anguish. *"Is there someone here who can give me some answers?"*

Simus looked at Riker—whose eyes widened at hearing the line he'd said earlier. They went even wider when he heard the next voice. *"This is Captain Jean-Luc Picard of the* Starship Enterprise," came the announcement over the ship's communications system. "Aventine, *you are ordered to stand down immediately. I repeat, stand down immediately, or we will fire!"*

Riker felt his mouth go dry. "I guess I should watch this."

Simus nodded. "I would."

STAGE TWO:

SHOWDOWN

"Better a city ruined than a city lost."
—Cosimo de' Medici

Twenty

"Captain, *Aventine* is not responding," Lieutenant Šmrhová said.

"Continue hailing," Picard ordered from his command chair. "Lieutenant Faur, put us between *Aventine* and the beacon."

"Aye, Captain," Joanna Faur said from the flight controller's station. "Eighty thousand kilometers and closing."

Picard watched unhappily at the scene magnified and depicted on the *Enterprise* bridge's viewscreen. His team had prepared several different action plans, contingent on who was waiting at the Corvus Beacon. It could well have been *D'varian* or no one. While Picard had considered finding *Aventine* there among the possibilities, actually seeing it firing on a Federation installation was chilling. Several segments of the beacon were ablaze, while a much smaller Starfleet engineering vessel sat nearby, unresponsive.

Worf reported, "Scans confirm vessel identity. It's *Aventine*. The other vessel is *Laplace*, under Captain Kwelm."

"Get me *Laplace*."

"Sixty thousand kilometers," the flight controller said.

A chirp indicated they'd connected with the engineering ship. "*Laplace, Enterprise*. Report your status."

"*Unharmed,*" replied a female Tellarite voice. "*Captain Picard, we are so glad to see you! Aventine arrived and began—*"

"*Hello, Jean-Luc,*" interrupted another, more familiar voice.

Picard looked back at Šmrhová. "On-screen!"

Admiral Riker appeared, head and shoulders visible before a black background. "*That was some way to say hello. 'Stand down immediately or we'll fire?'* " A hint of a smile crossed his face. "*I've had better greetings.*"

Picard was momentarily dumbstruck. He'd been hoping that it was all a mistake, a misunderstanding. He'd hoped to find something that could explain away the visual evidence from the Ferengi station. Even on seeing *Aventine*, there had remained some small room for doubt: outsiders had commandeered Federation starships before.

But he wasn't expecting to see his former first officer sitting there calmly, while *Aventine* continued to fire on the beacon. "Admiral, you're attacking a Federation station!"

"*That is what this looks like,*" Riker said, sounding mildly apologetic. "*Aventine is on an important mission, Captain. There's no time to explain, but we could really use your help.*"

"Help?" Picard blinked. *Help?*

"*The Corvus Beacon must be taken down. The crew has already been safely evacuated, so between the two of us, we should be able to make short work of it.*" Riker spoke matter-of-factly, as if he were suggesting nothing out of the ordinary. *"I recommend* Enterprise *target the far edge, working its way in. We'll meet at the center. Working together, like old times."*

Old times? Picard couldn't believe what he was hearing. "Are you ordering me to fire on a Federation scientific outpost?"

"I told you, there's no time to explain. But it's of critical importance."

"To whom? To you?" Picard shook his head. "Will, Starfleet is reporting a number of attacks like this one on communications outposts. I can't believe you're involved. What possible reason could there—"

"I'm following orders. I'm sorry you can't do the same."

"Orders? Whose orders? Admiral, if you'll just stop and talk—"

"Wrong strategy, Captain."

Picard blinked, startled by Riker's tone. "What do you mean?"

"I know you're buying time talking to me until I'm in range. We're done here. Riker out." The admiral vanished, his image replaced by the sight of *Aventine* pummeling the beacon, while *Laplace* sat off to the side.

Picard looked at Worf. "That—that was Will, wasn't it?"

Worf looked bewildered. "It seemed so."

Shrugging off what had been one of the stranger conversations he'd ever had, Picard called out to *Laplace*. "You're right there. Why haven't you acted?"

"It's a Federation ship," Kwelm said. *"And we haven't wanted to engage, for fear of damaging the beacon!"*

Picard frowned. "Raise your shields, *Laplace*, and move to interdict."

"They're faster than we are—"

"Get in the game, Captain Kwelm." He looked back to Faur. "Range?"

"Twenty thousand kilometers."

"Raise shields," Picard said gravely. "Let's do this."

AVENTINE

"Security team to holodeck one," Dax said. It was the third time she'd given the order. But every time she touched her communicator badge, she was serenaded by jazz great Dizzy Gillespie. Or at least that was who Bowers thought was playing the music. It would have been comical had the situation not been so dire.

Kedair had left her tactical station, which wasn't responding to her commands anyway, to deal with something equally unresponsive: the turbolift doors, which had seized shut. The powerful woman had been joined by three other bridge officers in trying to force the portal open, after the manual override failed. *"Aventine*'s in a mood all of a sudden!"

"No mystery who caused it," Dax said. Riker's takeover of her communications systems had sealed it for her. "You called it, Sam."

"I didn't predict *this*," Bowers said. Her first officer was going from station to station, futilely entering commands.

"You still think he has some kind of secret admiral-only override?"

"I was kidding. We've lived this ship every day for years. We'd have known if something like that existed."

Whatever Riker had done was a recent addition to *Aventine*—but that didn't make sense to Dax, either.

"The Admiral would need a team of the brightest minds in engineering in there with him to do all this."

"Hell, I don't know. He's in a holodeck," Bowers said. "He could have Montgomery Scott and Zefram Cochrane working side by side down there!"

"We could use them up here," Kedair said, struggling. "They could help us open the damn door!"

ENTERPRISE

"Captain, *Laplace* is moving to ram *Aventine*!"

"Target *Aventine*'s nacelles and fire if she attempts to evade." Picard gripped his armrests and watched as the starship skimmed just beneath the engineering vessel's hull, very nearly clipping one of the broadcast towers on the Corvus Beacon. It was a wild, sudden move on *Aventine*'s part—not in the direction Picard or his security officer were expecting. "Pursue."

Laplace had gotten into the game, all right—putting up a belated but spirited struggle to protect a scientific outpost her captain was clearly passionate about. But where *Aventine*'s dodge merely resulted in missed shots from *Enterprise*, the engineering vessel found itself soaring into a spherically emanating cloud of burning wreckage from a previous assault on the station. Weaker shields allowed colossal girders to slam against the forward section of *Laplace*'s hull, leaving one sparking gash, and then another.

"*Laplace*, status!"

"*Shaken*, Enterprise." He could tell from Kwelm's voice that there wasn't any need to ask if *Laplace* would continue the fight.

"Photon torpedoes incoming," Worf said, clearly startled. *Aventine* hadn't fired at them before, but now three of the shining projectiles rocketed outward from the aft launchers.

"Evasive action." *Enterprise* lurched. *Aventine* had fired them not to strike the ship, but to delay its pursuit—closing off an avenue of approach. *Enterprise* cut between two of them, Flight Controller Faur trying to keep the ship in *Aventine*'s wake. But the torpedoes detonated in space, delivering simultaneous twin jolts to *Enterprise*'s shields.

"Shields down to eighty percent," Šmrhová said over the noise of the barrage.

"Target *Aventine*'s . . ." Picard began. But there was nothing for *Enterprise* to target. *Aventine* resolved itself into a bright blur, redshifting out of observable reality.

"Mark that departure vector," Picard said. "Trace it!"

"Klingon space," Faur said.

Worf was puzzled. "Why?"

Picard ordered reverse angle onto the viewscreen. *Aventine* had left a trail of destruction, indeed. Only the skeleton of the Corvus Beacon remained intact amid the burning wreckage. The facility's tender, *Laplace*, loomed above, a visitor at a grave.

"We're being hailed by *Laplace*." Šmrhová completed the connection.

Captain Kwelm appeared on *Enterprise*'s viewscreen. There was smoke in the image, and Picard could see light structural damage had been done to the ship's bridge. The engineering vessel, not meant for combat, had acquitted itself admirably.

"We're in better shape than I thought we'd be in, Captain Picard," Kwelm said. The seated Tellarite was misty-eyed not from the smoke, but from surveying the remains of the station. *"Riker destroyed everything."*

Picard nodded. "That appears to be the case," he said, choosing his phrasing carefully. It wasn't the time to debate Riker's guilt or innocence—not here, not before *Laplace*'s crew.

And certainly not when he lacked a shred of evidence absolving his friend.

"I—we will try to go on, Captain. Thank you for saving what you could."

"Do you require assistance?"

"No. One thing," Kwelm said, standing, *"I want that human stopped. Stopped before he does this again."*

"We shall. *Enterprise* out."

He looked to Worf, grim and speechless—and then back to Faur. "Follow *Aventine*'s last heading. Full speed."

Clearly aware of the captain's mood, Dygan turned to him. "Captain, there are other vessels making attacks in this region. Wouldn't it make more sense to go after one of them? We can certainly stop a Ferengi ship faster than we can stop *Aventine*."

"I don't think so, Mister Dygan. One of our own did this," Picard said. "We will stop the *Aventine*."

"Aye, aye, sir."

Faur looked at the captain. "Warp speed available."

"Engage."

Picard didn't know how he would keep his word to Captain Kwelm. But he would try.

Twenty-one

*Y*ou don't realize how fast something is until it's not, Dax thought. *Aventine* was an incredibly fast ship, and it had a speedy and efficient turbolift system. Now, with many of the turbolifts offline, she had been forced into an unscheduled tour of her ship's Jefferies tubes.

She had just clambered from one into another featureless hallway when Bowers emerged from a maintenance hatch. "He's making us waste time," she said.

"He's doing a good job of it. The approach to EPS distribution is protected by a force field," Bowers said. "Riker's got half the ship thinking the hull has been compromised. We need to tell Leishman we've got to try something else."

Without thinking, Dax tapped her communicator badge—and was greeted by an up-tempo melody from a warbling clarinet. *"Damn it!"*

"Artie Shaw," Bowers said. "I think this one's called 'Honeysuckle Jump.'"

She glared at him.

"I could be wrong," he said meekly.

"Not something we need to worry about right now," Dax said. "Come on."

They made for a doorway that had been propped open at the end of the hallway. The access point beyond sat in the middle of a Jefferies tube, with ladders stretching up and down, out of sight. Looking up, Dax spotted Kedair sliding quickly downward, straddling the outside of the ladder with the insteps of her boots.

Dax stepped aside as the athletic Takaran hopped off and made a three-point landing on the metal deck. Standing upright, she looked winded. "He's killed artificial gravity on the decks above and below holodeck one," she said, wiping the sweat from her scaly brow. "He keeps alternately pressurizing and depressurizing the Jefferies tubes that run anywhere near the place."

"Gravity boots and oxygen masks, then."

"It helps to bring your own," called a muffled voice from behind Dax. She turned to see Leishman clambering out of a hatch. The chief engineer's face was barely visible behind her oxygen mask and night-vision eyewear. She had a pair of gravity boots hanging from a yoke around her neck.

"You look like you've been diving the dark ocean," Bowers said.

"I feel like it," Leishman said, pulling the mask down from her chin and lifting her goggles. "Every place we try to engage the overrides, he cuts the lights and messes with the air and the gravity." Exhausted, Leishman pulled the gravity boots from over her shoulders and threw them to the deck with an angry clank.

"He's eavesdropping," Kedair said. "He knows where we're going. You've got to manually kill the internal sensors."

Leishman looked at the security chief with tired

irritation. "We've been doing that. But there are only so many points from which we can try to get control of the ship back." She looked sorrowfully at Dax. "We've been trying to establish an ODN bypass from engineering to the bridge. But we couldn't get the systems on either end to accept the interface."

"Something blocked you?"

"I tried like hell to hide what it was we were up to. An ODN bypass—that's not something the average admiral knows about. But it's almost as if he knew we'd be trying this specific thing." Leishman looked at Dax. "Who games out every possible countermove?"

Dax patted the engineer's shoulder. "I honestly think he's baiting us, trying to get us to waste time while *Aventine* takes us—*wherever*."

Actually, Dax already knew where *Aventine* was headed—sort of. The main viewscreen on the bridge had shown her ship turning toward Klingon space just before the slipstream drive was engaged. She wasn't expecting a warm welcome.

Bowers walked around the circumference of the small room and tried a door. It worked. "The admiral has nothing against port accessway storage B," he said, after peeking in. "The lights work."

"He wants us where he wants us," Dax said. She gestured for the others to follow her inside.

Port accessway storage B had a variety of cubes and cylinders stacked up—and, remarkably, two chairs. "What are these doing here?" Bowers asked. "Anyone want a seat?"

Leishman had already slid down against the inside wall to sit on the deck, spent. Kedair was stalking about, going through the stored goods. And Dax was too wired to sit.

"All right," the first officer said, flipping the chair around and plopping down in it.

Dax looked up. "Sensors?"

"Still active," Leishman said.

"Then *he's* here," Dax said. She raised her voice. "Aren't you, Admiral?"

"I hear you," Riker said, his disembodied voice almost god-like from above. *"I know you must be concerned, Dax, and I fully understand why."*

Dax's eyes darted to Leishman, who scrambled to her feet. Together, the engineer and Kedair casually began searching for sensors. "If you're concerned," Dax said, "then give us command back!"

"That's not going to happen. I have a mission—and it can't be interfered with."

"A Starfleet mission?" Dax's eyes narrowed. "That won't fly, Admiral. You told us your mission was to prevent the spread of Takedown. But we no longer believe Takedown exists." Dax paused. It was a small matter, given the circumstances, to take the next step. "You fabricated those orders from Akaar, didn't you?"

"It was important to my mission that you cooperated, while I completed preparations."

"Preparations for what? To take over my ship?"

"She's Starfleet's ship, Captain. Don't get attached."

Dax was flabbergasted. "If she's Starfleet's ship, then give her back!"

"I will—when my mission is complete. And let me spare you a little dramatic scene: I've disabled the self-destruct systems aboard Aventine."

Dax and Bowers looked at each other. It wasn't something they'd considered yet, but it was certainly on the list of options. Or it had been.

Across the room, Leishman had guided Kedair to

a small bubble-like protrusion in the far corner of the room where the walls reached the overhead. Kedair turned and gave Dax a silent thumbs-up sign, while Leishman casually worked her way to the opposite corner.

"I realize this is uncomfortable for you to have to sit and watch," Riker said. *"If I had time, I'd beam your crew off. Someplace safe."*

"We're not going anywhere."

"You wouldn't have a choice in that. But Enterprise's *shields were up, and I'm not about to leave you stranded where we're headed."*

"Thanks for caring," Dax said. She wanted to say something worse, but for some reason, she had trouble swearing at the admiral. Some vestigial respect for his rank? She didn't know. "We're headed to Klingon space. Why?"

"'Ours is not to reason why,' Dax. Didn't you ever learn that?" He chuckled—a strange sound, when coming from all around. *"Never mind. I forgot who I'm speaking with."*

"Maybe *you've* forgotten, something, Admiral. The William Riker I knew would never follow orders blindly, whoever they came from."

A pause. *"I don't forget anything. Not now."*

Dax didn't know what to say to that. It was Riker's voice, for sure, but he sounded as if he'd aged decades in a week.

"I have to go. You can tell Kedair and Leishman they can destroy the sensors now. I understand people like their privacy."

The room went silent, and Dax saw the women looking to her for guidance. Dax ran her finger across her throat. Simultaneous crackling flashes later, the sensors were dead.

"There aren't any more in here," Leishman said, clambering down from the boxes she was on. "He can mess with the systems all day, but I don't think he had time to install more hardware in storage B."

Phaser still in hand, Kedair looked at Dax, astonished. "Did you hear what he said, there? He actually thinks he could run the vessel without any crew at all."

Leishman waved dismissively. "That's a nice dream, but it's simply not possible."

Dax remembered something. "Didn't Riker say he'd served on the task force that worked on quarantining holodeck functions from the rest of starships' systems?"

"The safeguards they put in place were many and complicated. I can't see a lone admiral undoing them, even if he did show a sudden talent for engineering."

Dax looked to Bowers, who was hunched over, lost in thought. "What about Sam's idea? That Riker generated a team of assistants down there on the holodeck to reroute *Aventine*'s functions there?"

Leishman shook her head. "Holodeck entities are only as intelligent as the ship's main computer—and they're bound by its functioning parameters. You can't program it to invent ways to subvert its safety protocols. That was one of the task force's reforms."

"Could Riker have created his own bridge crew to help him run the ship? We're seeing a lot of decisions being made at once," Dax asked.

Leishman thought for a moment. "It's possible. Holodeck characters act out running bridges all the time. But they wouldn't have been able to invent the method to connect their fake bridge to *Aventine*. An outside party would have been required—if such a thing was even possible." It was clear that Leishman still didn't think it was.

"That means Riker brought people on board with him." Dax bit her lip, trying to remember. "Sam, he was beamed directly to the holodeck from *Titan*. Was he alone?"

"Yes," Bowers said, looking up.

"Could others have transported over then, that we didn't know about?"

He shook his head. "No. No way."

Putting her phaser away, Kedair frowned. She took a breath before asking, "What about *our* crew?"

Dax looked at her. "What do you mean?"

The security chief gestured matter-of-factly. "Maybe he didn't have to bring anyone across. The ship's already crawling with engineers."

Leishman's temper flared. "What are you saying, Kedair? That one of my team is helping Riker?"

"You've got a huge crew down there," Kedair said, violet eyes piercing. "People are coming in and out all the time to work on that drive of yours. Maybe he planted people here ahead of time."

"My team's loyal and by-the-book, *Lieutenant*. I keep a good eye on everybody."

"Do you? Like the little guy we nabbed for messing with the replicators?" Kedair's eyes narrowed. "Is anyone missing on your team?"

"I can't exactly take a head count right now." Leishman stuck her finger at Kedair's pointed chin. "And if your people could get us onto the same floor with Riker, we wouldn't have this problem!"

"Enough." The captain was smaller than either

woman—and yet both of them shrank back at her presence. "We are not going to argue our way out of this. Finger pointing is useless."

"Dunsels," Bowers said. "An entire crew of dunsels." An old Starfleet term, it referred to parts unnecessary for running a starship. He opened a crate, apparently looking for anything that could be useful.

Dax watched him as he stared into one. "Find something?"

"Boatswain's whistles," Bowers replied, lifting two handfuls of the small handheld musical instruments. "Two hundred of them. Replicator gone wild?"

The three women erupted in laughter.

"Hey," Leishman said, "at least we've finally found a communications method that's not on the grid."

The tension having broken, Dax began to pace the small area. "Instead of trying to take our ship back from pirates, we need to be the pirates taking the ship. That means we should accept Riker's control of the ship as a given. We should look at whatever functions that the main computer can't do for the ship. The engineering mission is finding what we can get control of—and taking it. The security mission is protecting the engineers while they try."

Leishman and Kedair both nodded, first to Dax, and then apologetically to each other. "Maybe something with the shuttles," Leishman said. "We won't be at warp forever."

"We'll get you in there," Kedair said.

Dax nodded. "Good luck." Harmony restored, Leishman and Kedair exited the room.

"And what's the command mission?" Bowers asked, getting up. "Figuring out why Riker's doing all this?"

Dax looked off into the corner, which was still

smoking from Leishman's phaser fire. "That's a problem for Starfleet—and they're on the scent now, if *Enterprise* is out there. That makes us the inside team. We have to find a way to communicate with her—or whatever ship is out there."

"What if it's the Klingons?"

Dax looked back at him. "I know the Klingons. They're not big on talking."

Twenty-two

Picard sat in *Enterprise*'s ready room, lost in contemplation as the stars blurred by outside the tall rectangular viewport. They had identified the destination *Aventine*—and now *Enterprise*—was heading toward: No'Var Outpost, a Klingon watchstation near the Romulan border. While most communications stations were situated in open space, the Klingons had sacrificed efficiency for security, hiding their outpost in an asteroid field. Worf had assured Picard the location was heavily armed. The Klingons would almost certainly be on their guard after all the chaos of the past few days.

The door chimed. "Come."

Dygan appeared in the doorway. "I think I've found something, Captain."

"Come in, Glinn."

The Cardassian walked to the chair across from Picard's desk and indicated a need to access the captain's computer. "May I?"

"Please."

Dygan turned the screen so both could see and called up an image on the monitor. Riker was speaking, before a black background.

Picard recognized it. "It's from our conversation at the Corvus Beacon."

"Pardon me, Captain, but it isn't. It's a holographic re-creation of Admiral Riker, based on recent imagery of him." Dygan entered a command, and the image split into two Rikers. "This is the Riker from our conversation. Our technicians have marked a number of tags, as they call them—extremely subtle indicators worked into the figure's design that establish that both of these Rikers are holographically generated."

Picard sat forward abruptly. "You're saying it might not be Admiral Riker who's responsible for this?"

"That's one possibility," Dygan said. "All this evidence confirms is that a hologram spoke to us. It would take no effort to have one appear in this manner, speaking across subspace channels, and it would appear like any other shipboard passenger."

Picard didn't have to be convinced of that. The holographic Moriarty had appeared on the viewscreen of *Enterprise*-D, many years earlier, speaking from the holodeck as if he were speaking from another starship. His spirits rose. "So someone wants us to think that's Will Riker?"

Dygan put up his hands in a plea for caution. "Again, it's just a possibility, Captain. Yes, the speaker was an imposter. But we don't know who he was speaking for. And whoever it is has evidently gotten the complete cooperation of *Aventine*'s crew in this. I find it hard to see how a holographic character— even a holographic admiral—could command a crew to commit acts such as we've seen." He paused. "Not a Starfleet crew."

Picard's heart sank a little as he followed the logic. Dygan watched Picard's expression. "Now, I'm sure there's another explanation. This evidence could easily absolve the admiral, at least—"

Picard stood. "There's no need to backtrack, Glinn. Thank you for remaining objective. It's why I wanted you on this."

Dygan rose and bowed. "We'll be at No'Var Outpost in ten minutes, sir. We may have another chance to find out more, then."

"Ask Hegol Den to join us on the bridge. If Riker—er, the Riker *character* reappears, I'd like our counselor to weigh in on what he has to say. Even if the person on-screen is a facsimile, he's speaking for someone."

"Right away, sir." Dygan quickly exited.

As the door closed behind the Cardassian, Picard felt more conflicted than before. The holographic Riker appearing on-screen might well mean that the real Riker was blameless. But it also might mean that his friend and protégé was being held against his will, on *Aventine* or elsewhere. That, sadly, seemed the most logical answer. And that raised so many other questions. Had there been a takeover of *Aventine*—or worse, a mutiny?

Picard shook his head and walked across to the replicator. There might just be enough time for a cup of tea before *Enterprise* arrived, and there certainly wouldn't be time later. He hoped it would clear his thoughts and help him focus on his strategy for the upcoming—

"Incorrect strategy, Captain."

Picard recalled the line from the encounter. It rang in his ears as he stirred the cup. Riker had said it, or the holo-Riker, or whoever he was. It was an error on the part of whoever had programmed it, Picard thought: that odd phrasing. *"Incorrect strategy,*

Captain." It didn't sound like Riker at all. It sounded, in fact . . .

. . . like *himself*. It was something Picard had said years earlier.

Or rather, that *Locutus* had said.

When the Borg assimilated Picard long ago, the Collective had taken control of his body and mind, giving him a new identity: Locutus of Borg. Riker, then a commander on *Enterprise*-D, had attempted to sever the Borg's hold over Picard—and the assimilated captain had told him that it was a futile gesture.

"Incorrect strategy, Number One. To risk your ship and crew to retrieve only one man . . ."

Picard remembered saying that—just as he remembered his every statement and action from that painful time. Others might want to forget such memories. He had been forced to do some very bad things; the assimilated Picard had helped the Borg devastate a Starfleet force at Wolf 357. It was not his fault. He had only found peace after the Caeliar transformation.

But he had said the words. How would anyone impersonating Riker have known that phrase? And why would they use it now?

He was about to discard it from his thoughts as a coincidence when the light shifted in his ready room. Looking back at the port, he confirmed the *Enterprise* had dropped out of warp. His badge chirped the second he put down his teacup.

"Picard."

It was Worf. *"Captain, we have arrived at No'Var Outpost. There is an engagement under way—and Aventine is in it."*

Before Worf finished his sentence, Picard was on the bridge, beholding it for himself. The outpost was a mammoth communications station in space, its arrays shielded by massive black cannons. Two Klingon *Vor'cha*-class cruisers blazed away with disruptors as they chased the *Aventine* through the surrounding asteroid field.

"Put us at Red Alert." Jean-Luc Picard almost hoped it was Will Riker running the ship, for *Aventine*'s sake. He couldn't see how anyone else might expect to survive.

Twenty-three

If rage were radiation, Picard thought General Kersh would have set off every warning alarm in the sector. The dark-skinned Klingon woman aboard the No'Var Outpost bared her jagged teeth as she railed against *Aventine*, the Khitomer Accords, and all things Federation.

That included Captain Picard. *"I should have known you would be involved,"* she declared, clenching her gloved fist. *"Troubles follow you everywhere!"*

I followed them, *this time*, he wanted to say—but he decided silence was the wiser course. *Enterprise*'s appearance at the edge of the asteroid-strewn region had resulted in one positive effect: *Aventine* had withdrawn. The Starfleet vessel was trying to work its way around to another vector of approach, but the *Vor'cha* cruisers in pursuit were leaving it few openings. The outpost itself was firing like mad, trying to get lucky despite the long range; Picard could see Kersh was in a war room, surrounded by eager gunners. So far, they were mostly striking asteroids. Picard thought the Klingon cruisers were in more danger of being hit than *Aventine* was.

"Are you here to join this cowardly attack?" Kersh

called over her shoulder to her gunners. *"Lock disruptors on* Enterprise. *Stand by."*

"That is not necessary," Picard said. "We are here to help."

"Then start firing!" Her gravelly voice took on a sneering tone. *"Or won't you attack your own ship?"*

"We will, if necessary. But we need to coordinate our attacks, General, else we might accidentally strike each other—"

"Where have you been? Friends and foes alike have been striking at each other all week!" She turned to her gunners. *"Bah! Fire on them both—and let Kahless decide who's in the right!"*

Worf, who had been out of the Klingon's view, stepped up to Picard's side. *"Kersh!"*

The general's dark eyes widened with recognition.

"You were attached to me as military liaison when I was ambassador," Worf said, a snarl in his voice. "You would dare threaten me now?"

"Hold," she ordered. Her tone turned more respectful. "qaleghqa'neS, *Worf son of Mogh. Welcome to our little war."*

"Listen to us, Kersh daughter of Dakh—or the war will grow larger!"

Picard breathed a sigh of relief as the general calmed. He was glad to let his first officer handle the situation. Worf looked to the captain, who nodded assent for him to continue to speak for *Enterprise.*

Hearing from Faur that *Aventine* was racing around the far side of the debris zone, Picard spoke up. "General Kersh, we read life signs aboard *Aventine* but do not know who is in control. We want to disable the vessel, not destroy her."

Fire flared in Kersh's eyes. *"If your Starfleeters cannot free themselves, they are not worthy of consideration. The same for the crews of any of the rogue ships that have been attacking. Even,"* she said with obvious distaste, *"our own."*

"Have Klingon vessels been involved?"

"The fool General Charlak has shamed herself by striking another of our outposts," she said. *"There is a cloud upon the stars. Madness has taken hold."*

"Charlak was a loose cannon even before," Worf said. "She lacks the discipline of a true warrior. She should not have been a threatening opponent."

"You pick at the wound, Worf." Kersh shook her head, disbelieving. *"The defenders who faced Charlak described a terror, a dagger slicing through space. She cut through all our defenses, destroying a communications system and departing, without even doing her victims the decency of killing them."* She looked up. *"I had moved my command to No'Var, hoping she would come here. Instead, it's your* Aventine—*but its captain seems to have the same talent. In a better ship,"* she added, grudgingly.

Worf was incredulous. "Charlak never had such skills. She is no Riker."

Picard had heard enough. "General, with your cooperation, we will engage *Aventine*. She is a Starfleet vessel and will face our justice. Will you listen if we discover something that will end this thing?"

Kersh paused to think for a moment—and then gave a Klingon salute. *"Qa'pla,"* she said and vanished from the screen.

"Place us astride any possible approaches *Aventine* may take toward the outpost. Keep them guessing," Picard said as he and Worf retook their seats.

"Aye, Captain."

The task would test Faur's skills at conn sorely, but at least they had Kersh's guarantee that they wouldn't get struck from behind as they weaved their way through the obstacle course of asteroids. The Klingons had employed years of engineering to make the region look as it did, the captain surmised; this was an asteroid-field-by-tractor-beam, specifically designed to stop invaders. Yet *Aventine* was trying hard to run whatever gaps it could find.

"*Aventine* is hailing us," Šmrhová said, surprised.

Picard was too. *Aventine* seemed busy at the moment. Casting a glance over to Hegol Den, the Bajoran counselor seated to his left, Picard nodded. "On-screen."

Riker appeared, again before the same black background. His hands were out of the frame, but he gave no appearance of operating anything. *"Captain, if you're not here to help, withdraw. You're putting* Enterprise's *crew at risk."*

"I am surprised that you care," Picard responded icily. "Given the jeopardy you are placing *Aventine*'s crew in—"

"They're in no danger. I can assure you of that."

Picard looked to Worf. Their eyes met, saying the same thing: *That means the crew is still aboard.*

The captain chose his next words carefully. "I . . . don't know what value your assurance has. I'm not sure with whom I'm speaking. I see and hear Admiral William Riker—but I know I'm interacting with a hologram."

A little grin crossed Riker's face. *"Don't confuse expediency with deception."*

"A pretty aphorism. What does it mean?"

"Do we have to go through the motions, to establish

my bona fides?" Riker asked. *"Fine. The day we first met, Jean-Luc, you asked a favor of me. You asked that I not allow you—"*

"Yes, yes," Picard said, gesturing for the figure on the screen to stop. Years earlier, worried about running a starship with families aboard, Picard had asked Riker to make sure the captain didn't make an ass of himself whenever children were around. Riker smiled as he recognized that Picard had remembered the moment.

That settled it for Picard. Clearly, whoever was behind the Riker hologram had access to Riker's memories somehow. "Let's not play this game when lives are at stake."

"It'll be over soon. I'll be going once this station is offline."

"You have to stop this—"

"You can keep following me, if you want. I'm sure you will, in fact. Watch where I go next."

Picard called on all his resolve. "You'll have to go through *Enterprise*."

"I didn't mean now. Watch where I go after I'm finished here. You may learn something."

The captain was still puzzling over that when the communication ended. *Aventine* was already making its play. Braking suddenly such that the Klingon ships sailed past, *Aventine* looped and lanced through an opening in the asteroid field aft of *Enterprise*'s position. "Phasers, now. Fire to disable!"

Enterprise's weaponry opened up, even as Faur brought the ship around to get a better angle. *Aventine*'s aspect changed suddenly, weaving between bolts from its fellow Starfleet vessel and the Klingon outpost it was racing toward.

"I've never seen anyone react so fast," Faur said.

Picard hadn't either. As a captain, he'd always strived for the ideal: a crew that worked hand in glove with the ship, reading and responding to surrounding conditions with little time wasted. *Aventine*'s movements were at once immediately responsive—and yet somehow graceful, making a three-million-metric-ton piece of equipment into a living creature, soaring the spaceways.

A destructive creature, as it turned out. Before *Enterprise* could follow, *Aventine* shifted direction again. The action brought the vessel in line with the outpost, just beneath the station's field of fire. Skimming just meters above the station's gridwork, *Aventine* lobbed one photon torpedo after another from its aft cannons.

Once the flash dissipated, Picard saw *Aventine* soaring away. The edge of the enormous square of communications arrays blazed orange. "He's struck the disruptor cannons along the northern end of the grid," Dygan said, checking his readings. "He's caused a chain reaction."

"The No'Var Outpost's shields are down," Worf said. "On his next approach, he will be able to destroy the grid."

Without killing anyone in the station, Picard realized.

"I'm sorry, Captain," Faur said. "*Aventine*'s got an edge in a place like this."

"Agreed," Picard said, wondering how much awe was in his voice. He'd known better than anyone what Riker's talents were—but this, if it was Riker, was a superlative performance. *Astonishing*, he thought. *I don't know what I've just seen.*

"Locate *Aventine*," he said.

"Making another circuit of the field," Dygan said.

"The *Vor'cha*s are on her again. They've made adjustments. It might slow her down some. Based on their past results, she'll make another pass in three minutes."

Kersh hailed. She wasn't the grudging ally who had signed off with a salute a few minutes earlier; the old ire was back. Her officers appeared less enthusiastic now, many of their viewscreens visibly flickering in the background. *"You call that a defense, Picard? Perhaps you should get out and stand on the array yourself, holding up your hand to make him stop!"*

Picard started to reply to the taunt when he paused to think. What was it Riker had said? He thought back—and nearly gasped with realization. *Could it be that simple?*

He pressed his badge. "Mr. La Forge to the bridge, immediately." He looked back to the viewscreen. "Stand by, General. We have another plan."

Twenty-four

"**C**aptain, the battle is growing more heated," Dax's companion said. The young Vulcan engineer in a spacesuit just like hers looked through the shuttlebay entrance. "Should we be trying to disable the ship while the Klingons are shooting at us?"

"Let me worry about that, Sovak." Dax snapped her helmet onto her spacesuit. "Let's go, Lieutenant." Both sealed their helmets and manually cycled the airlock.

Ezri Dax wasn't fully up on the history of space battles, but she imagined there hadn't been many where a ship was under attack from both without and within at the same time. She was in one now. Since *Aventine* had emerged from slipstream, Dax had been working her way to shuttlebay one, trying to teach her errant starship a lesson.

Riker had deactivated the artificial gravity for the deck except for the footprints of the shuttles—and for good measure, he had decompressed the landing bay and turned out the lights. That had served Dax's purposes well, since she was planning on blowing a hole in the hull anyway, and she didn't want Riker to see. She and her spacesuited, gravity-booted companion tromped the short steps through the dark to the shuttlecraft *Meuse*.

When parked and deactivated, it and the other shuttlecraft weren't connected to the main computer; control of the bay doors was enough of a security system. But years before, a being named Arithon had stolen the runabout *Seine* by using microtorpedoes to destroy the bay doors. Dax had hoped to replicate the feat. At a minimum, outside *Aventine*'s hull she'd be able to send for help; at best, she might disable the ship enough for its pursuers to stop it.

Meuse's hatchway was open: an invitation. She and the specialist Leishman had provided entered the craft. Quickly, they activated its systems without using the vessel's usual data connection to the *Aventine*'s computer. They shut off their gravity boots. *Meuse*'s spotlight casting on the bay doors ahead, Dax reached for the weapons controls. She wasn't going to let the responsibility for the act fall on anyone else's head. *Aventine* was hers to preserve or destroy as necessary.

"*I wouldn't do that if I were you,*" came a bored voice over *Meuse*'s comm.

The engineer touched Dax's arm, alerting her. They'd deactivated their suit communicators for fear of tipping Riker off—but words weren't necessary now to show her what was going on. *Meuse* tipped forward, its stubby snout drawn quietly but irresistibly to the deck. It struck the deck with a clang that resonated throughout the shuttle.

He's messing with the artificial gravity outside, Dax realized. The ship naturally perched atop its nacelles; by somehow altering the settings for just the deck panels beneath *Meuse*'s prow, Riker had ensured that Dax's weapons had a good bead on the floor.

Undaunted, she fired up the engines, trying to lift the shuttle from the deck. *Aventine* renewed its pull, causing the shuttle to wobble improbably on its nose in the dark, its leading edge attracted to the insistent deck. *Meuse*'s internal artificial gravity, accustomed to compensating against planetary gravity wells, struggled to make sense of the bizarre environment outside, causing the shuttle's occupants to lurch back and forth. Only Dax kept her balance, fighting to gain control of the little ship—and yet attempting to change attitude only succeeded in sending *Meuse* sliding around in the dark. The craft struck something, and then something else. The shuttlecraft finally stopped with a colossal jolt against the starboard wall of the bay.

"Are we done now?" Riker said over the upturned shuttle's speakers. *"I'm a little busy at the moment."*

Reluctantly, Dax powered down and clambered out, followed by the engineer. The lights in the shuttle-bay came back on, and artificial gravity normalized—showing her the angry path *Meuse* had scraped across the deck. The entire episode had lasted less than three minutes.

Angry and dispirited, she made her way to the exit. She didn't want to blow a hole in her ship. She wanted to put one in Riker.

ENTERPRISE

Picard only had moments to fill in his first officer on his plan. The Klingon had met the idea with a skeptical upturned eyebrow—but hadn't questioned it. There was no time. The plan was already in motion when Geordi La Forge arrived to take the engineering station.

"Give me energy consumption readings on both

Aventine and the outpost," Picard said. "Inform me the minute anything changes."

"The outpost?" La Forge wondered about it, Picard saw, but the engineer knew better than to ask.

Dygan called out. "*Aventine* has found a lane and is making another attack run."

Not hearing a command, Faur asked, "Move to interdict?"

"Make it so." Picard knew they weren't likely to hit *Aventine* hard enough to divert her from pummeling the now-defenseless arrays attached to the outpost—presuming *Enterprise* could hit her at all. But that didn't matter. He could feel the ship turning and the batteries firing. It was important to make a good show of it before—

"Change at the outpost," La Forge announced. "Emissions from the communications arrays just spiked and went to zero!"

"Picard to Kersh. Status!"

Only audio came through, weak and crackling. *"Damage from the last attack. The ODN for the transceiver array is fried,"* she said. *"Our whole system is dead!"*

On-screen, he saw *Aventine* diving toward the defunct grid, its weapons array glowing as *Enterprise*'s volleys went harmlessly past. This time, *Aventine* did not fire. It veered, suddenly, skirting past the side of the outpost and disappearing behind it.

"*Aventine* is powering down her weapons systems," La Forge said.

Dygan reported, "*Aventine* is moving to leave the vicinity. *Vor'cha*s are giving chase."

"They won't catch her," Picard said. He looked to his right and the empty seat vacated by Commander

Worf. "Track *Aventine* closely. I want to know her precise heading as she leaves."

When Kersh had suggested getting out of the ship to personally protect the outpost, it had dawned on Picard that a way existed to do exactly that. Riker had said it: *"I'll be going once this station is offline."* The station now disabled, Riker had been as good as his word. *Aventine* activated its slipstream drive and vanished from the system, leaving them all behind.

Picard didn't really need to wait a few moments before hailing the outpost, but he did so anyway. "Report."

"The outpost's communication system is powering up again," La Forge said.

On the viewscreen, Worf appeared alongside Kersh. *"Enterprise, it worked. Disabling the station ourselves seems to have satisfied Riker."*

Kersh looked disgruntled. *"Playing dead!"* She spat on the deck. *"No way for a warrior to win!"*

Picard grinned. "I don't know that we won, General, if it makes you feel any better. We just took the worm off the hook."

The Klingon woman didn't seem to know what he meant by that—and the captain realized it was an inapt analogy anyway, since the No'Var Outpost was by no means a trap for *Aventine*. But it was possible to accomplish Riker's intent for him—or to at least make it appear as though his earlier efforts had succeeded. Picard didn't want to transmit the idea to Kersh where Riker might hear, so he beamed Worf over personally instead, taking advantage of the fact that the outpost's shields were down. Evidently his first officer had sold the Klingon general on the plan.

La Forge gestured to get his attention. "Captain,

there was a strange reading from *Aventine* just as she left. A distortion in the energy output while it was generating the slipstream corridor."

Picard stood and walked over to the engineer's side and examined the data. "The slipstream drive?"

La Forge nodded. "They've been pushing it too hard. The corridor they created is going to collapse before they get where they're going."

"Are they in danger?" Picard asked.

"No. But they're going to drop out into normal space before they get anywhere near their destination."

"Do we have a way of tracking where they'll wind up?"

"No. Just somewhere on the heading. They'll have to wait a few hours before continuing." La Forge pointed to a location on the starmap on his monitor. "No doubt on the heading, though. He's going for the Adelphous Array."

Picard turned back to the screen. "Do you hear that, General? *Aventine* is returning to Federation space."

Kersh laughed. *"He's your problem now."*

The captain didn't much share her amusement.

Twenty-five

Worf wore a sour expression when he materialized on *Enterprise*'s bridge. Picard had thought it best to bring him quickly back from the outpost. He needed his first officer's strategic expertise.

And Worf had already thought through the next steps, as Picard had expected. "Captain, there's a lot of territory between us and the Adelphous Array. Admiral Riker could emerge anywhere on that route—and he could go in any direction from there."

"There's no reason for *Aventine* to go there anyway," La Forge said. "That installation hasn't been crewed since the Borg Invasion. It's already out of commission."

"Riker would know that. I wonder what he's getting at?" Picard looked to the counselor, who had been watching in silence from the chair beside Picard's throughout the engagement. "What did you make of him, Doctor Den?"

"It's the strangest thing," the young Bajoran said. "Everything in Riker's voice exudes confidence—and not just the superiority of rank and experience. He's speaking to us like he'd talk to children. He's a level beyond, or at least he feels like he is. He had not the slightest doubt that he would disable the station and head on to his next destination."

"And yet his next destination is someplace he knows is defunct."

"*Watch where I go next,*" Den said, citing perfectly from memory. "The man who attacked us does not waste words. He meant you to heed them."

"*Watch—and learn,*" Picard said, paraphrasing. Taking his seat, he scratched his head. "I don't know what I am to learn."

But it was clear there was *something* to learn. What had sounded like bluster and bravado to Picard at the time now presented itself to him as another clue. He thought back again to the line from the Corvus Beacon encounter. Was Riker trying to communicate then that he was someone else's thrall?

"You say he's showing that he's in complete control, Doctor. Is he in control of himself?"

Den templed his fingers and considered the question. "He's presenting himself as he wants to be seen. That may be the reason for the holographic image."

"You mean, it may be Riker's mind, but his body may be changed?"

"Or captive, somehow. We've seen outside influence manifest itself in many ways."

Outside influence. It clicked for Picard. Riker had attained his goal and departed immediately, not following up on the obvious possibility that he had been deceived. Perhaps Riker was following only the letter of the law, when it came to his mad mission. Enough to satisfy . . . whom? What?

Starfleet had seen many cases of individuals being compromised by outside influence; it was inevitable in an organization that brought dramatically different species into contact. The effects of such influences ran the gamut, from subtle, almost unnoticeable changes in behavior to complete sublimation and loss of all control. Picard had been near the far end of the spectrum with the Borg—but even with his personality submerged, he had been able to provide Riker and *Enterprise*'s crew with the clue that saved the Federation.

Will Riker had—*possibly*—given him hints that he was under someone else's sway and that he only needed to disable the outpost's communications. And he had invited Picard to follow him. Either it all meant something, or not.

Picard had to find out. And the answers lay in both *Enterprise*'s future—and Riker's past.

"We're going to the Adelphous Array," he announced. "But first," he said, "give me General Kersh."

The Klingon woman appeared on the viewscreen, clearly bothered to have her repairs interrupted. *"What now?"*

"We are going to give chase," Picard said. "But first I'd like to route a communication through your array, if you'll permit it." A crumpled smile crossed his face. "Before another rogue ship notices it's still operational and attacks, I mean."

Kersh growled. *"Let them come. It will be the only way for a couple of my cruiser captains to restore their honor."* She rolled her eyes and shrugged. *"Go ahead."*

AVENTINE

"That's it," Dax said, staggering into port accessway storage B. The surveillance-free room had become the official staging area for her senior staff—and every member of it had retreated back to it in defeat. She didn't reject the chair that Bowers offered this time. She looked around at her officers. "I'm about to start taking a laser torch to the decks."

"If we could get to one," Bowers said. "Last torch I saw, he beamed away."

Dax queried Mirren, who had been tasked with watching the show from the bridge. "Did he destroy the Klingon outpost?"

"Disabled it. It looks like he took it down with the first volley," the Russian woman replied. "I've never in my life seen flying like that. That encounter put all our earlier raids to shame."

"The ones where we were in control, you mean." Bowers popped open a vial of water and passed it to Dax. "I think we're officially unnecessary," he said, opening another for himself.

Dax took a sip and looked at Leishman. The engineer was sitting on the floor, hard at work making notes on paper, of all things. Padds still connected to *Aventine* as of Riker's takeover were seen as vulnerable to compromise. "Mikaela, any progress on getting us a way to talk to each other while we're between decks? Riker—or whoever he's got in there—seems to be intercepting anything sent over the air."

"We're trying," Leishman said, clearly exhausted. "It's problem number twelve right now."

Leaning against the wall, Kedair shook her head. "It should be higher on the list. My people are relaying hand signals so as not to telegraph their moves—and we're not sure he's not reading those. How can this guy be watching everything at once?"

"I guess he didn't just replicate a bridge crew,"

Bowers said. "He's got a whole Romulan surveillance operation in there with him." He took a swig of water from a vial. "Maybe he's hiding them in the bedroom."

Dax asked, "What's the closest you've gotten to taking down the holodeck?"

"I had three people approaching a power distribution line from beneath," Leishman said, picking up a set of blueprints from near her ankle. Riker had blocked access to any schematics that might be found in the main computer. "As soon as they got within sight of it, Riker beamed them all to their quarters." She looked up at Dax. "Their individual quarters."

Bowers couldn't help but chuckle. "He sent them to their rooms. You know *he's* a parent."

Dax was past being amused by the absurdity of the situation. She focused again on her chief engineer. "What have we got that works? That we've got control of?"

"The tractor beam."

"That's a big help," Dax said. Then her eyes narrowed. "Wait. How do we have control of the tractor beam?"

"Well, 'control' might overstate the case," Leishman said. She shuffled through papers. "The thing's been glitchy since the damage we took from *Tuonetar*, as you know—it's been giving us energy fluctuations that feed back into the ship's systems. We detached it from the ship's power grid to quarantine it while we ran tests. We could switch the unit on while it has no power—so soon as we plugged it in, so to speak, it would activate."

Dax frowned. "But it won't stay on, once Riker notices it. He'd just cut power to the subsystem."

"That's right. We can turn it on—once, for maybe half a second. And he won't let us turn it on after that."

"That's not much help," Bowers said. "Maybe we can use it to capture a psychiatric team for the admiral."

"We wouldn't hold them for long," Leishman said. "I told you, the unit wasn't quite working anyway."

Another dead end. Dax drained her vial. She was hungry, but with the replicators off-limits to them, the only food was combat rations.

Feeling she needed to do something, Dax began to rise—then a violent quake shook the room, sending canisters and boxes tumbling to the deck. She looked to Mirren. "Are we fighting anyone?"

Mirren shook her head. "No, the slipstream drive was activated."

"Accent on *was*," Leishman said, sitting up straight. She brightened. "That was the sound of *Aventine* dropping out of the corridor unexpectedly. I knew it—he's been pushing the drive too hard!"

Dax took a deep breath. This was something. She knew it would be a while before Riker would get the ship moving again—but it wasn't clear what that time would buy them. "Oliana, you said *Enterprise* was still after us?"

"Like a dog on a trail. But I can't see how she'd find us. They'd know our heading, but would have to drop out of warp repeatedly to find us. And if Riker doesn't want to be found, he could make us very hard to detect."

Dax knew all that. But she also knew *Aventine*'s crew needed help. And that *Enterprise*—or someone—

would run across them again. She looked to Leishman. "Cancel the order for finding a way to communicate inside the ship. We need a way to communicate *outside* the ship."

"To do what?" Bowers asked.

Dax thought for a moment. "Tell me what was wrong with the tractor beam, again?"

Leishman let out a deep breath. The engineer clearly didn't see why it mattered. "There are sensors that identify, for our graviton beam, the mass of the item to be hauled. But if any of the matter we're grappling is transmuted to energy in a matter/antimatter reaction—as might happen in the engines of a fleeing vehicle—we get a greatly magnified feedback pulse instead of information. The incoming charge shuts down the unit. Pretty much defeats the purpose of a tractor beam."

The explanation had brought something else to mind. "You know, maybe there's something there," Dax said, rubbing her hands together. "There was something Worf did during the Dominion War. The Detapa Council was aboard a Cardassian ship being attacked by Klingon cruisers. We were on *Defiant,* trying to rescue the Council, but we were down to our last trick. Then Worf had an idea—to diffuse *Defiant*'s tractor beam so as to function as a partial shield, disrupting the disruptor fire. It worked—and we saved the Council."

Leishman nodded, which Dax took as confirmation she had it right. "What are you thinking, Captain?" the engineer asked.

"If we could target our tractor beam on incoming fire, the energy might do more than knock out the tractor unit. We might kill power to the whole ship."

The chief engineer shook her head. "It can't be phaser fire. Whatever we turn the beam on has to have mass." Leishman thought for a moment. "Now something like a torpedo—*that'd* do it. We hook onto one of those just as the matter/antimatter reaction starts and it's lights-out. For a moment anyway."

"How do we get someone to fire a torpedo in the tractor beam's arc, right when we're there?" Bowers laughed. "Maybe we ask the Klingons nicely next time."

"We can't ask anyone," Kedair said. "What are we going to do, stand in the ports and wave?"

"We can't," Mirren said. "Riker has set them all to opaque. We can see out. That's it."

"Which is why we need a way," Dax said, "to communicate outside the ship."

"Communicate outside, communicate inside." Leishman knelt and gathered up her papers in a clump. "I'd better go before I get any more requests."

Dax sighed as the engineer stood. It was true: the conversation had circled back, a sure sign they were spinning in place.

"Okay, Mikaela's right. One problem at a time," she said. "Let's try to get our ship back. Dismissed."

The staffers filed out into the circular area, ringed with hatches in the walls and ladders leading up and down. The last to emerge into the area, Dax surveyed the faces of the drained people standing there. They were good officers, and she had tried to lead them well—as well as she could, as well as anyone could in the situation. But they were at their limits.

They needed a break. And right now, she didn't care where it came from.

Behind Bowers, a hatch cracked open. A wild-haired human tumbled out of the darkened tunnel, his several tool belts clattering as he hit the deck.

"Oh, hello," Ensign Riordan said, noticing the crowd. "Er—am I interrupting something?"

Twenty-six

It was a good thing, Picard thought, that La Forge felt certain *Aventine* would need significant time to get back under way. Because it had taken far longer than he'd expected to put through his call. That, more than any Starfleet briefing, told him what he needed to know about the situation in this sector and beyond.

The subspace communication networks of all the powers operating in the region were damaged, with many of the normal routes for relaying messages dead. Certainly, there were thousands of talented engineers out there on all sides working on repairs—but not one of the installations Riker had struck was back operating, as near as the Klingon outpost's systems could tell.

And *Aventine*'s victims were only the beginning. Combining what *Enterprise* had learned from Admiral Akaar with the Klingons' information, Worf had counted no fewer than thirty strikes against communications hubs. The attacks were distributed across political lines: Khitomer Accords signatories, Typhon Pact members, and various nonaligned powers had been targeted. And, again, there was that strange inclusion of deep space facilities devoted to pure science.

The number of ships suspected to be involved in the incident was now between five and ten, although nobody could tell for sure. Defense forces around the region had been jumpy—and there were clearly already freebooting opportunists out there, taking advantage of the lack of communications coverage. Dygan and his team had struggled to separate the real from the imagined, the connected from the incidental. Many of the displays in his evidence room had been filled in, and names of several ships and their captains were now known.

As *Enterprise*'s chief security officer had remarked, this conspiracy—if it was one—involved players from more powers than the one against the Khitomer Peace Conference, years earlier.

"That's progress," Picard had darkly joked. "Inclusivity, that's our goal."

Now, having finally made a tenuous subspace connection, Picard learned that his joke had a special irony. "Let me get this straight," the captain said as he, Worf, and Dygan sat before the viewscreen in the observation lounge. "You're telling me all this may have begun at a *peace conference?*"

"*It's possible,*" Christine Vale said. The *Titan* commander was one third of another trio, gathered around another observation lounge table many light years away. Commanders Tuvok and Deanna Troi had joined Vale.

Needing to retrace the path of both Riker and *Aventine*, Picard had chanced trying to reach *Titan*. Even given the poor connection, Picard could spot the obvious worry in Troi's expression, caused by the unhappy news he had been forced to deliver earlier. On its exploration mission to the Genovous Pulsar, *Titan* had been completely out of contact with Starfleet Command as a result of the attacks in its neighborhood.

"Admiral Riker transferred his flag to Aventine *within hours of the Summit of Eight,"* Vale said. She was clearly unnerved, as well; she had paused the conversation earlier to order a security team to reconstruct Riker's movements. *"He left, and we left for Genovous. That's the last we've heard—from anybody, really. It's a mess out there."*

The Summit of Eight. It was the first Picard had heard of the meeting; it was clearly a secret Akaar had either not been able to share, or had not yet considered relevant when they were cut off. The account Picard had already heard had astounded him.

"Eight powers—four Khitomer and four Typhon—called to this Far Embassy. And we don't know who made the invitation?"

"We thought our invitation came from the Romulans," Vale said. *"As I understand it, the Tzenkethi thought their invite came from us."*

"Someone has been setting up blind dates," Picard said. "How could the Federation agree to attend—and on a station whose origin they could not confirm?"

"When the battlefield is this wide," Tuvok said, *"even a small chance at peace is worth the risk. The admiral did not fear it."*

He wouldn't, Picard thought. He wondered if his friend, new to the ambassadorial role, hadn't found the prospect of a diplomatic coup enticing. "How long was Riker on this station, this Far Embassy?"

"Three hours, five minutes, six seconds. The others

appear to have been there for approximately the same amount of time. We are sending you the list of vessels we saw in attendance."

Picard looked at the padd on his table. The information appeared. The few renegade vessels he knew specifics about were not on the list, he saw. But Riker's first act was to transfer to a faster ship. The others could have done the same. And there was Klingon General Charlak on the list of known attendees. Kersh hadn't mentioned any conference, but perhaps she hadn't been told of it yet, either.

None of this could be a coincidence, Picard thought. Whatever happened, the conference appeared to be the start of the problem.

"So either the eight of them formed a cabal and concocted this plan while there—in three hours—or something else happened." Picard looked up at the monitor. "Have you any other information you can share with me? Anything at all."

Tuvok read from a padd. *"Our security team appears to have found something curious. Our transporter chief reports that Admiral Riker requested that he be beamed to holodeck one on* Aventine.*"*

Picard's eyes narrowed. "Why would he do that?"

Troi spoke up. *"I know he had been talking about designing a holodeck program replicating his office and quarters here on* Titan. *He said it would save time on packing."* She paused. *"I thought it was a joke."*

A joke, perhaps, Picard thought, *but a perfectly marvelous idea.* He'd spent innumerable hours over the years getting admirals and ambassadors settled into their surroundings, having to deal with them when things weren't just so. *Bravo, Number One.* "Had he designed this program before departing *Titan*?"

Tuvok again consulted the padd. *"Our security team's reconstruction of Admiral Riker's movements indicates he did visit our holodeck before departing, recording a program. He could have taken it with him. We did not run the program in the interests of protecting his privacy—"*

"I think we're past that now," Picard said.

"We'll take a look at it," Vale said. *"Stand by,* Enterprise*—if the connection holds. We'll be back."* She and Tuvok disappeared from the screen.

Troi settled into the frame, replacing Vale. She looked anguished, and understandably so. *Titan* had heard a little about what Riker and *Aventine* had been involved in; getting confirmation had been devastating for her. But Picard could tell she hadn't surrendered to despair—yet.

"Captain, I think there may have been some reason he didn't want to take me with him."

Picard nodded. "If this is Will we're facing—and if he was already intent on this escapade, for whatever reason—he would want to protect you from the danger." *Or the repercussions,* he thought, but he chose not to add that.

"I don't think that's it, Captain. Even when he was on Titan*, he seemed anxious to send me out of his presence."*

This was something. "Do you believe," Picard asked cautiously, "that perhaps he knew something was . . . *wrong* with him, something that might infect you too?" This seemed like a worthwhile straw to grasp at; it explained Riker's actions while going some distance to absolving the admiral from blame.

Troi thought for a few moments. *"No. He wasn't trying to protect me. I know what that feels like. I didn't sense that in him."*

Picard shook his head, deflated. "Then why would he want you apart? Simply so he could do what he intended to do in solitude?"

She bit her lip, formulating an answer. *"I almost think his concern was that I, specifically, could sense that something was different in him."*

Picard looked to Dygan, who was noting all of this intently. "Certainly," the captain said. "As a counselor, as a Betazoid, as a wife, you would be trained to—"

"It's something more. I think if I could get near him again, I might be able to solve the mystery. I need to go to him."

Picard looked uncomfortably at Worf. "That's not really possible—not right now. We're in pursuit, and *Titan* is far away." There was no chance that *Titan* could catch up with *Aventine*—and if *Enterprise* waited to rendezvous with Vale's ship, Picard might well lose his quarry.

Troi looked to her left and edged aside. Vale returned to the screen. *"We've examined the holographic program,"* she said. *"It's exactly what Counselor Troi said it was: a facsimile of his quarters on* Titan, *minus the occupants. With a computer system identical to what he has in his personal space there."*

Picard frowned. "That sounds like a dead-end."

"Perhaps not," Tuvok said. *"Because while we have no access to his personal data files here, we were able to see just how quickly he designed the holodeck program. He built a complete facsimile of his quarters, apparently from memory, in thirty point seven seconds."*

"Commander Tuvok, inappropriate as it may seem, admirals' personal quarters are a popular holodeck setting. Certainly it was preprogrammed," Picard said.

"I do not mean he drew it from the computer's memory

files. It was new. He programmed it with a combination of vocal commands and key presses made simultaneously on two adjacent holodeck interface panels."

Vale nodded. *"It's uncanny, sir. It's just like the real room. The only things missing are Deanna and Natasha."*

Picard sat forward in his seat. He didn't know what to make of it, but somehow, he thought he'd just heard something important. "Can . . . can you do a biometric analysis of the admiral, based on the pattern you beamed to *Aventine*? For comparison to a baseline on file."

Vale and Tuvok looked at each other. *"We had not considered that, but it should be possible,"* Tuvok said. *"What do you suspect?"*

"I'm not sure. How long will it take?" Picard wasn't sure they could wait in Klingon space much longer. *"Aventine* will be moving again soon."

"I would estimate—"

The screen went black. Picard, alarmed, clicked his badge. "Lieutenant Šmrhová?"

The security officer preempted his question. *"The connecting station has dropped out, Captain."*

"Is this temporary? Do you think it will come back up?"

"Nothing else has."

"Just when we were getting somewhere," Dygan said, disappointed.

"We *are* somewhere, Glinn." Picard stood, his energy restored. "The eight powers they mentioned— all represented in your evidence room. A mysterious summit, on a mysterious station. An admiral who shows a sudden ability at high-speed holodeck pro- gram design, apparently working from memory." He walked to the port, excited. "I don't know what it all means—but we know it means something."

"Sir?" Worf asked. Picard looked back to the others. They didn't seem to share his elation. Dygan was still puzzling through everything, and Worf was considering the blank screen. "I do not see the connections."

"Will has said nothing without meaning in any of this." Picard paced back behind the desk. "He told me he is heading to the Adelphous Array, and that I would learn something from that. What would I 'learn' from that fact?"

Worf straightened his baldric. "The Adelphous Array is a major installation, larger than any he's struck before. We've seen one, just like it—a hundred light years or so from here, near the Cardassian border."

Dygan's face lit with recognition. "The Argle Array, isn't it?"

"*Argus*," Picard said. "What would Riker expect me to learn from that?"

"Perhaps," Worf said, "he means to say there is no place safe from their rampage. It is a warning that they intend a strike there, too. Perhaps he is encouraging us to set a trap at the Argus Array."

"That's awfully far from here," Dygan said. "By the time the rogue ships have fought their way there, half the Federation will be cut off from the other half."

"Even telling us to watch where he's going next isn't much of a warning," Worf said. "He knows *Aventine* will get there first. It might attack and leave before we arrive." He corrected himself. "Or it would have, if the slipstream drive problem hadn't failed him."

Picard shook his head, his smile returning. "No, Number One. When up against an opponent who isn't making any mistakes, it's reasonable to assume the mistakes he does make are purposeful. Like leaving when an array isn't really destroyed. And like pushing a drive so hard that it fails predictably—allowing its pursuer to catch up."

With that, he marched toward the door to the bridge. Worf and Dygan, startled, rose and followed.

"Captain," Worf said, walking through the now-open doorway. "What are your orders?"

"Admiral Riker's giving these orders, Commander. I think I've just figured out what he's trying to tell us." He walked to his chair. "The Adelphous system, best speed."

Twenty-seven

Dax watched in amazement as Ensign Riordan wolfed down another protein bar. The lanky young engineer hadn't eaten in two days, or so he had said—although it wasn't for a lack of food. One of his several toolbelts was festooned with MREs. He'd just forgotten.

Immediately after his sudden emergence from the darkened hatch, Leishman had brought Riordan into port accessway storage B. They had tried twice to extract the ensign's story from him, but his reporting abilities ranked just beneath his social graces. Dax had, so far, picked up bits and pieces of a winding travelogue, a tour of *Aventine*'s innards by narrow Jefferies tubes by night-vision goggles.

Dax tried again to steer him on course. "Once more, Ensign, how long have you been crawling around in the tubes?"

He answered between chomps. "You ordered me to serve out the rest of my sentence working on the exterior lighting problem."

"Didn't you notice the Red Alerts? Or the fact that we were in combat?"

"I noticed them . . . uhm . . . Captain. I even saw some of the fights, out the viewports." Mouth half full, he shook his head. "You guys really are going for the court martial to end all courts martial, aren't you?"

Leishman rolled her eyes while Riordan wiped the wrong side of his face. "Ensign . . . ?"

Bowers took the ensign by his uniform. He had little patience for Riordan and had been the one to throw him in the brig. "Did it occur to you, Mister, to present yourself in main engineering when the shooting started? As a courtesy to your commanding officer."

"I'm not on the duty roster." The first officer released him, and Riordan shrank back a little. "I'm still on report. I'm not part of whatever's going on."

Dax sighed. *I wish I had that excuse.* "*Aventine*'s systems didn't try to block your passage?"

"Oh, yeah. That's why I've been gone so long." He cast the empty wrapper onto the deck and drew pictures in the air. "I'd go one way and get stopped by a force field or a hatch slamming down. Another way and the tubes would start depressurizing. I've had to get pretty good at defeating the lockouts on hatches in the dark." He looked at Leishman. "I think something's wrong with the ship, Lieutenant."

The chief engineer put her hand over her face. "Captain, if you can spare me from this fool, I have things to do."

"Wait, Chief. Ensign," the captain asked, "where were you when the ship started acting up?"

"Ah, yeah. One of the engineering crawlspaces on the underside of the saucer section. I found a flutter in the power distribution router by the port registry lights.

"A *flutter*?" Bowers asked. "Is that your report?"

"I don't want to tax you, Commander."

Bowers stared coolly. "That's decent of you."

"Anyway," Riordan continued, "I took the control unit for the lights off the main grid and transferred it to my portable engineering padd. I was in the middle of a test when the ship went after the Corvus Beacon—I guess that's what it was—when everything went wacko. So I got moving."

Dax's eyes narrowed. "But what happened with what you were working on? Did you put the lights back under control of the main computer?"

Riordan laughed. "Hell, no. I was busy trying to figure out how to wiggle backwards through a meter-wide tunnel in the dark." He caught Bowers's expression. "I mean, '*Hell, no, Captain, sir.*'"

"So the engineering padd is still in there, with complete control over some high-profile lights on *Aventine*'s hull. And they were disconnected from the main computer before Riker took over." Dax looked to Bowers and Leishman. "That could be it, couldn't it? That's our way to communicate outside the ship."

Bowers laughed. "What are we going to do, flash Morse code at people? I don't think anyone's trained on that, even on *Enterprise*!"

Dax frowned. In the warp age, starships and starbases had such advanced sensors that exterior lighting had become, in large measure, superfluous as a means of communicating a vessel's position and bearing. One of the major reasons it continued to exist was as an aid for spacesuited workers during extravehicular activity. Some of the more comical—and embarrassing—stories from busy spacedocks were tales of engineers who'd done modifications on the wrong ships. It was like a doctor doing surgery on the wrong patient.

Leishman didn't think it would work as a means of ship-to-ship communication, but not for the reason Bowers said. "The big lights use a lot of juice. The admiral—or whoever has him—has shown he's wise to any change to *Aventine*'s power usage. We haven't even been able to recharge phasers. Switching the marking lights off and on—I can't help but think that something as simple as that would be noticed."

"No, no, no. You're missing it," Riordan said, excitedly. Catching his supervisor's look, he slowed down. "I'm sorry, Lieutenant. But we don't have to turn them on and off. A light is an emission—and *Enterprise* has got to be scanning the living hell out of *Aventine* for those. All we have to do is fiddle with the frequency and wavelengths of what we're putting out. There won't be power spikes." He smiled. "You'll be talking in pretty colors."

"Turning speech into modulated light." Dax turned the idea over in her head.

"Which can be transmuted back into speech. Free-space optical communication," Riordan said. "It's serious old-school. Alexander Graham Bell used it in his photophone. He always thought it was going to be the thing he'd be remembered for."

"I can tell you what we'll be remembered for if we don't come up with something," Dax said. She looked to the chief engineer. "Can you make it work?"

"We can certainly try it," Leishman said. "But if Riker isn't going to notice us sending a message, I don't know that the people you're trying to reach will notice, either."

"It's what we've got," the captain said. And if any ship in the fleet had personnel capable of figuring out what her crew was up to, it was *Enterprise*. "Ensign, can you rig the lights to send our message?"

Riordan nodded. He ran his hand through his

hair. "We'll also need to position spotters at the viewports, with tricorders capable of reading the same kind of signals in return."

"We'll see if we have any that are off the grid," Bowers said. "But the data rate's going to be slow. This is a step above smoke signals."

"We don't need to send a holonovel." Dax pointed to the first officer. "One of us should go back with Riordan to the control interface, to make sure the right message goes out."

Bowers put his hands before him. "You know what you want to say, Captain. And I might accidentally send him back to the brig before we got halfway there."

She cast a look at Riordan, who had wandered off from the conversation and was rummaging through the boxes in storage. He found the crate of boatswain's whistles and drew one out. "These are neat," the ensign said. "Can I have this?"

She looked back at Bowers. "Okay, I take your point. I'll go with him. I need you to set up a relay line of messengers between me and the bridge, to be ready to let me know when there's a ship outside for us to hail."

Bowers frowned. "It'll be tough to make that look casual."

"Sam, it's got to be easier than trying to fly a shuttle off a ship that doesn't want to let go." Dax felt more enlivened than she'd been in hours. "People are the one thing we control right now. Let's use 'em!"

Twenty-eight

All her life, Nerla had wanted what many other Romulans wanted: advancement. Beraldak Bay was far from the halls of power, but she had seen what power could do in the way the locals treated the formidable individuals who vacationed there. She had determined then not to follow her loathsome family into their low trade, seeking hospitality work instead in the hopes that someone would notice her fire and intellect. They would then deliver her from her sunny purgatory.

But she soon learned that no one came to a holiday retreat looking for administrative talent. She was no one's prospective *anything*, and that had proved ruinous to her plans. Only Bretorius had been willing to entertain taking her on as an assistant—something that should have been a tip-off right there. She'd heard his sob stories and hadn't minded: Nerla figured she would be the operator, the power behind the senator. But Bretorius was poor clay to work with. She couldn't turn nothing into something.

Worse, she found that rather than opening doors for her, working for Bretorius had shut them all. In the last few weeks, she'd given up completely, waiting out the end until she returned to the bayshore.

But now, here Nerla was, in an interrogation room in the high-security ward of a Romulan warbird, injecting a stimulant into the neck of the commander Bretorius had deposed.

Things had taken a strange turn.

Commander Yalok, strapped to the chair, looked up at her with bleary eyes. "You . . . won't get away with this."

"I'm sorry for the discomfort, Commander. It is the senator's idea." She paused to check Yalok's restraints again, though it hardly seemed necessary given his state. "It's *all* been the senator's idea."

"This will go badly for you, too," the woozy man said. He fixed his eyes on her and tried to focus. "You're . . . an accomplice to piracy and torture. If you release me now . . . I'll see that you are spared the harshest punishment."

The cuffs checked, she pushed at the metal frame. "I'm not releasing you. I'm just repositioning you so you can hear the speaker better."

Bretorius's voice came over the room's comsystem. *"Good morning again to you, Captain."*

"The honorable senator," Yalok said. "What's the matter, Bretorius—won't face what you've done in person? Where are you hiding?"

"I'm right down the hall, actually. But I'm much too busy to pay a call right now. Nerla will confirm, it's been an active period."

"Indeed." Yalok began to strain at his bonds. "I've heard crashing about. My crew is trying to break into here to free me!"

"Hmm? Oh, yes. Some have been trying to enter, I suppose. But this deck's defenses are formidable. Between the force fields and the paralytic gas dispensers, we're quite alone."

Yalok turned, as best he could, to look at Nerla. "What are you trying to accomplish with this madness? The Imperial Fleet will not be broken to the will of some fool senator, even if he did once helm a warbird!"

Nerla cautioned him. "Captain, I wouldn't—"

"Wouldn't what? Vex him? I don't fear death, not by his hands!" He looked up to the ceiling, where the senator's voice was coming from. "You were a terrible captain, Bretorius. The laughingstock of the fleet, a laughingstock of a senator. You were a nothing then, and a nothing now!"

"I don't think the Federation thought so, when I struck their station," Bretorius said. *"Or the Klingons. Or the Gorn."*

Yalok's blackened eyes widened. "The Gorn! They're our allies!"

"If that surprises you, you may be interested to know that as we speak, D'varian *is completing a strike on Thenta Karos."*

Yalok couldn't believe it. "That's—that's *our* station!"

"It was. I have to say, the Imperial Fleet did its best to protect it. But I know all their maneuvers, their tactical biases. It was a small matter to think several steps ahead of them."

Yalok said nothing for long moments. Then he spoke in low, grave tones.

"Bretorius, you have brought shame not just to yourself, but upon every member of the crew of *D'varian*. Quarlis will rue the day she ever yielded to your demands!"

"Subcommander Quarlis isn't involved anymore. None of your precious crew is. I am making decisions and seeing them implemented."

"I can't imagine how." Yalok looked again to Nerla—and then back up to the speaker. "You're delusional."

"Then you're living the delusion with me," Bretorius said. *"Frankly, it doesn't matter what you think. It is happening. And I am speaking to you now because I need something else from you."*

Yalok swore. Bretorius ignored it and went on. *"You see, I'm committed to a certain mission now—and I will execute it faithfully. But I can see many new possibilities arising once it is completed. Romulus has been weakened since the Shinzon affair and the subsequent civil war. Our empire is in need of a strong leader, a leader with vision."*

Yalok laughed—though the act appeared to cause him pain. "And I suppose you nominate yourself."

"No, Yalok. The people of the Empire will nominate me by acclamation once they fully understand what I can do. And there is no reason to stop there. I will lead all the Typhon powers and more."

The captain turned his head again toward Nerla, who was staring blankly into space. "How can you serve this madman, Nerla?"

"Just let him finish, Captain. It's easier."

Bretorius went on. *"I have plumbed the D'varian's systems for its secrets—but there are some that only you hold, Yalok. I did as well, when I had your position. I know, for example, that you have knowledge of secret arsenals and refueling stations scattered across this region. Romulus has relocated them since my time, but you know their present whereabouts."*

Yalok was incredulous. "What good would that do you? You are one man—and insane. Do you plan to load the torpedoes yourself?"

"There are many disaffected peoples in the Empire who would serve a strong leader," the senator said. "It is simply a matter of making the connections with them—and showing what I am capable of doing. And what I intend to do, once I have completed that to which I am committed."

The captain rolled his eyes. "This is ludicrous. Is that all? Anything else?"

"Yes. You have served as escort for both the praetor and the proconsul. You know the locations of their protective retreats and the codes for bypassing their defense stations." He paused. "Nerla?"

Yalok turned his head again to see her at one of the cabinets against the wall of the interrogation room. "What are you doing?" he said, seeing the hypospray injector in her hand. "What is that?"

"A drug that will make you more cooperative. Please try to speak clearly; Nerla will be listening, and so will I. Even if you don't hear me."

Yalok fixed his eyes on the ceiling and glared angrily. "You will die for this, Bretorius!"

"I used to fear death," Bretorius said, as Nerla approached the captain. "I feared a lot of things. But I have learned much since then—and I have much to do now. Good-bye."

Yalok looked up at Nerla as she administered the drug. His eyes pleaded with her. "Nerla, this is wrong. This . . . is wrong . . ."

"I'm sorry about this," she said—and she was. "Bretorius. He's—he's changed . . ."

Twenty-nine

So much of space was lifeless. It was a natural condition, nothing to provoke despair in the experienced traveler. But Jean-Luc Picard had seldom found any place lonelier than when visiting a system where life *had* been—before being snuffed out.

The population of Adelphous IV had been destroyed several years earlier during the invasion in which the Borg had changed its tactics from assimilation to annihilation. Picard had visited the system on *Enterprise*-D before the destruction; it was a routine stop about which he remembered absolutely nothing. That saddened him deeply. There were so many worlds out there; no one could know about all of them. The Borg had wiped out so many. Yet seeing the remains of that golden world glistening far in the distance off *Enterprise*-E's bow, he felt like he should remember.

He'd once experienced the last days of a long-dead world called Kataan through the eyes of its residents, thanks to a probe that took control of his mind. It was meant as a memorial, and he now felt privileged to have learned about them; not all episodes of alien control were necessarily negative. By contrast, the Adelphousians were known to the Federation, having offered their system as host to the massive communications array beyond the fifth planet. Records of the people and their lives existed. But Picard knew it was no substitute for walking among them, and that would never happen now.

The Adelphous Array was exactly like the Argus Array on the far side of Federation space: a giant gray honeycomb of hexagonal subspace telescopes networked together. Interferometry had been practiced by the earliest radio astronomers on Earth, using facilities like the Expanded Very Large Array in New Mexico; sites like Adelphous had applied descendants of those techniques to subspace in order to peer farther than any ship could currently go. But the workers at the offsite operations center on Adelphous had died with everyone else, and while the Federation had plans to bring the Adelphous Array back online, it hadn't yet done so.

"It's a shame they're taking so long with it," La Forge said from the engineering station on *Enterprise*'s bridge. His artificial eyes were locked on the space station growing larger on the massive main viewscreen. "There's still a lot of good this place could do."

Picard agreed. "I believe they're being respectful of the sympathies of the Adelphousian refugees."

Worf, seated to his side, observed, "A watchtower would honor those who died."

Picard felt the same way. The fact the array was out of service explained something else: the absence of Federation vessels ready to defend the place. That wasn't unexpected. Of greater concern was the absence of a certain Federation vessel attacking the place. He'd played a hunch that he would find *Aventine* here; now, he worried that his thinking all along had been wrong.

His first officer would never voice his disappointment, but Picard could tell the Klingon was frustrated. Picard thought he might as well give Worf a chance to get his thoughts out into the open. "Recommendations, Number One?"

"Perhaps we should backtrack along our route. If *Aventine* has been disabled so long that we could beat her here, she might be unable to move at all."

La Forge stepped into the command well. "Slipstream's new enough—fixing it might take a minute, it might take a day."

Picard looked to his chief engineer. "*Your* recommendations?"

"When he does get it going, he can probably continue to use it for several more jumps without stalling again. Maybe we ought to—"

A tone sounded from the tactical station. Šmrhová announced, "*Aventine* has entered the system. Eighty thousand kilometers from the array and closing."

"Red Alert," Picard said, calmly. "Just in time." *Aventine* was four times *Enterprise*'s distance from the facility. He spoke to be heard over the alert clarion. "Lieutenant Faur, full impulse to the Adelphous Array, now."

"Aye, Captain."

"Silence the alarm," Worf ordered. The Klingon leaned in and asked, "You are not going to confront him?"

Picard shook his head. He'd shared some of his suspicions with Worf, but not yet all. "The wrecking crew is coming. We're going to chain ourselves to the building."

Ahead, the Adelphous station nearly filled the screen with its dark, unlit mass. It was time. "Shields up,"

Picard ordered. "Orbit at our minimal turning radius. Hug the array." He looked to Worf and smiled gently. "They have the speed—but we have the shorter route."

Such a strategy wasn't possible at the Corvus Beacon, where *Aventine* had arrived first. Nor at the No'Var Outpost, where the asteroid field—not to mention the Klingons' disruptor cannons—made it difficult to maintain an inner track.

Picard was also banking on Riker not wanting to shoot at *Enterprise*.

That proved a bad bet. "Photon torpedoes," Dygan snapped. "Coming in fore and aft."

"Shields to maximum!"

The viewscreen went white. *Enterprise* shook madly as it sailed through a miasma of destructive power. His mind told him the torpedo wasn't aimed directly at them. His bridge crew gripped their armrests, struggling to stay at their stations.

"He's just trying to shake us loose," Picard said.

"*Aventine*'s shields are up. Still diving straight toward us and the station," Dygan said.

"Hold steady."

Another barrage—and then, after the universe stopped shaking, another call from Dygan. "He has broken off. Now circling the station at four hundred kilometers away, firing phasers."

"Circle at one hundred kilometers away," Picard said. "Keep our shields between *Aventine* and the array."

Enterprise quaked again. "We are taking damage without fighting back," Worf said, a little unease in his voice.

"The array can't fight back. We can take the damage better than it can."

The stalking continued for a few minutes before a hail came in. Picard ordered it put on-screen. The holographic Riker appeared, again before the black backdrop. *"I see you came back for more."*

"You invited us." Picard spoke in even tones. "You do realize this array is not operating?"

"A deactivated phaser is still a phaser," Riker said.

Picard found that puzzling. "The array is not a weapon, Admiral."

"It depends on your point of view."

"And what is your point of view?"

Riker looked a little pained. *"You figure it out. I'm busy."*

Picard needed to keep him talking. He wasn't ready to play his trump yet. "This will not end like the other times, you know."

Riker grinned. *"Captain, are you going to fire on a superior officer?"*

"Do I need to?"

"You outgun me, but I can outrun you," Riker said. *"Do you ever get the feeling we're developing a new training program for Starfleet Academy?"*

"I hope to be alongside you giving the lecture," Picard said.

Riker smiled wanly. *"I'm guessing that probably is not going to happen."* He looked off to the side. *"Not now."*

"It could, if you stop your engines. We could talk—"

"I know we could. But I already know what will happen instead. If you don't fire, your shields will reach their limit, and I will destroy the station. If you do fire, I will execute an evasive maneuver you're not expecting that will put me on a clear vector. And I will destroy the station."

"You didn't destroy the Klingon outpost."

"This location is different. Don't bother asking how." Riker shook his head. *"Now, it's time to—"*

"I spoke with Deanna," Picard said.

Riker paused. For a moment, the captain felt a break in the phaser fire striking *Enterprise*'s shields. Then it resumed.

"Deanna is concerned about you and the way you left," the captain continued. "I know about the Far Embassy, Will. I know."

All emotion left the face of the figure on-screen. *"I have work to finish."* Then he vanished, the comlink cut. The viewscreen reverted to the scene from outside, as *Enterprise* lurched around, keeping between *Aventine* and the array.

To Picard's left, Hegol Den touched his arm to get his attention. "I think you got through, Captain. If a holographic character can show emotion, that is."

"This one does." Picard looked over to La Forge, who had been scanning *Aventine* without pause since it had arrived. "Intensify your life-sign scan of *Aventine*, Commander."

"No change in the number of occupants, Captain."

"See if you can scan deck by deck," Picard said. "I am particularly interested in the number of people in or near holodeck one . . ."

Thirty

Ezri Dax thought captains should know every square centimeter of their ships. Yet Riordan had found crawl spaces she never would have considered entering. She hadn't minded, though: Riker had demonstrated that he had knowledge of what was going on in most of the Jefferies tubes. Riordan had found accessways so ill-suited for use that they'd stumped even the admiral's surveillance capabilities.

Still, she had somehow assumed that their destination would have been a larger opening. It had certainly been a hope, after shimmying through hundreds of meters of darkness, stopping only to deal with a turn left, right, up, or down. Instead, the area where Riordan had abandoned his diagnostic equipment was large enough for him and him alone. She'd been forced to remain on her stomach, lodged in a meter-wide shaft like a Trill mudcrawler in a burrow.

As low-tech as the signaling system Riordan was now working on, her own link to the bridge was even more primitive. The boatswain's whistles they'd found in storage B had been distributed to more than sixty different crewmembers, stationed at intervals all along the route between her and the bridge. The surveillance equipment aboard ship would certainly hear the alert sounds, which was why another sixty individuals scattered all around the ship had the instruments as well. Riker might hear all the tooting and tweeting, but only one line of signalers actually led anywhere.

From behind her in the crawlspace, three short, shrill chirps told her *Enterprise* was in view of *Aventine*'s underside. Four would have meant another Starfleet ship, five a "friendly."

Finding the whistle around her neck, she blew a couple of fast notes. *Acknowledged. Stand by.*

Curled up in his cubbyhole, Riordan made adjustments to a small equipment case by the light of the SIMs beacon strapped around Dax's head. The padd was connected to a port in the floor. "I've taken the audio input from my combadge and connected it to a transducer," Riordan said. He paused long enough to look back at her. "Don't worry about the details. It involves some steps I don't expect you to understand."

Dax groaned, feeling the confines of the shaft pinching at her. "You're a real charmer. You do realize there are ranks above ensign, don't you? You could try for one—by being a little less . . . *you*." She gave an acidic smile. "Just a little."

Riordan ignored her. "Okay, here we go," he said, unspooling a coil of wire connected to the combadge. "I wasn't able to get the transmission rate in real-time, so you've got to keep it *very* short. Will *Enterprise* figure it out?"

"We'll find out," she said, pulling the combadge close to her mouth. *"Worf . . ."*

*   *   *

ENTERPRISE

Another phaser barrage struck *Enterprise*'s shields. With the protective energy barrier down to fifty percent—and the bridge officers straining to keep the ship in the right position amid the din—Picard found the observation from his chief engineer bizarre: "There's something odd with *Aventine*'s ventral registry lights."

"We noticed that before. Some of them are intermittent."

"They still are. But they're oscillating in a nonrandom pattern." La Forge's fingers flew across the controls. "This might be something."

Or nothing, Picard thought. But anything different was good. "Mr. Faur, keep us oriented with a ventral view of *Aventine*."

La Forge sounded tentative. "I'm running the oscillations through a decryption algorithm," he said, studying the data on his console. A minute later, he looked back at the captain, triumphant. "It's speech!"

Speech? "Let's hear it."

Over the sound of phaser fire, a woman's voice reverberated throughout the bridge.

"Worf . . ."

The Klingon's eyes widened. "It is Dax!"

"Detapa . . . Council . . . tactic."

"Detapa Council? That's a Cardassian body," Dygan said.

"Torpedo . . . to . . . aft."

Picard looked to La Forge. "Is that all?"

"It's still coming in," the engineer said. "It took a minute to receive just that much."

"It appears to be a message to you," Picard said to his first officer. "What does it mean?"

Worf appeared lost in thought. In the meantime, the voice continued. *"Phasers . . . twice . . . ten . . . second . . . gap . . . to . . . acknowledge. One . . . minute . . . then . . . torpedo."*

The message began to repeat. La Forge turned down the audio. "I think that's the whole thing."

Dygan looked at Worf. "The Detapa Council—and Jadzia Dax. You were there?" Picard only knew a little of the matter: Sisko's team had acted to protect the Cardassians from the Klingons. It would have been a difficult episode for Worf. Dygan put the pieces together. "You even saved Gul Dukat."

Worf glared at the Cardassian. "Everyone makes mistakes."

As another barrage reduced *Enterprise*'s shields further, Picard put up his hand. "This tactic Dax is signaling to you about. Is there a chance that Riker could know about it?"

"I don't know." Worf thought for a moment. "It was a sensitive matter politically. Did the report reach the *Enterprise*?"

"No," Picard said. "What do we need to do?"

"Captain Dax wants us to fire on them. And I know why."

AVENTINE

Just as Dax began reciting her prepared message for the fifth time, the world went topsy-turvy around her. The fact that she couldn't see much of the world didn't make it any better.

"Something hit us!" Riordan said, as *Aventine* continued to reverberate. He put his hands on the low overhead to balance himself.

Dax struggled to recover her bearings. She'd lost her whistle in the impact, which had knocked her around in the shaft like an ice cube in a glass. "That wasn't a hit on us," she said, clutching onto the edge of the opening. "That was—"

Another noisy quake shook the ship. This time, she was more prepared for it. "That was two phaser shots to our shields. That's the signal!"

"I thought we had spotters with tricorders at the viewports."

"We're in a firefight. I needed something I could count on—and that didn't require the couriers to send the word about." She'd recognized what the shots were—and Leishman and her team waiting at the tractor beam certainly would have, too. "Two shots. Worf understood."

"That, or we've finally made them mad."

ENTERPRISE

"Ready photon torpedo," Picard said. *Enterprise* hadn't used the most destructive part of its arsenal on *Aventine* before now; only phasers, with the intention of reducing the vessel's shields. Where phasers were precise, torpedoes were a blunt instrument capable of damage far beyond what was intended, in certain circumstances. He looked to Worf. "Number One?"

"Aye, Captain." The Klingon was back at the tactical station, preparing the weapon. They had been keeping a countdown since firing the second phaser. "The torpedo is targeted for a location just outside the shielding area—and just inside the aft tractor beam arc."

"Ten seconds," La Forge said.

"Detonation under your control, Number One." Picard looked at the viewscreen, which showed *Aventine* continuing to rain harassing fire down on them. "Fire!"

Enterprise launched the weapon. It appeared on the viewscreen a moment later: a shining star, closing in on the vessel far above. "Readings on *Aventine*, Mr. La Forge."

"Nothing . . . nothing . . ." The engineer paused. "Tractor beam active. It has the torpedo!"

"Detonate!"

Thirty-one

*A*ventine lurched violently, shaking Dax completely out of the shaft and sending her tumbling into Riordan. The young engineer's jaw hit the side of the bulkhead as she collided with him.

A moment passed in the darkness as Dax cast about for her light-giving headgear, lost in the fall. "Ensign, are you all right?"

Riordan struggled to right himself. "That . . . hurt."

"Sorry." Bowers would have liked the chance to pop the guy, she knew. But there were more important issues at the moment. "Did it work?"

Riordan fumbled for his padd. Its lights were all dark. "Power's out," Riordan said.

Finding her SIMs beacon, Dax felt a momentary weight off her shoulders. And then she didn't feel any weight at all. "Gravity's out!"

Lifting in the narrow space and jostling Riordan in the process, Dax fought to swim back toward the darkened opening. Systems were down—but for how long?

*   *   *

ENTERPRISE

"Power consumption is zero on *Aventine*," La Forge said. "That's knocked them for a loop."

Picard believed it. He had never seen anything like it. Milliseconds after *Aventine* took hold of the photon torpedo, the weapon exploded—and suddenly the matter it was trying to grapple was moving at relativistic speeds, being both propelled and consumed in a reaction with antimatter. The tractor beam, normally visible in the electromagnetic spectrum as a cool white, blazed red—a sudden attack of heartburn.

He would ask La Forge about the particulars later. What was important now was that *Aventine*'s major systems appeared to be down. She was heading outward from the Adelphous Array, its circular path widening. It was no longer firing, its shields were down—and the registry marking lights, which had either been intermittent or used for Dax's unorthodox messaging, were extinguished.

"Systems should start to reboot in a few minutes," La Forge said. "Life signs are unchanged. Location of readings is changing, though. Some motion toward holodeck one—but it's slow."

"Then we'll go there ourselves," Picard said, standing. He already suspected what had happened to Riker—and he knew the clock was running. "Mr. La Forge, you and I will beam to *Aventine*."

"Ready, sir."

Picard had run his theory past the engineer on the way to Adelphous. It was a long shot—but if it was true, then he and La Forge were ideally suited to deal with the situation.

Worf was conflicted. "Captain, I wish to object again. We should send across a security team first."

"Number One, if my theory is right, they have security aplenty over there. What they need is experience of a sort only *we* can provide. And if I'm wrong, I'll need you here to protect the array." Standing next to La Forge, he clicked his badge. "Picard to transporter room. Two to beam directly to *Aventine* holodeck one. Energize."

AVENTINE

Picard had materialized in some strange places before, including some that had been considered a breach of etiquette. It wasn't always possible for the transporter team aboard *Enterprise* to know when it was beaming individuals into an awkward situation planetside. He had materialized in the middle of a Bolian domestic argument once—and then there was that time that the pleasure-world of Risa turned a beam-in zone into a changing area for the baths without telling everyone.

But beaming into a Starfleet admiral's bedroom was a first. Shining his light around the room, Picard saw all the accoutrements of a well-appointed boudoir. Gravity felt normal here. His artificial eyes seeing even more, La Forge clicked his badge. "*Enterprise*, are you sure we have the right place?"

"*On target. Holodeck one, portside aft corner.*"

Picard wasn't surprised. "*Titan* told us he had developed a program with his rooms." He touched the bed. "There must be some power to the holodeck, or this furniture wouldn't be here. The lights are simply off." He waved his hand before a bedside lamp. It lit up, casting a warm glow across the room.

"Something's in there," La Forge said, pointing toward the entrance to the bathroom. He moved his hand to his phaser.

"It won't be necessary," Picard said in low tones. Besides, it would be awkward enough to catch an admiral in the shower without being armed to boot. He edged toward the open door.

Inside, they saw the admiral was indeed in the shower—except he was in full uniform, and the shower and the rest of the bathroom, in fact, were missing. Riker stood motionless before a black background. Across the room from him, a small spotlight in the wall was unlit.

La Forge examined the unmoving admiral. "Holographic matter. This is who we've been talking to, I suspect."

"Holo-Riker." Picard examined the spotlight in the wall. There was a small input beneath it. "The admiral's studio."

Holo-Riker broke his statuesque pose. "This is an invasion of privacy," he said. "I protest."

"Relax, old man," the captain said. "You're not who we're here to see."

The artificial admiral shot Picard an offended look before resuming his frozen pose.

Picard led La Forge back into the bedroom. His badge chirped. He tapped it. "Picard here."

"*Aventine is continuing on the heading it was on when the torpedo detonated,*" Worf reported. "*Shields remain down. I have put security teams with gravity boots in main engineering and on the bridge.*"

"Activate our tractor beam. *Enterprise* won't hold her long if she really wants to move, but we'll know it."

"Acknowledged. Do you want a security team to your location?"

La Forge pointed. "Captain, there."

A flickering light came from the parlor beyond the door on the far side of the room. Picard nodded. "Stand by, Number One. Picard out."

With the captain leading the way, the two crossed the room toward it. Before they reached the light, however, a red brick wall appeared in the doorway.

"This isn't necessary," Picard said to the air. He turned back toward the bathroom and called out to the holo-Riker. "Tell him this isn't necessary."

A moment passed—and then the wall disappeared. Picard and then La Forge stepped through the doorway.

The room beyond was like any other VIP quarters aboard a Starfleet vessel: a tastefully appointed sitting area, this one with various musical instruments and pieces of Betazoid art on the walls. But in place of the usual desk and chair, there was something else entirely. A human figure sat in a sophisticated-looking chair with consoles at each arm—while above him, tiny lasers danced between his head and a half-globe emitter in the ceiling.

Picard walked before the high-tech throne and beheld the real William Riker. *"WELCOME ABOARD, CAPTAIN."* The voice came from *Aventine*'s main computer, and echoed around the room. Riker's lips did not move, nor did his expression change. *"SORRY I CAN'T GET UP."*

"As I suspected—just like Reginald Barclay." Picard stared up at the flickering lights. "The Cytherians are back."

Thirty-two

Eyes closed, Will Riker held his face in his hands and took long, labored breaths.

"Are you unwell?" Simus asked.

He raised his head without opening his eyes. The fuzzy feeling he'd felt on waking into Simus's earlier simulation of *Titan* had turned to a full-blown headache as he'd remembered more and more about recent events. His conversation with Simus had moved from the Corvus Beacon to the No'Var Outpost to the Adelphous Array, jogging his memory each time—and each time bringing a new wave of discomfort.

And now, with one word, his headache had a name.

"*Cytherians*," Simus said. "What do you know of them?"

Resigned, Riker raised his eyelids. "I think you know how much I know of them."

Simus regarded him quietly. "Yes, that's very true. But I'm not interested in what I would learn about them from a database. I would like your account."

Riker glanced around at his surroundings. The holographic representation of *Laplace*'s deck had been replaced several times over the course of the day by settings depicting other locations, showing moments reconstructed by internal sensor feeds. Riker had seen the recorded events that took place aboard the bridges of *Aventine* and *Enterprise*, and even the wrenching communication Picard had with *Titan* and Deanna.

He stood as one of two Rikers in the holo office aboard *Aventine*. His counterpart from the recent past sat frozen in time in his makeshift throne, being confronted by a concerned Picard and La Forge.

It was hard to look at. "Simus, I'll tell you what you want to know," he said, gesturing to the other Riker. "If you can make him go away."

"Certainly." Simus pressed a button on his wrist control unit, and the statuelike figures from the past vanished, including the bizarre chair the other Riker had been sitting in. Two comfortable chairs replaced them. "I think these match your decor," Simus said.

"It's a holographic version of a holographic version of a room. Close enough."

"I hope you'll sit," Simus said, settling into one of the chairs.

"Something tells me I've already been sitting too much." But tired bones having their say, Riker collapsed in the chair.

Simus clasped his hands together. "What do you remember about the Cytherians? Your first encounter, I mean. I know it was years ago."

Riker took a deep breath. He couldn't imagine that Simus didn't know it all already, but he clung to the hope that talking might ease the headache some.

"They're an incredibly advanced race—if race is the right word. They live in isolation near the galactic core, never venturing outward. Not until years ago, when the *Enterprise*-D discovered a probe."

"At the Argus Array."

"At the Argus Array." Riker thought back on the experience, many years before when he had been first officer under Picard. "The Cytherian probe was designed to instruct outsiders on how to reach their system, but not in the way you'd think. The probe attempted to integrate with the array—and after that, with one of our shuttlecraft. Both attempts failed. Next it pursued *Enterprise* through warp, emanating so much power it nearly destroyed us."

"But it didn't," Simus said, unclasping his hands. A withered finger pointed to Riker. "You've left out a step."

"If you know the story, why ask?"

"I want to hear it from you. Who saved the *Enterprise*?"

"Reginald Barclay, one of our engineers," Riker said. "The Cytherian technology hadn't been compatible with the array or the shuttle. But unbeknownst to all of us, when it tried to interface with the shuttle, it transformed Barclay instead."

"Transformed. Transformed how?"

"It made him hyperintelligent. And driven to visit the Cytherians."

Simus leaned forward with obvious interest. "How did he achieve this end?"

Riker took a breath. He'd known this was coming. "Barclay took control of *Enterprise* from an interface he designed on the holodeck. That chair you just saw. We never did figure out how it worked. And he went beyond that, altering our propulsion systems in order to permit a one-time trip across half the galaxy to visit the Cytherians."

"That must have been frightening."

Riker looked down at the floor. "The Cytherians were peaceful. Strange, but peaceful. They manifested in our dimension as giant floating heads."

"Heads?"

"Like yours and mine." Riker touched his forehead. "With crystals right here."

"That physiognomy seems odd."

"I don't think that's what their bodies really look like—if they have bodies at all. I think their appearance was for our benefit. We stayed there a few days and had . . . well, I guess you'd call it a brief cultural exchange." He rolled his eyes as he finished the sentence.

"Why that reaction?"

"Well, the exchange was mostly one-way." Riker shrugged. "I don't know that we understood any more about their culture after we left. They didn't have a Prime Directive of their own. However, they didn't let us keep the advancements Barclay had developed for *Enterprise*. But they certainly seemed pleasant. It was a nice visit, once we got our bearings."

"And yet the trip to visit them was not so pleasant," Simus said. "Tell me, how did Lieutenant Barclay describe what he experienced?"

Riker stared. He certainly remembered. "He told Deanna they *reprogrammed* him."

"Like a computer? Or a robot?"

"Or a tool." Riker then followed up quickly: "But they let him go. Returned him to normal, with no trace of what they'd done."

Simus scratched his cheek. "But they left him his memories of the event."

"You knew the story already."

Riker put his elbow on the armrest and rubbed his

temple again. It wasn't hard thinking that far back in time—but every time his thoughts danced near the present, he got wobbly. Simus's next question took him further off balance.

"Tell me, did you like Lieutenant Barclay?"

Riker looked up. "He's all right."

"But back then?"

"He was a bit of a problem. He was always a little out of step with everyone else and it showed." Riker smirked. "He also had a thing for my wife."

"But you thought Barclay was sane."

"Any sane man would be attracted to Deanna."

"Amusing, but not what I meant. Did you think Reginald Barclay was the same person after the events you're describing?"

"Yeah. Maybe even a little better for the experience."

"Better, how? Did you suspect he retained skills given him by the Cytherians?"

Riker shook his head. "Nothing like that. He picked up a little confidence after what he'd been through. It was natural growth. Human growth." He looked pointedly at Simus. "No offense."

"None taken."

"He was definitely sane."

"Ah." Simus leaned back. "And was he sane when doing the Cytherians' bidding?"

Riker thought for a moment. "He was acting rationally. We just didn't understand what he was trying to accomplish for the Cytherians."

Simus nodded. "You said he was their *tool*."

"Yes." Riker felt himself growing tired again. He didn't know where this was going. But Simus clearly had a direction in mind. The older man leaned forward and looked directly at him. "A tool can be a weapon, can it not?"

Simus touched a control on his wrist, and the chair Riker was sitting in transformed with a flash. The Cytherian interlink chair was back, only now Riker was the one sitting in it. He looked around, feeling lightheaded. Was this another game, or . . .

No.

"Simus, am I still aboard *Aventine*?" He looked up at the half-dome and its crackling lights. "Am I still in the Cytherian machine?"

"That," Simus said, bringing his hands together in a prayerful pose, "is for *you* to tell *me*."

STAGE THREE:

SHUTDOWN

---

*"Wars begin when you will, but they
do not end when you please."*

—Niccolò Machiavelli

Thirty-three

Admiral William Thomas Riker had longed for several things during his existence, but one stood above all the rest: the desire to occupy the center seat aboard a Federation starship.

He had gotten that opportunity first as a junior officer on the third watch of his first ship—and finally his own command: *Titan*. Those moments had meant a lot to Riker. But now he knew how shallow and meaningless those experiences had really been. Now, he *truly* sat at the center seat aboard a Federation starship. And from his interlink chair in *Aventine*'s holodeck, he controlled it all.

His mind had raced without stopping since that moment at the meeting table in the Far Embassy when the brilliant light enveloped him and the other envoys. He had been given directives, a familiar feeling for an officer in an interstellar fleet. But he had struggled to put them into effect. His mortal form was a dam, forcing the flood of his intellect into the narrowest of channels.

That was when the mission had been the most difficult. His new gifts came with obligations that had to be met, tasks that could not wait for him to find more effective ways to put his thoughts into reality. Yet at the same time, he could not reveal his new capacities while others could still thwart him.

He had been forced to lie.

The most difficult lie was the first one. Deanna Troi posed a double threat. She had more knowledge than anyone of Riker before the change and she had most closely observed Reginald Barclay after his mind had been touched by the Cytherians. Her skills as an empath were something he did not have; they represented a threat to his assignment.

Riker's solution, arrived at not long after he stepped away from the table at the Far Embassy, was brilliant in that it did something else to improve his chances. *Aventine* was faster than *Titan*; it was a better fit for the missions he knew were ahead. And while Riker did not know Ezri Dax as well as he knew *Titan*'s Christine Vale, he calculated that the former's recent brush with Starfleet justice would make her less willing to question his authority.

Commandeering the holodeck aboard *Aventine* had allowed him the privacy and the opportunity he needed to design his interlink chair. It was an easy thing for one of his intellect to subvert the safeguards that he, himself, had played a role in designing; it then became a simple matter of choosing the moment to take control. When *Aventine*'s crew balked at attacking the Ferengi station, the episode hadn't caused him a moment's concern. He just walked back to the holodeck—and started his life anew.

His first moments in the interlink chair had lasted a seeming eternity—and they had been agonizing. But not painful: the procedure was the very definition of non-invasive. Through the holodeck, which for its purpose needed to know the disposition of every molecule on its grid, *Aventine*'s main computer had scanned the location and condition of every neuron in Riker's brain. That had enabled his thoughts to escape the artificial confines of his skull. One by one, his neural pathways had been extended to connect with the main computer interface he had constructed. That hadn't hurt at all.

No, the agony had come from Riker's repeated realization, as each microscopic connection had been made, that he had spent his entire existence as a prisoner. In place of five senses, he now had a seemingly endless array. And in place of his body, he had the perfect form for living among the stars.

The beings aboard *Aventine* were foreign bodies in his bloodstream, now—but he could not simply eliminate them, any more than he could wantonly kill those at the targets he had been sent to disable. Such went against Riker's human morality and against his patrons' desires. Dax and her crew had done everything in their power to take back control of the starship. Riker had played the patient parent—something made *pet-owner* seem an inappropriate term—redirecting his charges to locations and activities where they could not harm him.

Then the *Enterprise* had appeared.

Riker could not be deterred from his appointed quest. But as an old Stratagema player, he was accustomed to considering multiple different courses of action at once—and now he could consider *millions*, all while calculating their odds of possible success. This, he realized, was what existence must be like for Data: steps could be planned far out into the future.

And even though Picard and *Enterprise* would be sure to oppose him, practically every scenario that included them resulted in less harm for any innocents involved. He could not permit *Enterprise*'s captain to stop him any more than he could allow *Aventine*'s; Riker's fate was sealed when he sat down at the table in the Far Embassy. His career was over. His life was over. But at least with Picard around, the damage Riker did might be mitigated.

Riker saw Picard and La Forge standing several meters away from him. His human sensory organs still functioned, but holodeck one's sensors necessarily kept track of everything in the area. It needed to know the locations of every molecule of actual matter in order to position its force fields, to replace photonic images with replicated matter when necessary. Through the room's systems, he knew everything about his guests, from their body temperatures to their genetic make-ups. He knew Picard was about to speak long before the sound waves went into motion.

It was then a matter of being patient. Picard's words only moved at the speed of sound, after all. He had calculated a strong possibility that they would be words of greeting, and they were.

"I KNEW YOU'D BE HERE EVENTUALLY," Riker replied, his voice echoing eerily through the room. *"I WASN'T ABOUT TO UNDERESTIMATE YOU."*

Picard nodded. "It wasn't all our doing. We had some assistance from Captain Dax."

Riker considered that. He had protected the holodeck with power reserves; his interlink chair had been unaffected by the torpedo detonation. But the shock to *Aventine*'s systems had been significant, and he was still struggling to bring them online even as Picard spoke. Sensing foreign objects moving through one of the ship's arteries he had access to, Riker calculated that one of them might be the Trill captain.

"THERE," he said. To La Forge's right, a flash of light indicated two figures beaming into the room. Both figures appeared prone, arms before them as if swimming, one after another, through a narrow underwater cavern—and both were half a meter off the deck. When they fully entered reality, both Dax and a young human—Riker identified him from *Aventine*'s personnel files as Ensign Nevin Riordan—plummeted the short distance to the floor.

"SORRY ABOUT THAT," Riker said as the startled pair got to their hands and knees. *"I'VE RESTORED GRAVITY IN HERE."*

"And you've got control of the transporters, evidently." Picard knelt to help Dax up. He looked back at Riker. "Will you be whisking us out of here now, or will you talk?"

"IF I HAD DECIDED TO SEND YOU AWAY, YOU WOULD ALREADY BE GONE," he said. *"WHAT WOULD YOU LIKE TO DISCUSS?"*

Thirty-four

Ezri Dax beheld Riker in his interlink chair. "What is *that*?"

"It's a Cytherian interlink unit," La Forge answered before Picard could.

"Cytherians?" she asked. Picard watched the dark-haired woman's expression go from puzzlement to surprise to recognition. Dax finally nodded. "I read the report on them." She let out an exhausted sigh. "That explains a lot."

"I'm not sure how," the young ensign said. He gawked at the power crackling above Riker's head, causing him to look like Zeus in his throne. "An interlink with what?"

"It connects the admiral's brain functions to those of *Aventine*'s main computer," La Forge said. He squinted at the chair. "That's not holographic matter, is it? It's real."

"GOOD EYE, GEORDI—AS ALWAYS," Riker said.

"Whoa!" Riordan said, looking at Riker—then at the ceiling and all around. "Admiral, your mouth didn't move at all, there."

Dax looked at Picard, almost apologetically. "This is Ensign Riordan. He helped us get in touch with you."

"Well done, Ensign."

La Forge was still staring at the chair. "Barclay's chair was generated by the holodeck. Why not this?"

"BARCLAY HAD NO REASON TO EXPECT A POWER INTERRUPTION. I NEEDED TO BE CERTAIN I'D MAINTAIN CONTROL, EVEN IF THE HOLODECK WERE MOMENTARILY DISABLED. I BROUGHT THE NECESSARY MATERIALS TO THE ROOM WHILE I WAS STILL MOBILE."

Dax frowned. "You mean the materials Leishman mentioned. The ones you requisitioned."

"CORRECT. THE HOLODECK HELPED IN THE ASSEMBLY."

"Wait." Riordan stared. "You mean outside that chair, his control of the ship is cut?"

"That's right," Picard said. The words were barely out of his mouth when the frizzy-haired youth started moving purposefully toward the admiral. "Ensign, wait!"

Before Picard and Dax could grab Riordan, a flash of light indicated a holographic creation in the space before Riker. A massive furry beast materialized, baring its fangs and growling at the engineer.

"Yahh!" Riordan dove behind his captain. "What is *that*?" he asked, repeating her words from earlier.

"That would be a bear," Dax said, frozen.

The creature let loose with a monstrous roar, and Riordan stumbled over his own legs heading for the far side of the room.

Picard looked back, befuddled. "Ensign, it's a hologram."

Riordan looked out from behind Dax. "He's running the ship, Captain. It's a safe bet he's killed the safety protocols!"

"NO HARM WILL COME TO YOU," Riker said. *"IF YOU KEEP YOUR DISTANCE."*

"*Some days you get the bear . . .*" Picard thought, remembering a line Riker had used before. "I think, Mr. Riordan, we had better leave things as they are."

"Gotcha."

The bear sniffed at the air and turned. It wandered to the side of the room. Riordan emerged, tentatively. "What's that thing again?"

"URSOS ARCTOS CALIFORNICUS," Riker said. *"THE CALIFORNIA GRIZZLY."*

"I sure didn't see any of those at the Academy."

"THEY'RE EXTINCT. AS I WOULD BE, IF I ALLOWED YOU TO DETACH ME FROM THE INTERLINK. IT'S JUST LIKE HOW IT WAS WITH BARCLAY. IF YOU REMOVE ME FROM THE INTERFACE WITH AVENTINE, *I WILL DIE."*

Picard recalled that too much of Barclay's persona had migrated into *Enterprise*'s data storage. It had taken the Cytherians themselves to safely disengage Barclay from the interlink. "You're regaining control of the ship's systems. Is it useless for us to try to prevent that?"

"IT IS," Riker said. *"I HAVE DISCOVERED MORE WAYS TO ROUTE COMMANDS THAN THE SHIP-WRIGHTS EVER IMAGINED POSSIBLE. AND DON'T THINK THAT WORF CAN STOP ME FROM LEAVING. I'VE CONSIDERED SEVENTEEN DIFFERENT MEANS OF ESCAPING* ENTERPRISE'S *TRACTOR BEAM."*

Picard became cross. "If you can escape, why haven't you?"

"BECAUSE I'M AHEAD OF SCHEDULE. AVENTINE IS FASTER THAN THE CYTHERIANS ACCOUNTED FOR. PERHAPS THEY DIDN'T KNOW WE HAD DEVELOPED

*SLIPSTREAM TECHNOLOGY. I ALSO DON'T THINK THEY
KNEW ADELPHOUS WAS OFFLINE—THEIR LAST CON-
TACT WITH US WAS BEFORE THE LAST BORG INVASION.
BUT I WAS ORDERED TO FIRE ON IT—AND TO SEE THAT
IT WAS DISABLED. I HAVE FIRED. IT IS DISABLED. AND
WHEN I AM DUE TO GO, I WILL GO."*

"So you have been compelled to do these things.
Do you know why?"

There was a long pause—which, Picard imagined,
must be an eternity for one of Riker's accelerated intelligence. *"I DON'T KNOW,"* came the response.

Picard paced around the room, only momentarily
noticing the bear gnawing on a Betazoid tapestry.
"You have an amazing tactical mind, Will—even
without all the enhancements. They've been sending
all of you to destroy these installations. You must have
some sense of their intentions?"

*"THERE IS SIMPLY A GREAT NEED TO DO WHAT
THEY HAVE DONE. THAT IS ALL."*

"Could this . . . could this be *benevolent*?" Picard
stopped and thought for a moment. "We parted in
friendship with the Cytherians. Could they be aware
of some threat—perhaps coming from beyond the
center of the galaxy—that might take advantage of
our communications systems?"

"IT'S POSSIBLE."

The notion chilled Picard. The Borg who destroyed
Adelphous had erupted into Federation space from a
location in the Azure Nebula, not far away. A network
of subspace tunnels terminated there, allowing their
entry into the region. "All of this chaos could somehow be a preventative measure."

"THAT IS WHAT I HAVE CHOSEN TO BELIEVE," Riker
said. *"'BETTER A CITY RUINED THAN A CITY LOST.'"*

Picard's eyes lit with recognition. "Lorenzo de' Medici."

"COSIMO, HIS GRANDFATHER."

The captain shrugged, a little amused by the correction. "Who am I to argue with the central computer?"

The lighter moment wasn't felt on the other side of the room. Since the bear ambled off, Dax hadn't stopped glaring at the man who'd taken over her ship. Losing control of a ship, Picard knew very well, was a hard thing for a captain. "You said they might be trying to help us," Dax said sharply. "But their intent could also be hostile. Isn't that right?"

"IT'S POSSIBLE."

"They could be planning to bring us brand new arrays for all we know," La Forge said. "They were a tough bunch to read."

Dax shook her head, disgusted. "This isn't benevolent." She stepped up to confront Riker, disregarding the growl of the suddenly interested bear. "*You* haven't been benevolent. You stole my ship. Made me and my crew pawns in your game!"

"IT'S NOT MY GAME." The figure in the chair remained motionless. *"I UNDERSTAND HOW YOU MUST FEEL. THERE WAS NO OTHER WAY."*

"No other way than to lie to us?" She turned to face Picard. "He wasn't in that chair in the beginning. He told us there was a hostile program called Takedown that was going to attack communications systems. But he really wanted *us* to attack them."

"THE CYTHERIANS REQUIRED QUICK ACTION, BEFORE I COULD ASSEMBLE THE MATERIALS I'D REQUISITIONED. I IMPROVISED."

Picard put up his hand. "I understand your anger. I felt it too, in your place. But when our crewman was touched by the Cytherians, they controlled his actions before he built his interlink chair."

Dax smoldered. "Barclay didn't cause an interstellar incident." Her eyes narrowed. "You made fools out of all of us—*Admiral*."

Riordan returned to her side, fingering his combadge. "He did choose some neat music."

Dax didn't look at him. "Ensign, shut up."

"Shutting up, sir."

"I DID THINK ABOUT YOU AND YOUR CREW, DAX. I DID EVERYTHING IN MY POWER TO LIMIT HARM. I HAVEN'T KILLED ANYONE," Riker said. After a long pause, he added: *"HAVE I?"*

Dax looked to Picard. "Not that we know of," he said. "But much depends on where you are going from here. Is it another communications target?"

A pause. *"NO. I WAS ASSIGNED SIX OBJECTIVES, JUST AS THE OTHERS. THOSE OBJECTIVES ARE ACHIEVED. NOW I AM ASSIGNED TO MEET THE OTHER SEVEN RENEGADE VESSELS AT A PRE-ESTABLISHED RENDEZVOUS."*

Picard was surprised to learn this much. "You are able to tell me this?"

"YOUR KNOWLEDGE IS IRRELEVANT. YOU CANNOT BEAT AVENTINE *THERE—THE SLIPSTREAM DRIVE IS FUNCTIONING PERFECTLY—AND COMMUNICATIONS IN THIS SECTOR HAVE BEEN DEGRADED PAST THE POINT WHERE YOU CAN ALERT ANYONE."*

Dax looked between Picard and Riker, alarmed. "There are eight hijacked ships? You're gathering for a mass attack?"

"I DON'T THINK SO—BUT I DON'T KNOW. THE CYTHERIANS IMPLANTED DESTINATIONS IN MY MIND BACK AT THE FAR EMBASSY. SOMETIMES WHEN

I ARRIVE AT ONE LOCATION, THE NEXT OBJECTIVE IS REVEALED TO ME."

"You said you were ahead of schedule," Picard said. "If *Aventine* waited here until the last moment to leave, could *Enterprise* reach there at the same time if it departed now?"

"IF I TOLD YOU WHERE IT WAS, YES. BUT I WON'T. I HAVEN'T TRIED TO DESTROY ENTERPRISE—*ONLY TO REACH MY TARGETS. BUT I CAN'T GUARANTEE THE OTHERS TRANSFORMED BY THE CYTHERIANS WOULD STAY THEIR HANDS."*

"We could not survive the onslaught of all of them."

"YOU COULDN'T SURVIVE ONE OF US. I'M THE LAST TO DENIGRATE STARFLEET, CAPTAIN, OR YOUR SKILLS. BUT THE WAY WE ARE NOW, EVEN DAIMON IGEL IN HIS FERENGI MARAUDER COULD TAKE YOU OUT AT ANY TIME."

As could you, Picard thought. It was nice of the transformed Riker not to say it.

Then he thought of something else. He walked up to Riker. "Why are you still here?"

Silence.

"You could leave at any moment; you've said so. You have a destination. If the slipstream drive is functioning perfectly, why are you still here?" Picard looked over at La Forge, who was studying the interlink chair from a respectful distance. "And how was it that you didn't know the slipstream drive would fail on the way from the No'Var Outpost? You seem to know everything. How did you not know?"

Behind Picard, Dax spoke up. "He did know."

Picard glanced back to the Trill captain. Her indignation past, Dax looked down at the deck, piecing things together in her mind. "He overtaxed the drive so it would fail, but not so badly that it would violate his obligation to the Cytherians. He did it so you could catch up." She looked up at Picard. "He's still here because you are."

Picard had suspected it—but he was still missing something. His eyes turned on Riker. "Is that it? What do you want me to do, if you won't let me stop what's going to happen?"

Riker said nothing. But across the room, the bear gave a curious growl—and disappeared.

It hit Picard. "You brought me here to kill you."

Riker's voice returned to the room. *"YOU KNOW THERE IS ONLY ONE WAY TO STOP MY ROLE IN THIS."*

"What? Remove you from the machine?" Picard looked around the room. "You have all the defenses the holodeck can generate. You would prevent that."

"I WOULD BE FORCED TO TRY," Riker said.

Picard blinked. "But you would not be forced to succeed. Is that it?"

"BETWEEN YOUR CREW AND DAX'S, YOU WOULD FIND A WAY. YOU ALWAYS DO." A beat. *"I TRUST YOU IN THIS."*

Picard half-grinned and shook his head. "No, no. This is absurd. You're telling me that the only way to stop this madness is to kill you—and that you will help us do that?" He shook his head. "Giving up is not the Will Riker I know."

"I'M NOT THE WILL RIKER YOU KNOW."

"Ludicrous. We will find another way."

"I HAVE TWELVE MORE HOURS HERE," Riker said. *"THEN AVENTINE LEAVES, WITH YOU ABOARD OR NOT."*

Picard looked to the others. "Then we most certainly should get to it."

Thirty-five

There was nothing at all wrong with food from a starship replicator, but Picard had rarely seen people lining up for it before. That was the situation he found in the forward mess hall aboard *Aventine*.

After an hour, when it had become clear that Riker wasn't about to engage the warp drive, *Enterprise* had released its tractor beam. The two vessels sat parked, side-by-side, orbiting the defunct array as a steady stream of personnel went back and forth between the vessels. Dax had taken the opportunity to get her exhausted crew fed real food, not MREs. Even though Riker had released his hold on the food replicators, she'd needed to send some people to *Enterprise* to get them fed immediately.

It had been engineers and scientists traveling the other direction to *Aventine*, assisting that vessel's specialists in studying how Riker was connected to the ship. La Forge had only been off holodeck one but a few minutes during the entire time. Walking through the mess hall with his tray, Picard caught the engineer during one of those times. The *Enterprise* chief engineer was stopped at a table where Dax, Šmrhová, Dygan, and Worf were sitting.

"Any change?" Picard asked.

"No, sir," La Forge said. "We've spent most of our time trying to figure out why the interlink works at all. We didn't exactly have time to study what Barclay designed."

Picard nodded. The device had vanished after the Cytherians had freed Barclay, and the record of its manufacture had vanished from *Enterprise*-D's holodeck logs. "He's letting you get close enough to study it?"

"We have to sort of play-act it," La Forge said. "If we do anything that directly jeopardizes the interlink, Riker beams the person out of the room. I don't think it's even intentional on his part; it's an autonomic response, like swatting away a gnat."

"I guess we're lucky he's not beaming people into space," Dax offered.

Picard shook his head. "He doesn't think they're gnats. There must be some moral dimension, even to the things he can't control."

Dax appeared to mull that over. Picard racked his brain for something else to suggest to La Forge, but came up with nothing. The only thing they'd flatly decided against was having Dr. Tarses mind-meld with the admiral. It was far too risky.

"I'd better get back to it," La Forge said. "We're running out of time." He departed, and Šmrhová rose to follow.

Dax offered Picard the now-empty seat beside her, across the table from Dygan and Worf. Picard's first officer and his investigators had beamed across to get full statements from *Aventine*'s senior officers, in the hopes of learning something more about the plot. Picard was surprised to see glasses and condiment jars arranged upside-down on the table, in a circular fashion.

"Glinn Dygan is playing with his food," Worf growled.

Picard watched the Cardassian moving them around with care. "I was going to congratulate Commander Worf and Captain Dax on their gambit with the tractor beam—but you've struck me curious, Mister Dygan."

Dygan looked up. "Sorry, Captain. It's just . . . being away from my evidence room, I got to thinking about the bigger picture in all this."

"Explain."

"It has to do with the specific powers that were brought to the Summit of Eight. Most of the affected powers are in a large area straddling the border between the Alpha and Beta Quadrants." Dygan gestured to the containers. "It oversimplifies things to say this, but if you were to draw a circle around a region of space, all eight of these powers would be sitting on the perimeter—Khitomer allies alternating with the Typhon Pact."

Picard looked at the circle, where drinking vessels alternated with condiment jars, and thought about the galactic map. Going clockwise on the Beta Quadrant side of the circle, Romulan space buffered the Klingon Empire, with the Gorn Hegemony farther down the line. Then Federation space, as the arc crossed into the Alpha Quadrant. Tholian, Cardassian, Tzenkethi, and Ferengi territory followed next. Much of the space inscribed by the very rough circle belonged to the Federation. But there were also plenty of neighbors in between, powers that did not attend the Summit of Eight: the Talarians, the Kinshaya, and others, all of which had seen their local communications assets attacked.

"We now know from Admiral Riker that the attendees at the Far Embassy function were transformed there," Dygan continued. "We also know from *Titan* that the invitations weren't really from the alleged senders. I suspect this Far Embassy was created by the Cytherians, just like the probe it sent to the Argus Array years ago—and that it was the Embassy that sent the invitations."

Picard nodded. "The Cytherians learned something of the political map and the players here during our visit with them. That might also account for the selection of the attendees. The Breen were not invited, because we knew less about the Breen. But they could be targeted as a secondary power."

Dygan shook his head. "I'm just still trying to work out the motive." He clasped his hands together and lowered his head close to the table, staring at the containers before him.

Worf looked distressed. "I believe I know."

"What is it, Number One?" Picard asked.

The *Enterprise* first officer steeled himself, appearing as if he were about to broach a distasteful topic. "Some Klingons of old used to make sport by placing jackal mastiffs along the edges of a circular arena. Targs placed in the center of the ring would have their shoulders cut, to drive the predators into a blood rage. The mastiffs would be released—and invariably, they would kill not just the targs, but each other."

"Gruesome," Picard observed.

"It was. It was banned, for the dishonor it does the animals." He pointed to the pieces Dygan had arranged on the table. "I believe that is exactly what has happened here. The Cytherians are trying to start a war that will debilitate everyone in the region."

"I have a hard time believing it. The Cytherians we met were peaceful. Certainly the one who sent for us." Picard remembered the giant white-haired head that first appeared to them on *Enterprise*'s bridge. "What did that fellow call himself?"

"*Caster*," Worf said. "He did appear peaceful, but we did not meet all the Cytherians."

We might have, and we might not have, Picard thought. He had never been certain during that visit whether Caster was a single entity or an agency representing many intelligences—or if that was even his real form. But nothing about that visit had been anything but pleasurable.

The men fell silent. Dax spoke up. "You know, I've been thinking about what La Forge said about Admiral Riker not harming the people trying to stop him." She opened her hands, palms upward. "*Aventine* hasn't suffered a single casualty during this whole incident. Not one."

Picard nodded.

"And in combat with other starships, he's been using the phaser instead of torpedoes," Dax said. "The phasers are a more surgical weapon, more precise in how and where they deal their damage."

Worf asked the *Aventine* captain, "You believe that even though he has no choice in whether he attacks, he has some choice in how?"

"The evidence supports it," the Trill said. "He's given us just enough control of our systems back that I was able to review some of our records—including the ones for phaser usage. If he hasn't altered those records—and I can't imagine why he would—he hasn't fired with full power every time. He's been judicious, sparing. Doing just as much damage as he needs, trying to limit collateral harm."

The *Enterprise* captain studied her—and then surveyed the table. "Strange that the Cytherians would force him to make these attacks and still grant him any latitude about them," Picard said. "It's an odd way to provoke a war."

"Everything about the Cytherians is odd," Worf said.

Picard grinned. "You said that about the Romulans."

Dax appeared to think for a moment—and then she reached forward with both arms, gathering the containers together in a bunch. It broke Dygan's concentration. "What?"

"We can't just save Riker," she said, eyes on the cluster of glassware. "Don't you see? We have to save *everyone*, or whatever they're trying will work."

Picard nodded. "You're right." He was stunned that it hadn't occurred to him that way before. "What do you suggest?"

"The Cytherians did this—and they're the only ones who can undo it," Dax said, drawing her arms back. "We know where they are. The Far Embassy. We just go back and make them do it."

Picard stared. "Will can't disobey his orders. But I don't know that we can do this without him."

"Then we figure out a way to do it *with* him." Dax stood up. "Right now he's the smartest human who's ever lived. I bet that'll help."

Thirty-six

Picard was talking about him, Riker knew. He had seen the captain speaking to the others in the dining room through *Aventine*'s sensors, though he had chosen not to listen in. It wasn't because he was suddenly subscribing to human boundaries again; rather, it seemed like an unnecessary waste of mental resources. As momentarily comforting as Picard's presence had been, the captain wasn't likely to come up with any solution Riker hadn't considered—and rejected—a thousand times in the last hour.

Neither would the engineers, working all around in the holodeck before his mortal form. Geordi La Forge had brought in several of his crack computer specialists in an attempt to reverse-engineer the interlink chair; together, with Leishman, they had moved to the outer hallway to take a quick sustenance break. It was one more thing Riker no longer needed, not when he could beam replicated nutrients into and unwanted products out of his body. He supposed the engineers had felt more comfortable dining without their motionless admiral staring blankly at them.

Only one had stayed: Nevin Riordan, *Aventine*'s aging *wunderkind*. He had been unaccounted for on the roster during Riker's renegade stretch and had apparently played a role in making the contact with *Enterprise*. Dax and Leishman had allowed the young man to aid efforts on the holodeck, though it was clear to Riker they had both regretted it. The guy was a hell-raiser, supporting all his ideas with equal fire, whether he was correct or colossally wrong. It didn't take a starship computer to see why he was eating alone.

Then again, Riker thought, maybe there was another reason. Riordan had eschewed the replicated office's furniture to eat while sitting on Deanna's prized Medaran rug—a place where he could continue staring up at Riker. It would have made the human Riker uncomfortable, but the admiral was past such things.

"WHAT'S ON YOUR MIND, ENSIGN?"

A little startled to be addressed, Ensign Riordan found his answer quickly. "Does it hurt?"

"THE INTERLINK? NO, NOT NOW."

"That's amazing," Riordan said. "What you've been able to do—I really envy you. I've been working with computers my entire life—and I'll never get as close to them as you are now."

"I'LL TELL YOU WHAT HURTS. NEVER HOLDING MY WIFE AND DAUGHTER AGAIN."

Riordan chuckled.

"YOU FIND THAT FUNNY?"

"No, that's not it." Riordan crumpled up a wrapper. "It's just that marriage and family are not in my program. So I think the wrong one of us got the chair."

"DON'T ASSUME THAT PRESENT CONDITIONS ARE PERMANENT. YOUR FUTURE MAY BE DIFFERENT THAN YOU IMAGINE."

Riordan shook his head, curls going this way and that. "You don't know me, Admiral. I've been called 'the human abrasive.' No one's about to pair off with me—and I wouldn't think much of anyone who would."

"THAT'S YOUR PROBLEM." Riker paused before continuing. *"THE FIRST PERSON TO SIT IN A CHAIR LIKE THIS HAD THE SAME PROBLEMS. YOU'RE DIFFERENT, FOR SURE—BUT TWO SIDES OF THE SAME COIN. REGINALD BARCLAY LACKED SELF-ASSURANCE."*

Riordan guffawed. "Haven't you heard? I've got shiploads."

"BARCLAY GOT SELF-ASSURANCE WHEN HE WAS TRANSFORMED BY THE CYTHERIANS. BUT I'M NOT SURE BEING IN MY PLACE WOULD GIVE YOU HUMILITY."

"If I had your powers, I wouldn't need it."

"WHICH IS ANOTHER REASON THIS SEAT IS NOT THE PLACE FOR YOU. POWER HAS ITS OBLIGATIONS, MISTER RIORDAN. PERHAPS WHEN YOU UNDERSTAND THAT, YOU WON'T BE STUCK AS AN ENSIGN ANYMORE."

Riordan nodded—then smiled awkwardly. "Did I just get a counselor chat from an admiral?"

"OR A COMPUTER, IF IT MAKES YOU FEEL MORE COMFORTABLE."

He looked up at Riker. "It kind of does. Thanks." He started to stand, tray in hands.

"LET ME GET THAT," Riker said. The ensign's tray vanished in a transporter glow.

Riordan laughed. "That's great. But I think if I were in your chair I'd have better things to do."

"I HAVE CHOSEN TO WAIT IN THE HOPES THAT TWO ETERNITIES THINKING ON A PROBLEM WOULD HELP WHERE ONE WOULD NOT. THE RESULTS ARE PREDICTABLE." His voice rose in urgency. *"CLEAN THE CRUMBS OFF YOUR COLLAR. THE CAPTAINS ARE COMING."*

Riordan straightened himself and looked toward the archway. Picard appeared with Dax right behind him. Riker had seen them discussing something just outside with the engineers. "Will, we need to talk," Picard said.

"MY OFFICE DOOR IS OPEN. I HAVE WHOLE MILLI-SECONDS WHERE I'M NOT DOING ANYTHING."

Picard stepped before him. "I believe there may be a way to free you from this—but we cannot do it for you alone. We must do it for all of those who the Cytherians have elevated. Else this madness will never end."

"I HAVE CONSIDERED THAT. WHAT DO YOU HAVE IN MIND?"

"The Far Embassy seems to be the key," Dax said. "Could we eliminate your . . . your gifts—and the gifts of the others—by destroying or otherwise deactivating the station? Is that even possible to do?"

"TO YOUR SECOND QUESTION: YES, IT CAN BE DESTROYED WITH RELATIVE EASE. WE FOUND THAT OUT WHEN WE DESTROYED THE CYTHERIAN PROBE WE ENCOUNTERED, ON THE D."

Picard nodded. "It had begun to pursue us—bombarding *Enterprise* with energy. I admit I never quite understood why it chased after us when it had already successfully interfaced with Barclay. Or why it was so easy to destroy."

"THEY HAVEN'T SHARED THAT WITH ME. BUT DESTROYING THE PROBE DIDN'T CHANGE BARCLAY'S CONDITION AND NEITHER WILL OUR DESTROYING THE FAR EMBASSY. I WILL REMAIN AS I AM NOW. THE GIFT, AS YOU CALL IT, REMAINS GIVEN UNTIL TAKEN BACK. AND THE GIVERS ARE UNTOLD LIGHT-YEARS AWAY."

"That is why they called for us," Picard explained

to Dax. The Cytherians could not, or would not, make the trip themselves. "The one named 'Caster' was called that because he cast out the lines to retrieve visitors."

"Glad I'm not the only one who was fished in," Dax said. "But maybe there's another play here. Unlike that time, the mechanism that transformed you still exists. Maybe we could get in and reverse the process."

"I HAVE CONSIDERED THAT, TOO. IT ISN'T POSSIBLE. SUCH A DEVICE, IF PRESENT, MIGHT NOT BE UNDERSTANDABLE EVEN BY ME. BUT IF IT WERE—AND A REVERSAL WERE POSSIBLE—I WOULD HAVE TO RE-ENTER THE STATION ITSELF. AND I AM CLEARLY NOT IN A POSITION TO WALK THROUGH ANY AIRLOCKS."

"I'm not going to give up on you just because you can't fit through a damn door," Picard said. "Would we be able to transport you inside, if somehow we kept the link to the main computer aboard *Aventine*?"

"THE FAR EMBASSY HAS A TRANSPORT INHIBITOR FIELD IN OPERATION AROUND IT." He paused. *"AND AS YOU HAVE ALREADY SAID, IT'S NOT ENOUGH TO DEAL WITH ME ALONE. WE WOULD NEED ALL THE OTHERS PRESENT. AND I DON'T THINK WE CAN GET THEM TO JUST—"*

Riker paused. Picard looked at Dax and then the admiral. "What is it?"

"I THINK I HAVE SOMETHING," Riker said. *"I WOULD HAVE TO LEAVE NOW, JEAN-LUC—LEAVING YOU AND* ENTERPRISE *BEHIND TO WORK ANOTHER PART OF THE PLAN. WOULD YOU BE WILLING TO DO THAT?"*

Ezri Dax's eyes widened—and her mouth dropped slightly open. Riker recognized the facial expression: "Not this again."

"I'm sorry," Dax said, shaking her head. "But we just spent a lot of time trying to get control of our ship back from you—and trying to reach Captain Picard. I'm not sure we really ought to beam him off and leave him behind." She looked up at Riker. "No offense."

"I UNDERSTAND. BUT YOU'D HAVE COMPLETE BRIDGE CONTROL THIS TIME—UNLESS WE ENCOUNTER A SITUATION IN WHICH MY EXPERTISE IS NEEDED."

Dax studied the seated Riker with caution. "And I would decide when those situations were?"

"OF COURSE. YOU CHOOSE WHEN YOU CALL ON AVENTINE'S COMPUTER NOW. THIS WOULD BE NO DIFFERENT. AND IF IT MAKES YOU MORE COMFORTABLE, BE AWARE THAT MY PLAN REQUIRES COMMANDER LA FORGE REMAINING ABOARD."

Dax thought about that for a moment and looked to Picard. She sighed. "All right."

Picard had been wearing half a smile since Riker got his idea. "Welcome back to Starfleet, Admiral Riker. We await your orders."

Thirty-seven

"Nerla, will you marry me?" Bretorius asked.

Nerla stared. No words emerged from her mouth.

"Ah, you're speechless," he said.

"That's not it," the senator's assistant replied. "I was just thinking that before this week, I would have laughed at you—and after I was done, I would have selected from a thousand reasons to say no."

"Ah. And now?"

"Now," she said, rising from her seat in the corner of the room, "I would stick with the main ones. You're married."

"No longer relevant."

"I have no interest in you."

"You are interested in power."

"All right," she said, walking around to face him. "Then how about this: you've willingly locked yourself inside a torture device—and there's lightning coming out of your head?"

Bretorius smiled. "You do amuse me."

She was right, of course. All the technical work he'd had done in the Tal Shiar office had prepared the brig for what he was doing now. He'd had ODN cables run from the agent's computer to one of the torture chambers. Then, once he'd secured the deck against infiltration, he'd done the rest of the work himself, connecting the equipment to the very special chair in the chamber.

It was called a Taibak Indoctrinator, named for the Romulan officer who had developed it. Taibak had used it, memorably, on *Enterprise*'s Geordi La Forge in a failed intelligence mission. *D'varian* and many other warbirds had them—and Bretorius saw in it the answer to his needs. In its basic design, the chair used probes to electrically stimulate neural implants surgically inserted in victims' visual cortices. La Forge—at that time—had implants and connecting ports already, simplifying the process. By using his newly gained technical prowess, Bretorius had constructed an interface allowing a mental connection with no implants. Most important, he was able to transform the Indoctrinator into a two-way device, allowing part of his intellect to migrate into *D'varian*'s main computer.

It did, however, require him to be immobilized within the macabre furnishing, with its metal forehead and chin restraints and wrist clamps to keep his mortal form from trying to escape. Birth was a painful process, and even birds of war sometimes wanted to remain in the egg. But once Nerla had been persuaded to help lock him in the device, the connection had been made—and he quickly bested the electronic defenses of *D'varian*'s main computer. Little had Yalok known when speaking to Bretorius earlier that the real commander of the ship was in the next torture chamber over.

Bretorius could have used the vessel's holodeck, he

imagined, but that would have sacrificed the protection the brig's location afforded. He also wasn't certain he would be able to survive detachment from an interlink created there—not that such a parting was remotely desirable.

The connection was more than sufficient for his needs, in any event. He had easily secured the deck by beaming all troublemakers to the farthest ends of the ship: one benefit to Bretorius of the *D'varian*'s twin-hull design was that it could be massively inconvenient to get from place to place. He had succeeded in disabling the six communications arrays assigned to him with plenty of time left over before the Cytherians' deadline to reach the rendezvous point.

He knew their names now. The computer had given him that after his connection. The Federation had met the Cytherians once in an encounter that Romulan intelligence had learned about. The file gave him the idea for his interlink device. In him, they had wrought something miraculous: the next evolutionary stage of the Romulan people.

That was deserving of awe—and consideration. "You still haven't given me a good reason why you won't marry me," he said to Nerla. He was still able to speak directly through his Romulan form; another benefit of using the Taibak Indoctrinator rather than another interlink method. "You needn't worry about carnal matters; I no longer think in those terms."

"That's a blessing."

"You would be empress to an emperor—or better still, the high priestess to a god."

"A god that can't go anywhere," Nerla said. "You're tied to the ship's systems!"

"I can go anywhere the ship goes. And I'm not so sure my physical form can never leave this room." He could already visualize a number of methods that might allow him to retain his Romulan body. That was a problem he intended to work on in the future—once he had dealt with more immediate problems.

Such as his deification. "We have had enough of praetors, proconsuls, and emperors," he said. "I was thinking of one of the ancient Terran traditions—"

"How do you know those?"

"I told you, I have full access to *D'varian*'s archives. They are quite encyclopedic in their study of our opponents. And it would please me if you would not interrupt me again!"

Nerla shrugged. "Sorry."

"As I was saying, in one tradition, each domicile had its own household deity—an icon or totem ruling over the home. I see the forces on the galactic map as houses, and now one member each of eight different races has been elevated. There can be no doubt in what the Cytherians have intended: a contest of champions, pitting our greatest against our greatest."

Nerla said nothing for a moment, trying to process the wild theory. But then she nodded. "If they're truly an elevated species, perhaps they see this as a way for the people in this region to fight it out one-on-one, without full-scale war."

"There's the rub. They may mean for my powers to expire after a time, after their aims are achieved. But I will not allow this."

"I'd be more worried about you expiring. I'm not going to stick around here and feed you—or anything else," she said, not hiding her distaste.

"I told you, I have no desire for physical sustenance.

The body is a thing to fuel the mind—and mine is fueled like a dwarf star in a warp core. And while my body will need tending to, I am certain caretakers of some kind can be found from among our billions of slaves."

Nerla shuddered. Every few seconds since he'd transformed himself, Bretorius had thought she might bolt for the exit. But he'd made sure she had nowhere to go. "What concerns you now?"

"This plan of yours to seize the Empire," she said. "Presuming the Cytherians do release you at some point—"

"Or I free myself."

"—or that, you're planning to win popular acclaim with feats against the Federation."

"And our more feckless allies." He smiled. She understood his plan.

"And then on top of all of this, you're going to use the information you got from Commander Yalok to remove the existing government." Nerla shook her head. "I don't see any Romulan being a party to that right now. Not after the years of hell we've been through."

Bretorius laughed. The sound resonated in the small chamber.

"What?" she asked. "You have an idea?"

"My dear, I have an agreement. One which I just made while you were talking. If only you could see what I see."

Nerla looked back to the large screen on the wall. "Show me."

Bretorius gave a mental command. The panel flickered and resolved into a split-screen image featuring two alien figures. "You're looking at Klingon

General Charlak, future emperor of that body—and Gul Rodrek, soon to rule Cardassia. They have agreed to assist me—in exchange for mutual considerations."

Nerla looked back at the two on-screen. "I thought the communications networks were damaged. Where are they?"

"Why, on their own ships—right off our starboard and port bow," Bretorius said, grinning. "We've reached the rendezvous point. A new Summit of Eight is about to begin. Only this one will end quite differently."

Thirty-eight

Whether the Cytherians had known it or not, the location they selected for the rendezvous had proved perfect for several of their agents. Located somewhere between the Azure Nebula and H'atoria, the Kalpaius system had several worlds at least minimally supportive of different kinds of life.

That had been a boon to the Cytherian-touched diplomats whose ships still had recalcitrant crew aboard. The other renegades faced the same limitation Bretorius did: for whatever reason, the Cytherians had compelled them to complete their tasks at minimal cost to lives. That meant they'd been forced to hold at bay any crewmembers they hadn't been able to win over or dupe.

But the Kalpaius system offered a solution. Bretorius had beamed down several hundred Romulans to the fourth world in the system. He'd determined, from their behavior and psychometric profiles, they would never willingly participate in his new order; and while the notion of using Taibak Indoctrinators to create puppets was one he'd consider again in the future, there was no time for that now. Others with site-to-site transporter technology had done the same; Zyene, the Tholian commander, had beamed her troublemakers to the infernal first planet in the system. It amused Bretorius that Subcommander Quarlis and the other problem children of *D'varian* were now on an island, up to their armpits in Klingons, Ferengi, and Gorn. Maybe they would all do each other in.

With most of the renegade ships having arrived, the meeting could begin. It was the improbable scene from outside the Far Embassy again: a vessel apiece from each major power floating around a central point in space. And the circle repeated on a virtual plane: Through ship-to-ship transmissions, Bretorius, using the Taibak visual interface, had logged into a meeting with the other Summit of Eight diplomats.

The senator didn't know whether it was a result of yet another subliminal suggestion by the Cytherians, but the mental arena in which they met was an identical representation of the meeting room aboard the Far Embassy. The exchange was entirely over short-distance comms—and yet it felt to Bretorius as if he were in the room with the others hearing them speak normally, their words automatically translated.

And how they had changed in the short time since their first meeting. Yes, there were the cosmetic changes: just as Bretorius appeared in his torture chair, several of the others were seated in various contraptions with electrical currents flowing to their heads. The Tholian had a variety of cables feeding into its helmet, all of them pulsating with light. The Tzenkethi representative, who went by what Bretorius considered the needlessly complicated name of Pikatha Tor Nim Gar-C, was a living rainbow, her skin coruscating with color as her throne channeled energy into her extremities. The species and their ships differed in many ways; the Cytherians had allowed them to find their own methods for implementing their assignments.

But more than their appearances had changed. Bretorius had gained confidence and authority since his transformation, and so had all of the others. Vekt, the Gorn, had gone from cautious to determined. DaiMon Igel was still a puny little greed-monster, but now the grandiose schemes he described had the ring of possibility. And while Gul Rodrek was still a cranky old man even with his mind fused to a warship, he seemed to have sobered up at least.

Only the Federation vessel had yet to arrive. Their true business could not begin, they all knew, until Riker appeared—or until one of them gained definitive knowledge that he had been taken out of action. It was another niggling thing that had been implanted in their minds by the Cytherians. Only a complete gathering would unlock their next assignment. Bretorius supposed it was a measure to keep their scheme running—and to prevent the participants from attacking each other.

But it could not stop them from making side deals while they waited. The seven had already worked up a variety of arrangements for a future time in which they would have more independence; most, like Bretorius's plot, involved taking control of their own peoples at home. But Riker's absence had led to a number of bargains at the Federation's expense, too.

"I want them out of our quadrant," General Charlak said. "I want everything along the old Neutral Zone."

"Everything to Algol is the Gorn's," Vekt said.

"You can have all the territory you want," Igel

piped in, "so long as I get my end. The mortgages, remember?"

Bretorius sadly did. The Ferengi had concocted a bizarre scheme in which he would conquer Federation space if he could rent certain planets back to their original owners at usurious rates. It had reminded Bretorius of the property he had not been able to reclaim from his wretched sponging in-laws, and even as far away as that life now seemed, it still pained him to think about them.

Figuring out what to do with conquered peoples would be a problem, if the predilection against deadly force the Cytherians had implanted in them could not be overcome. The limit had chapped General Charlak most of all. "It's obvious why they don't want us killing," she said. "The Cytherians—thanks for sharing the name, Bretorius—intend all this so they can soften us up for invasion. They want all the slaves left intact."

"I won't allow it," Rodrek said. "I'll destroy them all—er, that is, if I'm allowed to destroy."

Bretorius sighed. He would never have considered either Charlak or Rodrek allies in their pre-elevated forms; if they had his same level of intelligence now, they lacked his cleverness and foresight. "The Cytherians do not travel. The Federation found that out. Whatever their intentions, they aren't—"

The Tzenkethi spoke up. "There is an arrival. A Federation ship."

Finally. Bretorius used *D'varian*'s external sensors to get a view of Riker's ship. "*Aventine,*" he said, as the vessel slowed to approach their circle. Just a moment later, the open space at their gathering was filled. Admiral Riker blinked into being, seated motionlessly in an interlink chair like the others had.

Bretorius had the first question for him. "What's the meaning of this, Riker? That's not the vessel you left the Far Embassy in."

"I transferred my flag," Riker said. "From the look of it, Bretorius, a lot of you appear to have done the same. So don't give me any lip."

"*Aventine*?" Pikatha's form seemed to crackle with the power she was bathed in. "*Aventine* is a vessel of superior speed. Why are you the last to arrive?"

"I'm on time," Riker said. "I have better things to do than sit around with you people."

Bretorius chortled. "I'll tell you what happened. Romulan intelligence files describe *Aventine*'s captain, Ezri Dax, as a firebrand. She was even recently imprisoned. I'd bet that our Federation colleague has been busy fighting to control his own ship."

"Think what you want," Riker said. "And I know a lot more than you do about some things. Like who the Cytherians are, and what they did to us."

Bretorius laughed. "And now here is the benevolent Federation admiral, here to tell us poor unfortunates how the galaxy works. You're too late. Some of us figured it out on our own, and I told the rest."

"You don't have to be obnoxious about it," Riker said. "I thought you'd be wondering."

Pikatha shimmered with ire. "What's noxious is that your Federation encountered the Cytherians and simply left them alone, knowing what they might do if they turned on us."

"There was no evidence they would," Riker said.

Bretorius gave an exasperated sigh. "I should think enslaving one of your officers and stealing your starship would have been the tip-off. But no matter. We are finally all here, and we know why we are here."

"I'm not sure I—"

The Gorn snarled. "Just shut up, Federation. And concentrate."

Bretorius did. And then he knew his future.

"That's it," Pikatha said. "We have all arrived, just as our patrons expected we would—and another door has been unlocked."

"Amazing," Igel said. "It just came to me: where we're all supposed to go next."

Bretorius considered the list of coordinates that had just seemingly popped into his head. "Interesting. They've had us wrecking the border between the Romulans, the Federation, and the Klingons. Now we're to go to the Alpha Quadrant, to territory between the Cardassians, Tzenkethi, and the Ferengi. Another flashpoint."

"Another six targets," the Klingon woman said.

"That makes forty-eight, for you laggards at math," Igel said.

"That's not the important thing," Pikatha said. "Do you sense it?"

"Yes," Riker said, after a pause. "This might be it. They're cutting us loose afterwards."

Silence fell across the group, as all contemplated the thing that they all now felt.

Bretorius was first to announce his conclusions. "I have given it much thought. It's likely that after we've completed this mission for the Cytherians, they will find some way of either removing our powers or making us irrelevant to their next steps."

"You said they wouldn't be coming to invade," Charlak said.

"No, but they almost certainly have an aim, to go to such trouble. But no matter," the Romulan said.

"We will prevent the mission from ending—ever. And in so doing, we will be able to pursue whatever things we desire." *And many of those things, Riker, you won't like at all.*

"We can't subvert the orders," Riker said, his voice troubled. "That goes against the directives."

"Why, Admiral Riker, I'm surprised at you. I've seen in our database how often you and other Starfleet officers have disobeyed directives. And are you so obtuse that you haven't seen how the Cytherian orders can be gamed?"

The Tzenkethi representative agreed. "We simply need to concoct conditions that prevent the execution of the final task. We cannot directly disobey our own orders, but we may certainly conspire to raise difficulties for one another."

"That's been their mistake," Bretorius said. "They've left too much to our own individual styles, to our creativity. And they are not here to police it."

Assents rose from the group. "We'll have time to figure out how to do it," Igel said. "It will take a while for our ships to travel that far, anyway."

"*Your* ship," Riker said. "I want in on this."

Bretorius laughed. "I don't recall inviting you. Perhaps you should just do away with your six targets and allow the Cytherians to decommission you, if that is what they intend."

The Tholian, who had said nothing the entire time, spoke in chilling tones. "Or we could solve two problems at once—if the rest of us together imprisoned you here, unable to ever complete your assignments."

That was a popular suggestion, from the sound of the responses. Bretorius liked it. If all eight needed to complete their assignments to trigger the next stage of the operation, likely all eight were needed for the project to terminate.

Riker laughed. "You see? It's starting already. The group of us can't get along even independent of the people we represent. Your little cabal might cooperate for a while—but eventually, sides will be chosen again. It'll all fall apart."

"Hardly," Bretorius said. "We all have the intelligence now to see beyond rivalries—to see what is necessary for each of us individually to thrive. *This* pact will hold."

Riker's voice rose in ire. "Under whose leadership? Yours?"

"Oh, no. You won't fool me into going there," the senator said. "We don't need a leader. To seal this bargain, we only need a sacrifice. You—and your bloated Federation. We'll rise to power within our own peoples by taking you apart. But first things first."

Bretorius gave a mental command—and *D'varian*'s weapons systems and tractor beams came on line. One after another, his companions joined him in the act. Here, for once, the Cytherian rules made sense. They had more than enough power to take Riker alive— and in doing so, they could prevent the sun from setting on their abilities. Riker could hardly complete his missions buried for all eternity in a cave beneath the surface of Kalpaius III.

"You can't do this," Riker said. He clearly saw the danger, as *Aventine*'s shields had just gone up. But it wouldn't matter. Bretorius would see to that—

"Incoming subspace message," Igel said, surprise in his voice. "A long-distance one."

Bretorius paused. They had destroyed most of the network in the region. *Could it be the Cytherians?*

It turned out to be something else entirely—something Bretorius had never imagined.

A subspace connection made, three interlink chairs appeared atop the large simulated table between the participants. The chairs' occupants, unmoving, sat like gods above the gathering. A human, a Klingon, and a Cardassian.

"Greetings to the members of the Summit of Eight," the bald human said. His mouth did not move. "Search your intelligence files, and you may recognize us as Captain Jean-Luc Picard, Commander Worf, and Glinn Dygan."

"That is who we *were*," Dygan said, his mouth not moving either. "Who we are now is something else."

"And," Worf added, "we are only the beginning!"

Thirty-nine

Bretorius couldn't believe what he had just heard. "What is the meaning of this?"

"What did you think," Picard said, "that no one would track your activities back to their origin? And that the rest of us wouldn't figure out how to use an airlock?"

"This must be a trick!"

"Track my signal. You will find it is coming from the direction of the Paulson Nebula—where the Far Embassy rests. I brought *Enterprise* to it and took control." The human captain paused for effect. "Clearly, we have discovered its secret."

Bretorius's mind reeled. Since the Cytherians had touched his mind, nothing had posed a challenge for his intellect. He had conceived of grand strategies; he had envisioned long strings of tactical moves and countermoves. But it had never once occurred to him that the Cytherians weren't done transforming people.

"We are not beholden to the Cytherians as you are," Picard said. "You are only the drones. We are the warriors."

"We have freedom of action," Dygan put in.

"And we can use all the force we want," Worf added. His expression was frozen in a growl.

Bretorius wasn't alone in being stupefied—or skeptical. "We've laid waste to much of the subspace network out here," Igel said. "How could they be coming to us so clearly?"

Picard's tone showed little patience. "The Far Embassy has its own transceiver. How else could our governments have learned of the summit? Now remain silent. Our message to you is brief."

Before Bretorius could object, Picard continued. "The Federation has control over the Far Embassy, and we intend to use it. A call has gone out. Soon our starships will be arriving here—and we will see that the best and the brightest of our citizens enter the station to join us. We will not tolerate intelligences such as yours to threaten the Federation. If there is to be an intellectual arms race, we will win."

Riker spoke up. "You've done it, old friend—and just in time. They were about to betray us all." His voice was jubilant. "The tables are turned, Bretorius. The Federation won't be threatened by the likes of you!"

Picard's tone was not welcoming. "Neither will the Federation tolerate officers who fall so easily under the spell of alien influences. You, Admiral Riker, are relieved of command."

Bretorius sat, stunned, as the humans squared off across subspace. Riker's voice grew angry. "You've exceeded your authority, Picard. Enough of this!"

"Enough yourself," Picard said. "I didn't appreciate you leapfrogging over me in rank, 'old friend,' not when you had been my junior. When I learned you'd betrayed your own people to secure the Cytherians' ends, I knew I had to do something." He paused. "We could not stop you, but as you can see, we have learned to counter you. You have been made irrelevant."

Riker said nothing for a few moments. When he spoke again, his voice was cold. "Why did you call, Picard? Why are you telling us this?"

"Because I want you to know that you have been passed over. I am the admiral of the only fleet that matters. In less than twenty-four hours, dozens of our ships will arrive at the Far Embassy—and you all become irrelevant. Good-bye."

The trio vanished.

Had it been a real room the eight summiteers were sitting in, it might well have shook under the cacophony of raised voices that followed. They all knew of Picard and *Enterprise*, of course; several knew of Worf, and the Cardassian knew of Dygan. The prospect of the races of the Khitomer Accords having sole control of the Cytherian station was intolerable. All had assumed that the Summit of Eight had been called explicitly to transform the eight, and no more. If Picard really had no list of tasks to complete, nor subliminal checks against his actions, then he and those who followed him would be supremely powerful.

"Does this mean I'm not going to get my rents?" Igel grumbled.

"Are you such fools you didn't realize the implications?" the Cardassian railed. "Forget your damned fool rents—and forget borders and races. The danger is to us. We are no longer unique!"

"Could Picard really have learned so much?" the Ferengi asked.

"I faced Picard at Epsilon Outpost 11," Bretorius said. "He would have been aware of us." Bretorius felt as though he'd betrayed himself. Had he shown up Picard so badly that he'd forced the captain to his current course?

"It is known that Riker passed Picard in rank," Pikatha said. "Our spies learned of it."

"I can see being humiliated by that," Charlak said. She let loose with a digital snort. "That Picard's a man after my own cold heart, Riker. He's shown you up, well enough!"

Riker, who had said nothing since Picard vanished, sounded humbled. "He's stabbed me in the back. I had an excuse, at least, in what I did." His tone grew morose. "It's all ruined now."

"*You're* ruined, you mean," Bretorius said. He wasn't about to give up so soon—to let this happen. "We have to take the Far Embassy back."

Charlak agreed. "And if we can't—then we must destroy it."

"What?" The suggestions appeared to have startled Riker. "Destroy it? That might revert us all back to what we were before."

Bretorius frowned. "You're lying. I've read your report from years ago, Riker. You destroyed a Cytherian device with no effect on the human it had granted intelligence to. You're just trying to protect your Federation's edge."

"That's not true. This is something we should talk about . . ."

The Federation admiral's suggestion was met with silence. The other members of the Summit of Eight were too busy laying in headings and preparing their ships to go to warp, Bretorius among them. Their collective programming had dictated that they travel to the Alpha Quadrant for their next mission; the Far

Embassy happened to be along the way. They could all go there—and act—while there was still time.

Fortune and the Cytherians had given Senator Bretorius a chance to stand out. He would never go back to being a face in the crowd ever again.

Forty

Dax had attended many entertainments in her many lives, but this had been a bravura performance to match them all. She had watched and listened to the drama, which Riker had patched through to the main viewscreen on the bridge; she had been amazed to see the other summit representatives in their new guises as galaxy conquerors. And she had waited until the last vessel went to warp before engaging the slipstream drive. *Aventine* would follow the same course as the renegades—and if all went well, it would arrive before they did.

Riker had concocted the entire plan in that second of silence back at Adelphous when they'd been debating what to do. When she'd learned of it, it had stunned her with its simplicity. Riker had realized that Adelphous existed on a direct path—at least, so far as the curious curvature of warp space was concerned—between the Far Embassy and the Kalpaius System, where he was to meet the others. Faking a signal from the Far Embassy was a simple matter of bringing a portion of the Adelphous Array back online in order to send a subspace broadcast.

It could not be done while Riker was present at Adelphous; that would have violated the letter of his instructions from the Cytherians, who expected the site to be defunct when he left it. It had fallen to Leishman, serving with *Enterprise*'s crew while La Forge was aboard *Aventine,* to get the array operational. They would need to establish a two-way message with the group at Kalpaius at the exact moment Riker had instructed: two minutes after he was scheduled to arrive.

That was the technical part—and it had gone off perfectly, thanks to *Aventine*'s talented chief engineer.

The next portion, which had required Picard as well to stay behind, was more of a gamble. It was also a daring bit of deceit, requiring some acting. Some captains might have been hard to sell on the notion, but Picard had quickly seen how the idea of a flood of rival supergeniuses, all on the side of the Federation, would work on the wayward diplomats. He'd caught the thrust of that part of Riker's plan without the admiral having to verbalize it. Dax figured it was good to have colleagues who thought alike, no matter how different their brains were.

The rest had been a matter for *Enterprise*'s holodeck. Holograms of the Cytherian interlink chair were easy enough to construct; it had taken Riker less than a second to send across a design for a nonworking version. The decision to use Worf and Dygan in the deception told the listeners that the Federation had not only used the power of the Far Embassy, but would do it again and again. And the fact that the three men were of different species would certainly play on the fears of several of the Summit of Eight members. Here was the Federation, ready to accelerate the evolution of themselves and their allies.

Now *Enterprise* was hurtling at top speed toward the Far Embassy, as was *Aventine*. Even with the slipstream drive, Picard would arrive first, but Riker had still more things to prepare in the meantime. Dax was looking at one, a high-tech gadget laid out on the worktable Riker had generated in holodeck one.

"What is it?" she asked Geordi La Forge. He was on a stool, hunched over and staring intently at the small device he was working on.

La Forge looked up at her and smiled. "It's something that shouldn't exist."

Over in his chair, Riker spoke. *"WE GOT THE SEVEN TO FOLLOW US BACK TO THE FAR EMBASSY, BUT THAT'S JUST THE FIRST PART. AT A MINIMUM, WE CAN TRY TO CONTAIN THEM THERE. BUT MY HOPE IS THAT WE CAN REVERSE THE PROCESS WHILE THEY'RE ALL IN THE AREA."*

"The admiral thinks he can make that happen if he goes back inside the Far Embassy station—but we can't detach him from the interlink chair. So we need something else." La Forge gingerly lifted the colorful blinking device he was working on. "I can barely believe this—but he's shown me how to build a mobile holoemitter."

Dax gawked. The mobile emitter was a piece of future technology obtained by *Starship Voyager*'s Emergency Medical Hologram. It permitted a holographic program to exist without holoprojectors, compact in a device that could be worn by a virtual person. It should've been impossible, given what they knew of the science. "I thought that was one of a kind," she said.

"That's right," La Forge said, bringing it before his shining eyes. "Fabian Stevens of the Corps of Engineers did a molecule-by-molecule replication of the original, but couldn't get it to work. I'd been meaning to try building one myself—I'd gotten the schematics from the Project Voyager files—but I never got around to it."

"GEORDI, YOU NEED TO CHECK INTERFACE 208," Riker said. *"IT'S ONE MILLIJOULE TOO HIGH."*

La Forge set the device back onto the workstation surface and waved a tool over it. "You're right. But I don't think I can adjust this one. It's too small."

In a flash of light, the holographic doppelganger of Riker appeared on the other side of the table. "Not a problem." Politely, he edged past Dax to take the instrument from La Forge.

"KEEP AN EYE ON THIS FOR ME," the holographic figure said in unison with the seated Riker. La Forge watched closely as holo-Riker made a series of incredibly minute adjustments.

La Forge checked the work. "Looks good." Holo-Riker set down the tool and walked to the real Riker's side.

"I COULDN'T JUST REPLICATE IT, BECAUSE THE EMITTER HAS TO USE REAL MATTER," Riker said. *"ANYTHING I WOULD GENERATE HERE WOULD LOSE COHESION AS SOON AS IT LEFT."*

Dax nodded. That was basic holoscience.

"It's amazing," La Forge said, peering at the emitter. "I can see the microscopic level on which we're working, but I'd never be able to do anything this precise."

"DON'T SELL YOURSELF SHORT, GEORDI," Riker said. *"I COULDN'T DO THIS WITHOUT YOU."*

Dax's eyes narrowed. "Admiral, how does this help you?"

The holo-Riker waved to her. *"THE MOBILE EMITTER CAN'T CONTAIN MY INTELLECT,"* the admiral's disembodied voice said. *"BUT MY DOUBLE WILL BE*

ABLE TO FUNCTION—AND AS LONG AS I HAVE A SUB-SPACE LINK TO THE EMITTER, MY HOLOGRAPHIC COUNTERPART CAN ACT FOR ME."

Dax nodded. "Envoy of an envoy."

"MY LIFE IS ONE BIG RECURSION CHAIN." The holo-Riker vanished. *"THAT'S GOOD WORK, GEORDI. I THINK WE CAN TAKE A BREAK NOW."*

La Forge smiled and rose from the stool. "I have to admit, Will—I never thought we'd be collaborating like this."

"YOU AND ME BOTH."

The engineer turned and looked back at the seated Riker. "We're going to get you out of there as soon as we can—I promise. But I can't deny I'd love to know what you know." He bowed his head gently, turned, and left.

Alone with Riker, Dax faced him and straightened. "We're making best time to the Paulson Nebula," she said, "though you already know that." She shook her head. The whole situation was bizarre, and it felt foolish to deny it. "I guess I could have made my report from my ready room."

"I THOUGHT WE SHOULD DISCUSS WHAT MIGHT HAPPEN ONCE WE ARRIVE."

"Fine." It didn't make sense why they had to do that here, either.

"AND THERE WAS SOMETHING ELSE," Riker said. *"I KNOW I EXPLAINED MYSELF BEFORE—BUT I REALLY WAS HOPING YOU WOULD ACCEPT MY APOLOGY. YOU AND YOUR CREW."*

Dax looked off to the side and let out an exasperated sigh.

"CAPTAIN?"

"Sorry—"

"DON'T BE. I'M THE ONE APOLOGIZING."

"I don't know how to react. A starship's never apologized to me before." She looked directly at him. "No ship of mine has ever needed to apologize before."

"HOW ABOUT A SUPERIOR OFFICER?"

"They've let me down a few times. And even thrown me in the brig." She paced past the interlink chair and looked at the tapestry the bear had chewed on. "Intellectually, I understand everything that's happened here—and I know you weren't responsible. But it still happened to *Aventine.*"

"IT HAPPENED TO ME, TOO."

"And I'm not denying that." She looked back. "Listen. You're a lot smarter than I am, Admiral. But I'm a lot older."

"AGREED."

"I've disappointed people in my life. Sometimes it was my fault, sometimes it wasn't. But that didn't matter. They were disappointed. And I've had to work to get them back." She stepped back in front of him. "And that really is the only way. You can't fix the past, but you can try to make things better in the future—by doing things like you're doing now. That won't work with everybody. There are people I lost that I can never make amends to. But the only way you're going to have a hope of getting yourself back is by staying alive, by continuing to fight."

"THAT'S MY PLAN."

"Good." Her expression softened. "Now, you were going to tell me your plan for when we get there?"

"ACTUALLY, IT'S YOURS . . ."

Forty-one

In his earlier life, Bretorius had never dealt well with anxiety. His stomach had a tendency to try to crawl up his throat whenever he had too long to brood about an upcoming event. He'd led the Romulan Senate in sessions missed because he was off being sick in the restroom.

Now, when even a minute was an eternity to Bretorius, he had spent the last several hours thinking on the encounter that lay ahead. And while the Cytherians' influence had greatly increased his confidence, their handiwork had brought him problems of a different sort. He was no longer worried about the unknown; he could easily think through any possible scenario, finding a solution that benefited him. But there, also, lay the quandary. He could imagine *so* many possibilities that it had become difficult to focus.

The Terrans had a figure of myth, Prometheus, who had sought the knowledge of gods and earned only hardship. Writing of him, an Earth statesman-turned-poet had said too much knowledge had caused misery. *Typical human response*, Bretorius thought. As a people, they were reluctant to grasp the opportunities before them, the same way they hid behind their Prime Directive so as to avoid the appearance and responsibilities of kingship. Romulans weren't like that. Yes, there were a multitude of factors in play and he was having trouble figuring out what his best course was. But Bretorius far preferred knowing about them to not knowing. It was why the future would belong to him and the Romulans.

He would make sure of that.

The others were heading to either capture or destroy the Far Embassy. They had left without coordinating, left without deciding which approach they would take. They would certainly succeed at either, so long as *Enterprise* was the only Starfleet vessel there with a Cytherian-elevated captain aboard.

But it did make a difference, Bretorius now saw, which thing they did. Once Picard was bested, Bretorius could easily see a battle breaking out between his partners. The Klingon and the Tholian were likely to want the Far Embassy destroyed, to prevent members of any other races from being elevated by the Cytherians; the Tzenkethi was likely to want to see it preserved, for use by her own people. The Ferengi would want to keep it around just to charge admission. It was a mess—and considering all the angles had taxed even his mind.

The answer had dawned on him. He had to be in a position to thrive whichever result happened. And that meant he needed help.

Fortunately, he already had it. "You understand the danger I'm in," he said, looking through the metalwork of the Taibak Indoctrinator at Nerla. "If the

Far Embassy is manufacturing masterminds, I will no longer be unique."

Nerla yawned in her chair, clearly exhausted by the recent days. "No longer unique. Right. So that's why you want to destroy it."

"I might, and I might not," Bretorius said. "If Picard is telling the truth, the Embassy is able to provide mental advancement without the conditioning—without the compulsions that I am under. If there is a way to remove these handicaps from myself, I want to know."

"So fly over when we get there," she said. She pointed backward with her thumb. "You said you can get out of this contraption if you want. Just beam yourself down to a shuttle and fly over."

Bretorius sighed. *A pretty fool, but a fool.* "If I leave *D'varian*, I will lose command of the ship. I will need an agent, just as the Cytherians made agents out of the other diplomats and me." His eyes focused on her. "I need you to board the Far Embassy."

"No!" she blurted. Then she laughed. "You want them to transform me, too?" She shook her head. "I told you, I'm not interested in marrying you. You don't need to turn me into—into whatever you are."

"I wasn't thinking of that. I don't want anyone else transformed at all. And that's why I would send you over—in case Picard has other people inside. You would be armed. You could stop any further use of the facility from inside, while *D'varian* prevents anyone else from boarding." He paused. "Once it is secured, you would be my eyes—and I would pry loose any remaining secrets the place holds."

Nerla leaned back in her chair, the backside of her head rolling against the headrest. "Bret, Bret—this is crazy. I've not your one-woman army."

"You've had military training."

"Six weekends a year ten years ago!"

"I believe in you, Nerla. And there's no one else I can send." That much was obvious just from the pounding that still echoed through the walls of the ship. Instead of quieting *D'varian*'s occupants, the sudden transport of so many of the crew off the ship had radicalized the rest. Bretorius had announced across the ship that the missing people had been beamed to a safe location, but his surveillance showed that almost everyone assumed he'd transported the others into the void of space. He wasn't in any danger from the crew—not while the deck still had defenses—but he couldn't expect any help from them, either.

And even Nerla's aid was in jeopardy. "What happens if I go in and the Klingons or whoever tries to blow the station up?"

"I'll prevent that. I'll be outside with the ship, remember?" He appealed to her as best he could from inside the restraints of the Indoctrinator. "You have to do it, Nerla. Or everything until now could be for nothing."

She let out a deep breath. "It *was* for nothing, Bret. You're just too smart now to see it." She stood and looked to the exit. "This whole thing has gotten too crazy. I've got to go."

"Go? Go where?"

"I don't know. You've ruined me so I can't go home. Just let me off somewhere."

Bretorius looked up at her and sighed. It was a shame—but he had planned for this, too.

"Very well. There should be a severance package." His eyes darted to the door. "Step across the hall. Something in the replicator should be ready for you."

Nerla looked at him, puzzled, before wandering outside.

A few moments later, she returned, her gaze fixed on the shiny thing in her hands. It was a breastplate necklace, with a ruby eye set in a golden medallion, suspended from a thick loop of the same metallic material.

"It would have been appropriate for the consort of an ancient king—or a modern one," Bretorius said. "I had intended to give it to you on our betrothal—but since that's off, you might as well have it."

Nerla turned the precious gift over in her hands. "It looks like gold-pressed latinum. But that can't be replicated!"

Bretorius grinned widely. "You did say I was smart."

Nerla looked at him in wonderment—and then back at the necklace. "Bret, if you can do things like this, why bother stealing starships?" She shook her head. "Even now, you never think this stuff through."

"Don't be so sure. You see, it's a much more valuable gift than you think. It has a secret. If you try it on, you'll find your body temperature will unlock a compartment set behind the jewel. Inside is the elusive replicator formula for latinum that you think doesn't exist. It does exist—now—and it is yours, for services rendered."

Nerla gawked. "And I don't have to board the Far Embassy?"

"You said no. So, no."

Mesmerized, Nerla pulled the ends of the band behind her neck and fastened them. She adjusted the fit for a moment and lifted up the medallion to look at it in the light.

Then she frowned. "It's suctioned to my neck," she said, pulling at it. "The chain."

"Ah," he said. "That's so the injector can have access to your external carotid artery."

"Injector!"

"Yes. For the fast-acting poison secreted inside the band. If you choose not to do as I ask, you will die."

"Stop joking!"

"I'm quite serious."

Nerla stared at him, stunned.

Then she punched him in the nose, causing his head to smack against the restraints of the Indoctrinator. "You are *such* an ass!"

Nose bleeding, Bretorius snuffled—and grew enraged. "I wouldn't do that again, Nerla. The injector might go off by accident. And if it didn't, I would cause it to."

She stared at him—and drew back.

"The stakes are too high, Nerla. You will do as I've asked—and you'll carry me with you, as there's a short-range subspace transceiver and camera in the medallion. Do as I ask and there's no reason you should be in any danger from anyone inside the Far Embassy—or from me."

Angry with herself, Nerla let out a pained groan. "I bet this isn't gold-pressed latinum, either."

"Of course not. I can't change the laws of nature," he said. "Though perhaps I'll work on that next, after this is over. But first things first."

Forty-two

Picard looked through the forward viewport as the shuttle approached the station. The Far Embassy was just as he'd seen it in the files provided by *Titan*. The vessel had been waiting on the scene when the *Enterprise* arrived. Christine Vale had backtracked to the place where, all now knew, the trouble had begun. The *Enterprise* captain had enough time to fill in *Titan*'s crew fully about what had happened and about what was expected once *Aventine* and the renegade ships arrived.

Aventine had made it in before the rest, as anticipated, giving them further time to prepare. Deanna Troi had wanted very much to see her husband, but he had thought it best that she didn't. Picard didn't blame him. There was too much already going on in Riker's mind, even with its enhanced capacity. And while the Cytherian influence provided added self-confidence—a commodity Will Riker was well supplied with—Picard could tell Riker simply didn't want to be seen by her or his daughter in his current state.

"They bought it completely," the holographic Riker

said from the seat opposite Picard in the rear of the
shuttle. He was wearing the mobile emitter, perfected
on the journey. "You, Worf, and Glinn Dygan make a
great acting company."

"Worf wasn't sanguine about the ploy," Picard
said. "But I agreed with you: if they were involved,
the renegades would be incensed." He looked at holo-
Riker. "You heard me speak the lines you gave me
about your promotion. I didn't relish that part. You
know I couldn't be more pleased for you."

Holo-Riker shrugged. "It was the right play. I don't
know a lot about the players on the other side, but
thwarted ambition seems to be a motive they understand. It worked. I don't know if they're coming to
conquer or destroy, but they're coming."

"We'll be ready," Picard said. "Or rather, you will."

It was one of the stranger situations the captain
had been involved in. Riker—or rather, his holographic stand-in—was sitting there being directed
remotely by the real Riker back on *Aventine*. At the
same time, the admiral was busy coordinating the
three ships' upcoming defense of the station. Only
one person could board the Far Embassy at a time
through the Federation's designated airlock; they'd
decided it should be Picard, who had been part of the
first contact with the Cytherians.

He would be bringing Admiral Riker along lit-
erally in his vest pocket. Holo-Riker again showed
him the controls of the armband. Picard would enter
the station alone, but both of them would be able to
work inside it—and provided the local subspace link
between *Aventine* and the mobile emitter remained
operational, the hologram would retain its live connection back to the admiral's mind.

A jolt shook the shuttle. "That's the automatic trac-tor beam," called Sam Bowers from the pilot's seat.

Picard looked forward to see Bowers and *Aventine*'s chief engineer, Mikaela Leishman, at the controls. They were here not simply as pilots; Riker and Dax had concocted a plan he called his "ace in the hole." The admiral had not been sure the scheme would work, nor did he know what circumstances would make him play the card, but it was something they could do to try to affect the station. If Picard had learned anything about the transformed Riker, it was that he planned for every eventuality.

"Do you think you can complete the assignment as the admiral laid it out?" Picard asked the *Aventine*'s officers.

Leishman's eyes scanned the approaching interface with the station. "It's doable. A Federation-style docking port and tractor beam, of a model from about twenty years ago."

Riker nodded. "That's when the Cytherians would have last seen schematics for them."

"Why were you showing them docking ports?" Bowers asked.

Picard answered that. "As an aid to them, in case they made contact with anyone in this sector."

Bowers stared at the docking port, growing ever-larger outside. "Well, they've definitely made contact." He looked back to Picard and Riker. "We'll start work as soon as you're inside."

"Thanks," Riker said, leaning forward to address the *Aventine* officers. "Stay sharp. Don't let anyone put one over on you—no matter who he says he is."

Bowers and Leishman nodded in appreciation—even as the shuttle turned to line up with the airlock. A second later, *Meuse* bumped the station with a metallic thud.

"Will the door open for me?" Picard asked.

"You're an invited guest," Riker said. "Try it."

Picard stood at *Meuse*'s hatch. The shuttle's door opened, revealing a gray portal beyond with an alphanumeric keypad at the center. Picard entered the passcode the United Federation of Planets had been sent. After a pause, the door opened, revealing the cramped turbolift car Riker had used on his visit.

"That's one hunch that worked," Riker said. "They didn't plan to use the airlocks again, so why change the passcodes?" He turned so that Picard could access the mobile emitter. "Captain."

Picard took careful hold of the armband, knowing that it would fall to the deck as soon as there was nothing to support it. "I've never deactivated a superior officer before," he said, carefully operating the controls.

"Very funny. I'll see you inside."

AVENTINE

So this is the place that caused all the trouble, Dax thought as she watched from her command chair. *Aventine* had taken up a defensive position alongside *Enterprise* and *Titan*, all three vessels preparing for the renegades. But her interest was what was in the shuttle, docked at the Far Embassy.

"Magnify," she said.

Meuse didn't look too bad for the beating it had taken in her attempt to break out earlier. Right on schedule, the shuttle's upper hatch opened, disgorging two figures in EV suits. Commander Bowers and Lieutenant Leishman scuttled across to the docking interface. They couldn't get inside, Dax knew. But they could access something else—perhaps the only part of the Far Embassy that wasn't designed by an advanced civilization.

"They're starting," Helkara said from the science post. "I'll be amazed if this works."

"I'm tired of being amazed," she said. "I just want to be right."

Behind, Kedair reported, "Proximity alarm. One, three—no, *six* vessels arriving from warp, on the expected vector."

"That's our friends," Dax said. "Red Alert. Shields up. Bowers, Leishman—finish and get out of there."

"It's everyone but the Romulan, Captain."

"It's plenty." The Trill looked back to Kedair, eyes cold and serious. "We're going to defend the Far Embassy, just like *Enterprise* defended the array from us. Listen for the Admiral's orders!"

Forty-three

Bretorius had figured it perfectly. While the other six renegade vessels were arriving along the same vector, he had dropped from warp short of the Far Embassy—only to engage on a route plotted to deliver *D'varian* on the opposite side of the station, well beyond the reach of the sensors of any Federation vessel nearby. He'd been expecting anything from a single starship to a flotilla defending the location; three ships were enough to confirm for him that the Federation indeed had plans for the Far Embassy. He had immediately engaged his cloaking device, cruising calmly and casually toward the station without regard for the battle now raging around it.

Things weren't going as well inside *D'varian*. What crewmembers weren't working to get at him were trying to disable the warbird. It had been a game of move-countermove for him. He would use the transporters as a defensive weapon, they would attempt to disable them. The crew would try to protect themselves by constructing transport inhibitors, he would beam the components into space. He had even been forced to expend valuable time trying to figure out how to replicate and beam knockout gas into the ventilation systems.

The whole thing would have been so much easier if anyone had followed him.

But there was still Nerla, bound to his will. From within the Taibak Indoctrinator, he looked up at her. "Cheer up," he said. "You're going on an adventure." Nerla looked miserable and angry in her spacesuit, equipment he'd beamed into the brig from storage. "I will beam you to a location near the Romulan docking port, just outside the range of the Far Embassy's transport inhibitors. The tractor beam will bring you to the hatch. There is a keypad with characters in our language. Use—"

"I know, I know," she said, snapping her helmet on. "Use the code you gave me."

"When you are inside, remove your suit. I will be able to communicate with you and see what you can see—via the necklace. The Far Embassy may be proof against transporters and most of *D'varian*'s sensors, but I already know from my first visit that we can get a subspace signal through. And don't forget the disruptor," he said, eyes darting to the weapon on the table nearby.

Nerla stared at it. "Who's over there?"

"I told you, I can't read life signs through its shell. Nobody can—it's why my colleagues are able to strike at it without it violating their conditioning. As far as any of us know, the place was uninhabited. I want to make sure it remains so. Use the disruptor to thwart anyone who attempts to gain power from the Cytherians. Or anyone who just seems too smart."

"Fine." Picking up the disruptor in her gloved hand, she pointed it at Bretorius. She glared at him. "You fit both descriptions, don't you?"

He sighed. "You *know* I wouldn't have replicated a weapon that I couldn't deactivate in an instant, right?"

Nerla rolled her eyes. "I'm so sick of this. And you."

She snapped the disruptor in her holster and shrugged. "Okay, whenever . . ."

FAR EMBASSY

Picard stepped from the cramped turbolift into the round room. It was just as Riker had described: large, domed, featureless—lit by a light seemingly coming from nowhere. And there was the large octagonal table, an impractical number of meters across, in the center of the room, surrounded by eight chairs of different configurations.

It was time; there was more than enough room for two here. He pulled the mobile emitter from his pocket, held it at arm's length, and activated it.

In a flash, the holographic admiral appeared. Holo-Riker looked up and around. "Genie out of the bottle," Picard said.

"We could trade archaic expressions all day," Riker said. "But I can tell you that our guests have arrived outside. Six ships against three. Dax, Worf, and Vale have launched the defense I designed."

"How long will that give us?"

"That depends," Riker said, walking toward the giant table. "My fellow diplomats won't be able to use deadly force themselves, but that won't stop people they've duped from using it. Nothing will stop them from firing on the Far Embassy if they get past."

"Or mounting electronic attacks," Picard said, wandering the room. "If they jam *Aventine* or the station, your link could be severed. I'm curious how we can get a subspace signal out when our sensors can't pierce the station's hull."

"That's how the Cytherians wanted it. The diplomats had to be able to call back to their ships on arrival—it made it seem less like a trap." Riker walked to one of the chairs at the table designed for a bipedal humanoid. "Where it all started," he said. He sat down in it and put his hands on the smooth surface. "This place hasn't changed an atom since we all walked out. They didn't even put the furniture away."

"They? Was someone here?"

"No. It was all functioning automatically." He looked about. "Our transformation was triggered when we all sat down—there was this bright light. Nothing's happening now."

Picard looked at the other seats. "Did we need to bring seven others to trigger the process?"

"I didn't have time to build emitters for a holographic menagerie, if that's what you mean. This was chancy enough without spending time creating our own fake diplomats."

Picard nodded. "Perhaps the mechanism senses you're a hologram. Perhaps I should try it."

Riker looked up at him. "I don't want this thing transforming you as it did me. I don't know that it would happen, but it happened to me."

The holographic Riker paused. Picard searched his face. "What is it?"

"*Meuse* is safely away—and the renegades have engaged our task force." As Riker said it, a low sound thrummed through the room. "That would be a close call delivered by a Tholian *Emerald*-class juggernaut. He ran his hands across the table and looked up and around. "We can't wait much longer. But even knowing what I know now, I can't perceive any mechanism in this room at all."

Picard walked around the table and surveyed the

place, even as another blast reverberated through the chamber. "Just a moment. Who called this place the Far Embassy?"

"The hosts, in their invitations," Riker said. "The Cytherians."

"The Cytherians are incredibly precise in their language, Will—you remember. They would not call something an embassy unless it was."

Riker nodded, catching the idea. "It's not an embassy for any of us. It's an embassy for them."

Picard's eyes lit up. "Precisely. And where there is an embassy—"

"—there is an ambassador," Riker said, standing up. "Well?" he called out to the air.

Nothing.

"You might as well show yourself," holo-Riker said, cupping his hands together. His voice echoed through the room. "The game is up. I demand to see the ambassador!"

A searing flash blinded Picard. When his eyes adjusted, he saw the giant floating head of a Cytherian floating ethereally, several meters above the center of the table.

Giant eyes focused on the humans. *"Disturbance unnecessary,"* the woman said.

"Madame Ambassador," Picard said, bowing.

"We have some things to discuss," Riker said, as another explosion rocked the Far Embassy. "And you'd better talk fast."

Forty-four

She was three meters tall from chin to her bundle of orange hair. The color matched the six-pointed jewel embedded in her forehead. The Cytherian's skin was old and drawn, and her eyes narrowed as she beheld her visitors. When she spoke again, the words she repeated boomed around the chamber, louder than before.

"Unnecessary disturbance!"

Picard and Riker had been in the presence of a Cytherian before—and had become accustomed to the race's parsimonious means of expression. Picard stepped forward, his palms open in a gesture of friendship. "I don't know if your people remember me. I am Jean-Luc Picard of the United Federation of Planets."

"Impatience. Slight regard." The floating head began to slowly revolve away from Picard.

"Remarkable," the captain said, staring at her with wonder. "But the Cytherians don't travel. Or they didn't before." He looked to Riker. "What do you see, Will?"

As a holographic character, Riker's doppelganger was not limited to human senses. Holo-Riker studied the alien face. "I can't tell you much about her. I don't have all the sensors I'd have on *Aventine*." He gestured to Picard. "Use your tricorder."

While Picard reached for the instrument, the giant head's eyes fell on the holographic Riker. She stared at him coolly. *"Simulacrum,"* she said and continued to rotate.

The captain activated his tricorder and directed it at the Cytherian. The readings didn't help much. "It's just like aboard *Enterprise*, with Caster. It's difficult to tell whether she's material or not. She could be here—or she could a holographic program."

"I can't tell either. But the Cytherians told us they didn't travel. Odds are she's a program."

The captain shut the tricorder off and started walking around the floating head, which continued to turn faster than he could keep up. It was like trying to maintain eye contact with a gyroscope.

Finally, he stepped into her field of view again. "And how should we address you?"

"Proctor."

The name made sense to Picard. Caster's name—at least as a term *Enterprise*-D's crew could understand—was in some sense a description of his role, or so the theorizing had gone. "You are a teacher?"

"Proctor." The Cytherian resumed her disinterested, slow turning.

Picard walked round to Riker's side, pocketing his tricorder as he did. "They don't give you much, do they?"

Riker glared. "It was like this years ago. It's like talking to a tarot card reader. They give you just enough and make you imagine the rest." He spoke to the back of her head. "You forced skills on me, Proctor, and a mission of destruction. I want to know why."

At once, the head spun a hundred eighty degrees. Proctor's eyes looked daggers at Riker. *"Impertinent vested intelligence."* The head seemed to bob angrily. *"Rejection of assignments. Failure."*

Picard scratched his head. "I think 'vested intelligence' means you, Will."

"I've only started to be impertinent. You haven't answered my question, Proctor. Why have you done all this?"

"Impudence. Misapprehension of station!" Proctor's voice boomed—and as it did, the Far Embassy shook again.

"We don't have time for this," Riker said. *"Your* station is under attack!"

AVENTINE

It was the most challenging tactical situation Dax had faced in her recent memory. And she wondered how Starfleet could ever train someone for it.

Six attacking vessels, from six different interstellar powers. It wasn't a simple matter of Lonnoc Kedair working against the profile of a Klingon battlecruiser. It was a ship identification seminar, all in one attack wave. The best defense against one wasn't the right move against another.

Complicating matters was something that had become quickly apparent: the six ships didn't seem to have the same objectives. The Klingon, the Cardassian, and the Gorn were clearly targeting the Far Embassy; the Tholian and Tzenkethi were buzzing around, evidently looking for ways to approach the side of the station with their docking ports. The Ferengi was dithering—waiting to salvage the pieces? She didn't know.

But the fact was, for the Starfleet vessels, this was an advantage. Dax was in command and leading *Aventine*. But Admiral Riker on holodeck one was providing the master plan for their defense of the station, coordinating *Aventine* with *Enterprise* and *Titan:* a commodore running a fleet action. Only this commodore had a nearly infinite capacity to process information and direct mental access to the ship's sensors.

Dax and her crew weren't just along for the ride. But Riker was acting as a force multiplier, and they needed one now more than ever.

"They've stepped it up a notch since Meuse *undocked,"* Riker said over the comm.

"The Klingons and the Gorn are unloading on the station. We're doing our best to deflect and divert," Dax said.

"They think because Meuse *left, the station's unoccupied. So now they don't have one arm tied behind their backs."*

Aventine swooped past the Klingon cruiser, cutting off its path and forcing it to angle away. "I don't suppose we could tell them we've got people inside?"

"They wouldn't believe us—or they wouldn't want to. They're all aching to act in ways their programming won't let them."

"It helps that they're not coordinating," Dax called out, straining to be heard over the din on the bridge.

"They are. There's subspace messaging going back and forth. They keep forming alliances—and breaking them and forming new ones in mid-battle. That's our advantage. We're not changing our minds."

While Riker was talking with her, another portion of the admiral's mind was focused on the battle and their next steps, and operating his holographic doppelganger on the Far Embassy. For the first time, Dax realized the full scope of what the Cytherians had given—or foisted on—him. Just how busy could a living mind be, if it had both the capacity and the means to effect action?

It took her breath away. *Glad he's on our side—now.*

"I've got *Meuse* hailing," Mirren said.

Bowers called over the communications systems. *"No way we can get back aboard with the shuttle, Captain. You're moving too fast."*

"Abandon it. Engineering, beam them to the bridge."

The two spacesuited officers materialized in front of the command chairs—and several seconds later, Dax saw the shuttle explode in a hail of disruptor fire from several of the renegade vessels.

Bowers looked back at the viewscreen, unnerved and astonished. "They weren't shooting at us at all before we left!"

"That's just it. You left," Dax said. *Riker was right*, she thought. A target with life signs could be harassed, but not destroyed. *Meuse* had been taken out the second it was empty.

"We've made contact with something," Riker said. *"We've got to keep the defense going."*

Like we have a choice, Dax wanted to say. But there was no point in carping now. "Look alive, *Aventine*. Another wave incoming!"

FAR EMBASSY

We're getting nowhere with Proctor, Picard thought. And she seemed to agree.

"Conversation futile," she had said. *"Queries irrelevant."* And now the latest, *"Pointless exercise."*

"Exercise?" Riker snapped his holographic fingers. "There's something."

Picard's hands clapped over the back of a chair to steady himself against the shaking of the station. "What have you got?"

"Something I was thinking before I came here the first time," holo-Riker said. "People exercise because a mind needs a body to be effective. But when I sat in the interlink chair, *Aventine* became my body—and I could suddenly do a whole lot more."

"Right."

"We've been thinking all along the Cytherians were far away—that this station was a trap to create drones for them, to give them a way to affect events here."

Picard figured out where he was going. "But if Cytherian power could make your mind merge with a starship—"

"—then this station isn't a trap. It isn't even a station. It's a starship, with a captain on board. And like *Aventine*, its captain's lost control!"

Disregarding the shaking of the deck, Riker climbed up on a chair and looked accusingly at Proctor. "Caster is here, isn't he? I mean, *really* here. He's aboard this ship!"

Proctor glowered at Riker for a moment. *"Impertinence intolerable,"* she finally said. *"Mission vacated."* Proctor turned, and her eyes fell on Picard. *"Federation."*

Her stare was so intense the captain actually took a step backward. "Yes," he said, not understanding. He put his hand to his chest. "I am Picard, of the Federation—"

"Existing vested intelligence inadequate. Federation agent required." And with that, a low hum emanated from the table.

Riker's eyes widened. "Wait a minute. This is where I came in!" He hopped down and pushed Picard back out of the way of Proctor's direct gaze. " 'Federation agent required?' I remember now. She's going to transform you, as she did me!"

"Federation agent necessary condition. Newbeing Picard necessary." Proctor's eyes began to glow. *"Resistance futile."*

"We've heard that one before," Picard said, defiant. He drew his phaser.

"Weapon irrelevant. You can do nothing."

"On the contrary," Riker said, a canny look materializing on his holographically generated face. "I'm doing something right now."

AVENTINE

"Captain Dax!" Riker called from holodeck one.

On the bridge, Dax looked up. "Yes, Admiral?"

"Play the ace. Disable the Far Embassy. Don't destroy it—disable it."

"Understood. Captain Picard is still aboard."

"Yes—but that's not the only reason. I can't explain now."

"Understood." Dax looked to Bowers and Leishman, who had quickly removed their EV suits. "Are we ready?"

Leishman nodded. "Can't say as I've ever purposefully broken a system that was working. But it should do what you want."

"Turnabout's fair play," Dax said, triggering a control on her armrest. "Attention, *Enterprise* and *Titan*. Play your ace."

Forty-five

"**A**cknowledged," Worf said. He turned in the command chair to look back at Lieutenant Šmrhová. "Photon torpedoes on my mark, full spread, targeting a point near the Far Embassy's Federation docking interface."

The chief security officer calmly answered, "Aye, aye, sir."

"Time their explosions for the instant the tractor beam takes hold."

"Aye, sir." Šmrhová looked down with trepidation. "I hope they know what they're doing."

"*Aventine, Enterprise* is ready."

AVENTINE

"*Titan's a go,*" Christine Vale reported over the comsystem.

"That's it," Dax said. "Fire!"

Aventine, under fire itself from the renegade vessels, launched a series of torpedoes in the direction of the Far Embassy. *Enterprise* and *Titan,* closer at the moment than *Aventine,* did the same milliseconds later. The hurtling bundles of destruction converged on a point not far from the docking ring of the station.

The torpedoes triggered the tractor beam at the Federation's entrance. At that moment, the projectiles in its grip detonated.

The brightness filters on *Aventine*'s main viewscreen were only barely a match for the flash that followed. The calamitous explosion lit the space all around—and sent the entire station tumbling end over end through the nebula, crackling with some kind of charge.

"Admiral," she called out to the air. "What's the status aboard the station?"

"Stand by."

FAR EMBASSY

Picard had known to expect *something*—but nothing like the shock that seized the structure around him. The thunderous impact was but one part: striking a region well above the meeting room's dome, it had thrown him up into the air. Landing roughly, he saw the next effects. The overhead lighting blinked out—and what he could only call lightning shot from the center of the table to the Cytherian. Proctor let loose with a horrific screech that pierced ears still throbbing from the sound of the blast.

Feeling the Embassy shuddering around him, Picard worried it would vent to space; a direct impact surely would have cracked it open like an egg. But it held together and so did Proctor—barely. The disembodied head slumped sideways, as if knocked to the deck.

Nearby, the holographic Riker was still standing, surveying the changes to a room now lit only by the weak luminescence given off by Proctor. "We've got gravity, but that's about it."

"Look there!" Picard said.

A glow emanated from the surface of the octagonal table. It grew in intensity for several moments—until finally, like a child being born, a second giant evanescent head popped into the space just meters above the watchers.

"It's Caster," Riker said. "But he looks bad."

It was indeed the Cytherian that Picard remembered. Withered, pale-skinned, and with white whiskers descending like shimmering tendrils. Only the violet jewel at the crown of his forehead was flickering, and the being seemed on the edge of consciousness. "Did our blast do this?" Picard asked.

"Partly," Riker said, walking closer to Caster. He put his hand up, reaching toward, but not touching, the being floating above. "If my control of *Aventine* could be shaken by a feedback overload through the tractor beam, theirs could be too."

Picard marveled at Riker's acuity. The docking interface and tractor beam had been the only portions of the Far Embassy based on Federation technology; Riker had reasoned, along with Dax, that the same glitch in *Aventine*'s tractor beam that permitted the feedback could be introduced into the tractor beam systems at the Embassy. Leishman and Bowers had made that modification, and the three Federation ships had done the rest.

They had two Cytherians now, their weakly radiant heads lolling in the dark. Picard was about to ask what could be done for them when he heard a noise behind him. One that told him everything was about to change again . . .

* * *

AVENTINE

"Playback," Dax ordered.

The viewscreen changed to depict, in slow motion, the exact moments of detonation. Just as the first matter-antimatter reactions were triggered, the tractor beam blazed grotesquely red. Then it winked out entirely, lost in the flash of destruction.

From holodeck one, Riker had confirmed that his double and Picard were unharmed—and that the tactic had not only prevented the Cytherian transformation from happening to Picard, but that it had revealed another Cytherian's presence. It hadn't returned Riker and the other renegades to normal. Riker had explained earlier that destroying or damaging the station wouldn't change his condition, but with half a dozen vessels charging at her, she'd dared to hope.

At least several of the renegades had backed off. Clearly not expecting the Federation ships to fire on the station they were protecting, the leaders aboard those vessels had broken off temporarily from their assaults to study the situation. The Klingon ship chased after the Embassy as if nothing had happened; *Enterprise* and *Titan* rocketed alongside it, keeping it from attacking.

"I mark anomalous readings in the region near the detonation," Helkara said. "I think it's our wayward Romulan."

The science officer put what he was looking at on the large viewscreen. Dax agreed quickly. "Are you seeing this, Admiral?" she called out. "*D'varian* is cloaked off the forward quarter."

"*I know. There's currently a Romulan holding a disruptor on the Captain and me,*" Riker said. "*The holo me.*"

Forty-six

Nerla's boss—her *former* boss, she needed to think—may have been insufferable, but he had been right on all the details. She'd been able to enter the Far Embassy fifteen minutes earlier in just the manner Bretorius had predicted.

That didn't make the entry any less frightening. She had materialized in space, a scary enough prospect for someone who had never donned a spacesuit before. But the first thing Nerla saw after opening her clenched eyes was a raucous battle being waged not far away. Half a dozen ships of various types were battling Starfleet defenders in an attempt to reach the Embassy. She had screamed, as any right-minded person would, and then activated her propulsion, driving her toward the station. The tractor beam had caught her, bringing her to the airlock. Once she was done throwing up, she had entered the code and fled inside.

Doffing the fouled spacesuit in the turbolift car that had delivered her, Nerla had made her way through the hallway to the destination Bretorius had described. However, before she reached the door to the meeting room, a cataclysmic boom sent the universe around her sideways—while putting out the lights.

It had taken her several minutes to calm down—and more to find her weapon and the door again.

Finally, she had emerged into the cavernous meeting room to find the two humans and the two . . . *whatevers* hovering over a big table.

"Walk closer, Nerla," Bretorius said, voice easily audible through the comm in her medallion. *"I can't see what they look like."*

"They're *things*," Nerla said, afraid to approach. "Big head things. They seem to be asleep."

She could make out the Federation officers, who were lit from above by the macabre somnolent heads: both resembled individuals Bretorius had briefed her about. "Welcome," the older bald one said. "There's no need for the weapon. Who might you be?"

"Her name is Nerla," Bretorius said over the necklace's comsystem. *"She is my representative at this meeting. A meeting uncalled for, I should say. Whatever secrets you are trying to gain from the Cytherians, advanced intellect will not protect you from a disruptor. Keep a bead on them, Nerla. Drop your weapons, gentlemen."*

Picard complied. Riker raised his hands, showing he was unarmed. "That's Senator Bretorius speaking, I presume."

"And that is Captain Picard beside you, Riker—out of his alleged interlink chair, I see. I smell a ruse." Bretorius's disembodied laughter echoed eerily in the near-darkness. *"An amusing play, Admiral. But then, you can't really be Riker if you're walking around over here, can you? Step closer to the light, so Nerla can have a better look."*

Shrugging, Riker did so—and then Bretorius laughed again. *"Wonderful. A mobile emitter—in actual use! I'd read about it in our intelligence files. Well done, Riker."*

"Thanks. I think." The Federation admiral eyed the disruptor clutched in Nerla's shaking hands. Nerla looked back at him, nervous.

"I'm going to want that emitter. I'm glad I sent you, Nerla. I was wondering how I would generate assistants in the future. I'd considered using our Indoctrinator chairs, but that's a messy business. But if I mass-produce those units, I could run quite an army from a ship's holodeck. Loyal help is hard to find."

"You could try actually instilling loyalty," Riker said.

"I'm here willingly," Picard said.

"Bretorius hasn't got a clue what you're talking about," Nerla said. Her voice quavered—but it gained strength as she spoke. "He's never known how to lead."

"I am leading now. Picard, you will deactivate Riker's emitter and toss it to Nerla. Do so and you will not be harmed."

"You've forgotten something. The Cytherians won't let us kill," Riker said, taking a cautious step toward Nerla.

"No, but like you, I have found a number of ways to get past the programming. Acts carried out by my agents seem to be a gray area. I have crafted a condition in which she believes it is either her or you. I do not feel responsible for her choice."

"Not—*not responsible?*" Nerla sputtered. "You've threatened to kill me if I don't obey!"

"I would be using the only tool I have available there for self-preservation—something else the Cytherians allow. You shouldn't have threatened me with that weapon earlier, Nerla. You entered another gray area."

"He's a madman," Nerla said to the humans. "You hear that, Bretorius? You're crazy!"

"He's not crazy," Riker said. "He's just had power handed to him. It seems not everyone knows how to handle it."

"Oh, like you, perhaps?" Bretorius said, indignant. *"It's been wasted on you. It always is on those who—"*

Behind Riker and Picard, the male Cytherian stirred. And the room responded, with lights beginning to come up.

"He's coming around," Picard said.

"I see. First things first, then. Nerla, destroy the Cytherians."

Nerla looked up nervously at the glimmering heads. "What are they? Are they even here?"

"They're advanced life-forms, Nerla," Picard said. "And I believe they are here—or at least, they could be harmed. You don't want to do this."

"Nonsense," Bretorius said, his voice urgent. *"We can't know whether they're alive and present or not. I feel no compunction against acting, Nerla—you shouldn't either. Do as you're told."*

"Senator, you don't know what shooting them would do to you and me," Riker said, cautiously approaching her now. A few meters separated them.

"I'll take that chance. Nerla, shoot them, now!"

"Enough!" Nerla removed her right hand from the stock of the weapon and clutched at the necklace. "I'm sick of you. I quit!" There was a moment of intense pain as something stabbed at her skin—and then she ripped the jewelry free from her neck. She threw it on the floor, pointed the disruptor at it, and fired. The necklace was instantly incinerated.

She looked over at Riker and Picard, speechless and surprised in the growing light. She felt the poison beginning to course through her system. "If this is an embassy," she said, wobbling, "I request asylum."

Then she fell to the deck, and said no more.

D'VARIAN

"Nerla? Can you hear me?"

She couldn't, Bretorius realized. He couldn't hear her or see any of the other goings-on aboard the Far Embassy. The necklace communicator had simply died—but not before sending the signal that said it had delivered its fatal poison.

That meant she was dead.

There was no time to feel regret, no time to feel guilt. Such a foolish woman, denying her chance to have everything. It was all up to him, now. There was no time to waste.

D'varian began moving under cloak toward the tumbling station. The Federation defenders were ahead, occupied in combat with the other renegades. He would not attack the Far Embassy directly; Picard's presence aboard it prevented him from acting with lethal force. But his allies in the other starships still thought the station empty—and he could help them by uncloaking in the right spot and breaking the line *Enterprise* had established with the other ships. Then his colleagues would destroy the Far Embassy, preventing the Cytherians from creating any more rivals for them.

He would beam the holographic Riker's body and the mobile emitter right out of the wreckage—and the future would be his.

D'varian neared the Federation line. Too easy.

*   *   *

FAR EMBASSY

Picard knelt at the Romulan woman's side. "She's convulsing," he said. "I think she's been poisoned. She needs sickbay!"

"*Aventine*'s sensors say the transport inhibitor went online again when the power started coming back," Riker said.

He turned. Caster was aware now, if woozy. Behind him, Proctor was only beginning to stir. Caster looked on the humans for a moment—and brightened with recognition. "*Picard. Riker.*"

The admiral wasted no time with pleasantries. "Caster, this woman needs help," Riker said. "We have to use our transporter to send her to our vessel. Will you deactivate your inhibitor field?"

Caster stared for a moment at Picard and the fallen woman, as if trying to focus. Then his eyes widened—and then narrowed, as he appeared to concentrate. "*Inactive,*" he said.

Picard hit his badge, ready to call back to *Aventine* to have the Romulan woman beamed to sickbay—when he saw her dematerialize. He let out a deep breath when he remembered that everything the holographic Riker saw, the real Riker saw. And he had access to *Aventine*'s systems.

Which meant he saw something else. "*D'varian*'s uncloaked behind *Enterprise*," Riker said. "Dax can't get to her. The line's broken. We're in danger—all of us."

"*Regret, remorse,*" the enormous floating head said. A blast shook the station. "*Newfriends offended. Difficulties unnecessary.*"

Picard got to his feet. "Our difficulties are outside—

in the form of the people whose minds were altered by your technologies. Can you *do* something?"

Caster's big white eyebrows furrowed in concentration. His voice rumbled. *"Something done."*

D'VARIAN

D'varian pummeled *Enterprise*'s shields from port and *Titan*'s from starboard—and from the brig, Bretorius watched as the Cardassian, Tholian, and Klingon ships broke away, racing for the Far Embassy. *Aventine* was giving chase, but it was a futile effort. The renegades were working together, he could tell, focusing their attacks on a point on the outer surface of the Far Embassy's drum. He would need to keep the other Federations ships busy for only another moment.

Then a funny feeling came over him. It was a bad feeling in the pit of his stomach. An old familiar feeling.

The feeling of being the old Bretorius.

"No," Bretorius said, seeing the lights go out on the Taibak Indoctrinator. "No, no! No!"

He struggled to get out of the restraints. In vain.

AVENTINE

"Ready fire on three targets," Bowers ordered. "I don't know if we'll make it, Captain. They've got too much of a jump."

Dax knew it. But something else had drawn her attention. "The renegades. They've stopped firing on the station." She blinked. "Keep approaching—but hold fire. I think something might have changed."

"Good instincts, Captain," Riker said over the communications systems. *"All Federation ships, cease fire. Hold position. Let's see what they do."*

Dax's eyes narrowed. "What do you know, Admiral?"

"Caster has just revoked the Cytherian powers granted to the seven other diplomats. Anyone running their vessels through a mental interface is out of luck. They won't be able to control a thing now."

"You said the seven others," Dax said. "Are you all right, sir?"

"No change down here in the VIP suite," Riker said. The disappointment in his voice was clear. *"I think I'm being kept after school for something."*

Forty-seven

Starfleet had learned long ago that while the universal translator could translate the words, it wasn't always able to capture larger meanings. Picard had experienced that most memorably on El-Adrel with the Tamarian named Dathon and his language based on myths and metaphors. By contrast, the Cytherians used the exact words they meant to; they just used so few of them that listening to a complicated story was an exercise in extrapolation.

Caster had spoken long enough that Picard and Riker had picked up the gist. When Proctor had roused—and realized the new situation—she had become willing to talk, too. Her perspective helped enormously.

The Cytherians were, as Picard had expected, beyond simple concepts like political factions. It wasn't even clear they were all distinct individuals. But the female face, Proctor, appeared to represent forces in their society opposed to contact. The Cytherians had things to attend to in their own realm; to Proctor, Caster's earlier activities sending out probes was a childish act. To her, he was like one obsessed with a game, wasting time trying to interact with creatures whose lives had no real bearing on what happened in Cytherian society.

However, nearly twenty years earlier, Caster caught a bite—and reeled in the *Enterprise*-D. And while Picard and his crew could not have known it at the time, their meeting had forever changed the Cytherians.

Two decades were both a heartbeat and an eternity to them. The dissension among the Cytherians—who might even have been different personality aspects of the same being, for all the two Starfleet officers knew—grew heated. And it only worsened as Caster, having learned so much from his encounter with the Federation, set upon a new plan.

The *Enterprise*-D had provided knowledge of many of the Federation's neighboring races in its visit. The Cytherian simply *had* to see them for himself. But he had learned that individuals didn't always like to be taken against their will to the center of the galaxy to meet curious aliens. It was only right and proper for the Cytherians to do the venturing.

Caster designed a new probe, intended to be inhabited: a first of its kind for the Cytherians. It was a starship designed to carry a fragment of Caster's persona, with a subspace link to the rest of it back home. Just as Riker, tied into *Aventine*'s computer, was able to make the holo-Riker act for him, Caster was able to partially inhabit the Far Embassy and its systems.

He designed the vessel for friendship. It bore no weapons, no shielding. He used the schematics *Enterprise*-D had shared to add docking interfaces for several of the cultures he expected to meet in the Alpha and Beta Quadrants. Caster had learned from his visitors exactly how to contact the Federation and its neighbors. He would arrive—and reach out to all in the name of galactic peace and harmony.

But reaching out ran afoul of what Proctor—and the forces she represented—thought was right and proper. Caster calling outsiders to the center of the galaxy to visit was bad enough; this presaged even wider contacts—and not all Cytherians thought that was a good idea. It wasn't that they were xenophobes; neither was it a case of a good-intentioned Prime Directive–style fear of negative consequences for the less advanced races being contacted. Even now, Picard couldn't quite tell what the reason was.

"It's almost like a hobby Proctor doesn't want to compete with," Riker said. But that wasn't quite right, either. Sometimes Caster spoke of Proctor as a teacher and mother; sometimes as a spouse; sometimes as a daughter or charge. Whatever the roles were in Cytherian society, they were multidimensional and jumbled.

And Caster's impending voyage promised to create enough havoc for the Cytherian family that Proctor had been moved to drastic measures. During the construction of the Far Embassy, she had implanted a fragment of her own consciousness aboard the vessel. She had triggered it to awaken on arrival in the Paulson Nebula, before Caster's being emerged from hibernation. Locking him out of the vessel's controls, she set about the next stage of her plan.

It was never Proctor's intention to harm any living being: that was anathema even to Cytherians who disagreed about everything else. But she could scare Caster's prospective friends away from ever wanting to interact with the Cytherians again, like a mother warning off the undesirable neighbor children. Or, as Riker put it, "She was lighting a fire to scare off the wildlife." The Far Embassy had arrived, and Proctor would start a fire with it. It would not cause death, but it would cause chaos—and it would ultimately be traceable back to the Cytherians.

That was key. *Of course,* the affected powers would discover the Cytherians' involvement. *Of course,* they would track the mischief back to the Far Embassy, and the false invitations she had sent to lure the locals to the assembly center. Everyone was *supposed* to turn on the Cytherians. They could never counterattack, not really; the Cytherians lived too far away.

But the peoples of the region would never again want to interact with them. And that would be the end of Caster's friendly exchanges.

As a secondary measure, she had sent her thralls to target subspace arrays—particularly those that might be able to pierce the long distances to the Cytherians' region of the galaxy. The Cytherians knew about the location of many of the long-range stations from their own observations; that was why they had sent their earlier probe to the Argus Array. They had learned about other stations from the *Enterprise*; quite a few were located near the Paulson and Azure Nebulae, not far from where Federation, Klingon, and Romulan territories converged. Every one of those arrays threatened Cytherian peace and order, as Proctor saw it.

The destruction of dozens of arrays would not block all future communications with the Cytherians. But it would reduce such contacts in number, all while turning the natives against the alien puppeteers.

It was a bold play, Picard thought. And efficient: attacking only communications arrays offered minimal casualties while provoking maximum panic. All of that fear and anger would bubble up, ready to boil over—just in time for the Cytherian hand to be seen. Picard thought about this as he looked up at Proctor, bobbing mutely above the table to Caster's left. He fully understood her strategy now. "She's Catherine de' Medici."

"Local-context comparative," Caster said, interested. *"Elucidate."*

Picard watched Proctor as she floated beneath the high ceiling. "Mother to three French kings on our planet Earth—and behind the scenes, the most powerful woman on her continent in her century." Picard explained. "Some believe she provoked the incident that led to the St. Bartholomew's Day Massacre, killing off her religious rivals."

Riker nodded in agreement, quoting: "'A false report, if believed . . . may be of great service to a government.'"

Picard smiled. "I didn't know you were aware of her story, Admiral."

"I've learned all sorts of things lately," Riker said. "I also know that the situation quickly got out of Catherine's control." He eyed Proctor. "You thought you could frame Caster and have the natives turn their ire on the Cytherians. But you didn't consider what the natives might do to each other in the process. You could well have started an interstellar war."

"Incorrect interpretation," Proctor said. It was the first words she'd spoken in a long time. *"Cytherian responsibility obvious. Risk minimal."*

"Minimal risk to you perhaps," Picard said. "But much has changed since you first learned of our peoples. This region has seen attacks by the Dominion and the Borg. Defense has become an important issue. Alliances have formed and shifted. Peace here is a delicate balance, easily broken."

"You should have known that," Riker added. "You

used a peace conference to attract the pawns you wanted." He stared at Proctor. "I don't think you cared how much chaos you caused us."

"Accusation misplaced." She raised her nose to the domed ceiling, defiant. *"Harm minimized. Precautions taken."*

The floating head of Caster turned to face Proctor. His eyes were full of horror. *"Newbeings threatened."* He raised his voice. *"Proctor indifferent!"*

Proctor looked away from him. *"Precautions taken!"*

"Precautions insufficient. Episode unnecessary." Huge sad eyes looked down on Picard. *"Friendships thwarted."* Then they turned to Riker. *"Friends harmed."*

Picard and Riker watched as Proctor, tentatively at first, sought Caster's gaze. *"Rationale established. Arguments made. Cytherian outreach unwise."*

"Disagreement and discord." Caster continued to look upon Riker. *"Shame and remorse, Riker Newfriend. Convey apology to others affected."*

"We will," Riker said.

Picard looked at the admiral. "I've been meaning to ask, Caster. Why didn't the admiral return to normal with the others?"

"Safety," Caster said. *"Reintegration requires hologram deactivation."*

Riker nodded, seeming to understand. "He wants my attention in one place for me to be restored, body and soul."

Picard touched his badge. "Picard to *Aventine.* Prepare medical crew to stand by at the interlink chair if needed."

"The admiral's already told us," Dax said.

Holo-Riker looked at Picard. "I could get used to

this two-places-at-once thing." He smiled wanly and bowed to the Cytherians. His hand moved for the control on the mobile emitter—

—and then stopped abruptly. "Wait."

Picard looked at him, concerned. "Is something wrong?"

"I'm still an admiral—for however long—and a peace envoy. I came to this station for a diplomatic summit. I intend to have it."

Dax, listening in via Picard's combadge, spoke up. *"The other powers are leaving, Admiral."*

"But the Cytherians remain," Riker said, approaching them. "And *they* are in need of a peace conference."

Or some family therapy, Picard thought. The Cytherians watched Riker, dumbfounded, as he climbed onto the table and stepped between the two floating heads.

"I offer the Federation's good offices in arbitration of your differences," Riker said, gesturing openly with his hands. A pause. "That is, if you think we mere humans can help."

Proctor and Caster looked at each other, astonished, and then back at Riker.

"Response . . . contingent," Proctor said. *"Fairness questioned."*

"If I'm not mistaken, while I'm near this facility, I'm an open book to you," Riker said. "You were able to restore the minds of your minions outside the station; I would suspect you can read mine if you try. You can trust me."

Another pause, while the Cytherians studied one another. Picard could not know what was transpiring between the beings, either here or far away, where the larger part of their intelligences resided. But after a few moments, something seemed to change. Both turned to face Riker again.

"*Agreement,*" Caster said, beaming. "*Appreciative agreement.*"

"*And humble regret,*" Proctor added, looking down. "*Peaceful goals uniform. Differentiation in methods reconcilable.*" Her eyes fixed on Riker. "*With helpful assistance.*"

Riker smiled—and held that expression as he looked back to the captain. "I guess we get a summit here after all."

Picard laughed. "Convenient."

Forty-eight

The Romulans who broke into the Ter'ak Pen had found their captain first, freeing him from his cell. Only then had they entered Bretorius's chamber, disruptors raised.

The weapons hadn't been necessary at all. He may well have been the easiest capture in the history of interstellar piracy. For when Bretorius had lost all his other knowledge, he had forgotten how to get out of the restraints of the Taibak chair as well. He was sitting there, haplessly waiting when the guards entered.

It may well have saved his life, because any anger they might have felt toward him melted into amusement. Yalok, looking grizzled and half-starved, had nearly injured himself laughing as he was helped into the room. *D'varian*'s crewmembers had taken their frustrations out instead on the cable and all the equipment Bretorius had attached to the seat, making absolutely certain that he had no more control over the vessel.

"Bridge," Yalok spoke into a communicator he had been handed. "This is Commander Yalok. Do you have control?"

"*Yes, sir.*"

"Full speed for Romulan space."

"Yes, sir."

Yalok turned his gaze onto Bretorius, still locked up. His voice was full of tired malevolence. "I may die for failing to resist you, Senator. But I'll go knowing I got to teach you a lesson first."

Another question came from the bridge. *"Do you need anything, Captain?"*

"No, do not disturb me," Yalok said. "This will take a while."

AVENTINE

As diplomatic negotiations went, the conversations with the Cytherians had transpired in record time. The Cytherians had taken advantage of the fact that speaking with holo-Riker was, essentially, talking with *Aventine*'s main computer; the discussions thereafter had taken place on an exalted, electronic level.

Riker wasn't sure he fully understood the Cytherians, or the issues between them, any more than a counselor fully understood the people being counseled. More than once, he'd wished Deanna had been in the conversation—but she was never far from his thoughts anyway, and the last thing he wanted was for her to suffer the plight he'd experienced.

No, Riker had worked through it, doing his best to find ways for human ethics to be relevant to the Cytherians and their differences. It helped that he had access to the wide swath of historical writings from countless worlds via *Aventine*'s database. *This* was a reason Starfleet vessels carried all this information.

In the end, both parties had been willing to give a little. Proctor had come to understand that exploration need not endanger a society's domestic production and tranquility. Caster had acknowledged that every opened door affected a house, and that each new step outward should be approached with some deliberation. And both had come to agree that it worked both ways. The true importance of the Federation's Prime Directive, known to the Cytherians from *Enterprise*-D's visit, became relevant for them. Whatever the Cytherians did in the future, remotely or in person, they would need to carefully consider the potential impact their visits had on the indigenous species.

Finally, after an understanding had been reached, Riker assured the Cytherians he would send for a first-contact team well versed in their culture. He said his good-byes, then, and Picard had touched the control on the mobile emitter, terminating the holo-Riker's presence on the Far Embassy.

Minutes later, the *Enterprise* captain materialized on holodeck one, in front of the interlink chair and the motionless admiral. Dax's senior officers were there along with La Forge and a group of medical professionals, preparing in case something went wrong following Riker's impending removal from Cytherian influence.

"YOU'LL BE PLEASED TO KNOW THAT THE ROMULAN, NERLA, HAS BEEN STABILIZED," Riker said, his voice echoing through the chamber. *"SHE SHOULD RECOVER."*

"Excellent," Picard said, acknowledging those around him. "It seems her shipmates left without her."

"They all did," Dax said. "We picked up a lot of strange chatter from the other ships while they were here—but I'm guessing the original crews all retook control. They were in no hurry to sit around telling us about it."

"I'm not surprised," Picard said. He looked to Riker. "I left the mobile emitter with the Cytherians, Admiral, as you instructed."

"I KNOW YOU'RE DISAPPOINTED, GEORDI," Riker said. *"BUT IT'S NOT OURS TO UNDERSTAND YET. CONVINCING THE CYTHERIANS TO ADOPT THEIR OWN VARIATION ON THE PRIME DIRECTIVE MEANT I HAD TO BEGIN WITH US."*

"A shame," La Forge said. "Still, we'll be meeting and talking with them more often now. I guess as we show we're ready for things, we'll learn more."

"THERE'S ONE EXCEPTION, OF COURSE," Riker said. *"THEY INSISTED ON HELPING REPAIR THE COMMUNICATIONS SYSTEMS DAMAGED BY THEIR ATTACKS. I EXPECT THEY'LL THROW IN A LITTLE DASH OF HIGHTECH TO MAKE SOME OF THE PAIN GO AWAY."*

Dax nodded. "There will be some embarrassed diplomats after this."

"Save one," Picard said, gesturing to the admiral in the chair. "The one who did the right thing."

The admiral turned over the compliment in his mind. It was heartening to hear. But seeing *Aventine*'s staff, he remembered the things he'd been forced to do—and he saw the multitude of possible futures that lay ahead of him. And he knew that the next few days wouldn't be simple for William T. Riker at all. Or good.

But it didn't take super intelligence to know there was no sense in trying to put them off.

"RIKER TO THE FAR EMBASSY. CASTER, PROCTOR— I'M READY. PULL THE PLUG."

FINAL STAGE:

LOCKDOWN

---

*"We read that we ought to forgive our enemies;
but we do not read that we ought
to forgive our friends."*

—Cosimo de' Medici

Forty-nine

Riker opened his eyes.

Simus sat in the seat across from him, watching intently, as the admiral sat in the Cytherian interlink chair. Riker flexed his fingers first and then moved his head. His neck was stiff, but the powerful gravity he'd felt keeping him in the elaborate armchair earlier was gone.

He stood. Simus watched him as he stretched. "You don't believe that chair is where you belong?"

"Hell, no. That's worse than the rowing machine." Riker looked back at the thing. "I should have generated a seat cushion."

Simus's face brightened. "I think that's enough," the old man said, forcing himself to stand. He touched a button on his wrist control device, and the office around them disappeared, to be replaced by the glowing holodeck gridwork. All that remained were the two men and Simus's cane, resting on the floor nearby. He gestured to it. "Can you get that for me?"

Riker walked over to it, glad to be moving. It felt as though his blood was pumping again. He picked up the old man's cane. "Simus, what happened here?"

"It was necessary to walk you through the entire experience," Simus said, accepting the cane.

"To restore my memories?"

"Among other reasons."

Riker looked behind him. The holodeck arch had reappeared. "So where am I, really? *Aventine*'s holodeck, still?"

"No. What is the last thing you remember?"

Riker concentrated. "I'd been freed from the Cytherian interlink. They'd taken their powers back. I'd been reunited with Deanna aboard *Titan*. We were bound for Betazed—Betazed Station 4, for some kind of service issue."

"This *is* Betazed Station 4. And the service issue, if you will pardon my using the expression, is *you*."

Riker chuckled. "Granted." But the details didn't make sense. "I don't remember getting here. Did I black out?"

"Something like it. Your body was greatly taxed by the experience. How long did you sleep last night, before encountering me?"

"Sixteen hours, I think."

"It was actually sixty-four."

Riker shook his head.

"Your medical team helped with some of the nutrients you'd lost, but this was something else—neither sleep nor coma."

"I don't get it," Riker said. "Barclay didn't get burnt out like this."

"You have a few more duties as an admiral than Reginald Barclay had. You were already fighting exhaustion when the Cytherians touched you."

Riker thought it was an odd turn of phrase, but it worked.

"And the Cytherians held you longer and caused you to do quite a few more things. A sleepless mind, constantly active, is stressful on the system."

"But why did I have such trouble remembering in the beginning? Barclay was fine immediately after the Cytherians withdrew their influence. And so was I—until . . . I collapsed aboard *Titan*."

Simus gestured toward the archway, and the two began walking toward it. "I think the difference is that unlike Barclay, you fought back against the Cytherian suggestion. What Barclay was asked to do was beyond the bounds of his authority as crewman, but he had no expectation that people would be put in physical jeopardy. Meanwhile, you were prodded to do things that endangered people—and your submerged personality fought and clawed the entire way."

"I don't know if I can take credit for that," Riker said. "Proctor didn't really want anyone harmed. The attacks we were sent on were chosen to maximize chaos but to minimize actual casualties."

"You should give yourself more credit," Simus said. "You were suffering from 'diminished capacity,' as the JAG has already determined. And yet you alone among all the Cytherian pawns left no injuries in your wake. None at all." Simus touched the arch controls, and the huge doors opened, revealing a bright white hallway beyond. "The difference between minimal casualties and zero was William Riker—and his sense of responsibility. You were a marionette who pulled against the strings just enough when you had to."

Riker looked into the hallway and took a breath of cool fresh air. His companion hobbled ahead of him.

"Who are you?"

"I am Simus." The man seemed willing to leave it

at that, for a moment, before turning. He smiled and offered his hand. "Doctor Simus, Starfleet Medical."

Riker shook Simus's hand. *A smiling Vulcan.* He'd seen everything now. "I take it that your practice is evaluating those who've been controlled by alien entities."

"There is much work to do in that line," Simus said, resuming his walk.

"Been doing that for a while?"

"Oh, yes. For more than a hundred years, in fact. My first assignment was someone who traveled aboard another *Enterprise*: Mira Romaine."

Riker goggled. "She was on James T. Kirk's crew." He thought back to his history lessons. "She was possessed by . . . the Zetarians?"

"I dislike the term 'possessed.' Rather, a guest consciousness took residence in her corporeal form. A hundred members of a lost race, in her case."

Riker whistled. "I guess I had it easy."

Simus made for an opening up ahead, and Riker followed. "When the Zetarians left Mira, she was judged fit to begin her duties on Memory Alpha. All the tests of the day—the Steinman analysis, her hyperencephalograms—said she was the person she was before. But even then, Starfleet was uncomfortable, worrying that she might still carry some artifact of the experience."

"Understandable," Riker said. "The Zetarians were powerful."

"I was young then, a doctor about to serve my first tour aboard Memory Alpha—when I was asked to keep a special watch over Mira. It sounded important to me: a clandestine mission of galactic importance."

Riker thought Simus looked almost wistful as he described those days.

"In fact, I became both counselor and friend to her. Over time, I learned a lot about what she'd experienced and what questions to ask those who faced a similar predicament. It has become the foundation for all my work since."

They rounded a corner into a large tree-filled atrium. This was the source of the breeze Riker had felt earlier: a large domed arboretum, lit from above by growlights. Paths wound between the foliage, and Riker could see towering viewports on either side showing outer space beyond. Betazed was down there, warm and blue. Here and there, the admiral saw others wandering the parklike setting in contemplation.

Simus led him toward a picturesque wooden bridge spanning a creek. "I have a feeling this place is more than just Betazed Station 4," Riker said.

"It is the Mira Romaine Center for Rehabilitation and Reintegration."

Riker laughed. "So they *were* sending me away for R-and-R. Just not the kind I had in mind." He looked to his host. "No offense to you, Simus. You've been good company."

"Once you knew I wasn't a Romulan interrogator," the old man said, stepping off the bridge. He turned, walking alongside the rivulet.

"You're a therapist, then."

"Of a sort. I suppose my manner is somewhat surprising—I have strayed more than a bit from Surak's teachings. But I have always felt that a more approachable personality is, in fact, the most logical choice for success at what I do here." He stopped and gestured to some of the other figures roaming the area. "We don't have a lot of guests, but we try to make things comfortable for those we do have."

Riker looked from face to faraway face. "How long do people stay here?"

"For some, the stay is brief," Simus said. "A lucky few might only return for an hour's talk now and again, when they feel they need it." He looked out the other large window, to the stars beyond. "For others, more deeply affected, the Romaine Center provides a safe haven for the rest of their lives."

"Why haven't I heard about this place?"

"You should know, Admiral, that many of the encounters of this nature are classified. Many people remember little of their episodes, but others remember quite a lot—and it's important that no one takes advantage of them and what they know."

"Who else is here?"

"Above your clearance, sir." Simus clasped his hands together thoughtfully. "There is another advantage to anonymity. Shared-body experiences are an occupational hazard, but they've been known to impact careers. It's important to me that anyone who needs to return to the Romaine Center for any reason be able to do so without fear. Physiological changes, phantom memories, or just the need to talk to someone: you will always be able to return here, as needed, no questions asked."

"That suggests I can leave."

"That is up to you . . . now." Simus turned and started to walk again.

Riker blinked as he puzzled over the old man's last statement. *Was there a time when it* wasn't *up to me?* He wondered how many of the people here were present by choice.

"Wait a second," the admiral said. His eyes narrowed, and he stalked after Simus. Clutching at the

Vulcan's arm, he turned Simus around to face him. "What was the business with tricking me into thinking I was aboard *Titan*, earlier? You were trying to make me think that my wife and child were in danger. What was that about?"

Simus was about to respond when someone called out from the wooden structure they'd crossed earlier. "I can answer that."

Riker turned to see Jean-Luc Picard standing above him, looking down from across the railing. "Join me, on the—er, bridge . . ."

Fifty

Simus had declined to follow Riker up to meet Picard, choosing instead to step away and speak to a Bolian patient seated in a nearby rock grotto. Picard smiled broadly as Riker scaled the curved bridge. "You seem better rested."

"Someone forgot to wake me up." He glared down at Simus, who cast only a casual glance back. "This is a strange place, Jean-Luc. The doctor says this is a halfway house for alien abductees—and yet I woke up this morning to a fake crisis, where Deanna and Natasha were in danger."

Picard nodded, knowingly. "Staged on a holodeck."

"Were you watching it?"

"No. But I have taken such a test myself."

"Test?"

Picard looked away apologetically. "I'm very sorry for all this, Will. But it's necessary, for one who's undergone your experience." After a moment, he returned his gaze to Riker. "You were immersed in what you were led to believe was a real-life experience, where you would have been motivated to do anything in your power to avert a disaster. Is that correct?"

Riker nodded.

"And in it, you were confronted with a technical problem that was far beyond your natural ability to solve."

The admiral slapped the railing, suddenly remembering. "The shield calculations that Tuvok was working on. I had to step in to do them—even though I couldn't have figured that out in a million years."

"No, you couldn't."

Riker's eyes went wide with realization—and then he silently cursed himself for not getting it earlier. "They were trying to see if I had retained any of the intellectual abilities from my time as a puppet."

Picard nodded. "I don't know if Deanna ever told you. But she noticed an improvement in Reginald Barclay's social abilities in the days after the Cytherians left his consciousness. It was enough that when Starfleet followed up on Reg's condition, they recommended he visit the center here, and he agreed. Simus worked with him to develop a testing regimen, to determine whether such post-possession changes were a natural result of having gained experience."

"Or whether you've retained remnant talents, that someone might need to be concerned about."

"Or not. Every experience is different."

"Something like this almost certainly has a name."

Picard chuckled. "It is known as the Barclay Battery."

"The Barclay Battery." Riker smirked. "I'm sure Reg loves being immortalized."

"I'm not so sure how I would feel about it myself. But it sounds better than 'Psyche Separation Analytics Package,'" Picard said.

Riker scratched his beard. "I guess I'm lucky I only had the one test."

"Don't be so sure there was only one," Picard said, looking covertly over at the Vulcan. "Simus was most certainly evaluating your ethical and moral decision-making during the entire time you talked."

"Wait. You said you took the test yourself." *Of course*, Riker thought. "But I don't recall your coming to Betazed after what happened to you. And Reg's experience took place after that."

"Oh, I didn't pay a visit until much later. An invitation to meet with Simus *was* extended after I was freed from Borg control, but I declined it." The captain shook his head. "Pure hubris. I had been deemed fit for duty. I had checked out perfectly on all the medical scans and passed the conventional psychological tests. It didn't strike me as wise to call any more attention to my experience than necessary by coming here—even to a secret installation."

Riker nodded. "I guess the higher-ups would know."

"I thought it would be a handicap. But it turned out that exactly the opposite was the case. I found that certain doors were closed to me in Starfleet. Some people felt that I was responsible for what had happened. Many suspected that I might still be compromised."

Riker nodded. He knew that a grieving Benjamin Sisko had given Picard a difficult time about the role Locutus, the captain's Borg identity, played in the death of his wife. During the Borg queen's attack on Earth, Starfleet had purposefully ordered *Enterprise* to avoid the fray because Picard had once been under the Borg's control.

"As we've seen in our careers, episodes of explorers being . . . *misappropriated* for use by alien intelligences are quite common," Picard continued. "Starfleet knows full well that it's an occupational hazard, especially when it comes to dealing with creatures that may have no other way to communicate. It's important to Starfleet—and to the Federation—that talented individuals not be lost to service because of incidents like these."

Picard looked again to the Vulcan, who was now patiently watching them from a distance. "Admiral Akaar knows of Simus's work here—as does the Federation president. The Simus seal of approval carries extraordinary weight. When I did finally visit, following the Borg queen episode, I found a lot of the road blocks had vanished."

Riker shook his head. "You saved the Federation."

Picard gestured to the forest around them. "While the public at large doesn't know about this place or Simus, when those at the top are satisfied with you, their confidence has a way of projecting to all."

Riker decided it was time for the frank question. "So the last few weeks haven't been career suicide?"

"We don't use that term here," Simus called out. Riker turned to see the Vulcan hobbling up the bridge. "No, you haven't any reason for concern. My report will describe a man who had a remarkable experience and who under extreme duress managed to use what latitude his captors gave him to mitigate damage. And more than that—he resolved the crisis."

Picard nodded. "We've had additional interchanges with the Cytherians since you've been here. They cannot repair our arrays personally, but they've provided technical guidance that will enhance our deep-space studies. The Federation has agreed to distribute the knowledge to all the injured parties and the rest of the Typhon Pact. It will net positive for everyone."

Riker was relieved to hear that. "And the political situation?"

"Starfleet Intelligence believes most involved will sweep the matter under the rug. It's been an embarrassment for many—and it's shown us all how vulnerable our communications arrays are."

Riker nodded. "I imagine a lot of people will be less willing to go to the next summit meeting." *Then again,* he thought, *fewer pointless exercises might be a blessing.*

"I don't know what will become of some of the others involved," Picard said. "I suspect Senator Bretorius's political prospects may have gone from zero to a negative number. If he lives."

"Which just goes to show," Simus said, "that Admiral Riker fared better than anyone." He presented his hand to Riker. "A number of other people have spoken highly of you over the years, sir. I've long been interested in meeting you. I am sorry for the circumstance, of course."

Riker returned the handshake. "Thank you, Simus. It's been an experience."

"Experiences are my specialty. You know where to find me."

Fifty-one

The *Enterprise* captain led Riker up a garden path to a plaza with a fountain. The trees were thick, all around, and the admiral could see several other guests of the center wandering in the woods. Who were they, and what might they have experienced?

Riker realized, then, how lucky he was to be leaving. The Romaine Center was a nice place, and Simus a helpful doctor—once he started answering questions instead of asking them. But certainly there were people here whose brushes with other intelligences had left them unable to function outside the station's confines. He had no lingering aftereffects that he could tell—apart from the physical toll it had taken. However, some of the people here were likely forever scarred by what had happened to them. He was glad that Starfleet had developed this facility. It wasn't easy living with two minds using one body.

And that made him think of someone else.

"One more thing," Riker said to Picard. "Captain Dax has had a rough time since the Andorian incident. I'm going to see that she and her crew get a commendation, a plum assignment, something."

"It's already happened," Picard said over the burbling of the fountain. "*Aventine*'s repairs are complete, and she's back in action already. Her crew's heroism was self-evident, but I'm sure whatever words you put together would be welcomed."

"As an admiral, Jean-Luc, I'm officially horrified to have another captain who is a member of the Order of Occasionally Disobeying Orders," Riker said. Then he grinned.

Picard chuckled—and mentioned someone else who had disobeyed a directive. "Nerla has recovered and been granted full asylum. She's expressed interest in being a resort planner."

"Good. After Bretorius, she's someone who needed a vacation."

Suddenly realizing the time, Picard looked down a path to the right. "I have to get back to *Enterprise*. We have a mission of exploration to resume." He gave a slight bow. "May I take my leave, Admiral?"

"Good luck, Jean-Luc."

Riker smiled as Picard walked away toward a brightly lit doorway. Out of habit he reached for his combadge. It was not there. "Hey! How am *I* supposed to get back?"

"Someone will come for you, sir," Picard called out, not looking back.

CITADEL VAR'THELDUN
ROMULUS

Being hung upside down was easier on the stomach when you hadn't eaten in days.

That was one of the very few conclusions that Bretorius had reached during his time in the suspension device, other than that the person who had developed the thing was a diabolical sadist. The table he was strapped to pivoted gyroscopically to a new position at random times. While perhaps not as hard on the body as being held upside down all the time, prisoners spent most of their time wondering when the thing would move next.

It was a device that told him he was in the hands of the Tal Shiar. And, truth be told, it was a better thing to be imprisoned in than their gravitic rack, which applied varying amounts of artificial gravity to different parts of the body. They'd given him a day in that before his digestive system told them he wouldn't survive another.

The table lurched again—this time, bringing him fully upright. When the world stopped spinning, he saw the door to the all-white chamber open. It revealed a middle-aged Romulan male with jet-black hair and a silvery uniform, holding a black padd. "I am Irliss, your handler for today."

Bretorius let out a low moan. "Another one?"

"Yes, another one," Irliss said, snappish. "You were expecting, perhaps, the praetor?"

"I don't know."

"Praetor Kamemor would not meet with you," the handler said. "She is not fond of harsh methods."

Two guards entered through the door behind Irliss. They walked to either side of Bretorius and began detaching him from his restraints.

"I feel as though I am in the presence of celebrity," Irliss said. "There has been quite the squabble trying to decide who gets control of you. The Military Affairs Division wants you for what you did to *D'varian*. Research and Development is interested in the modifications you made. Internal Security is going mad trying to find out how such a thing could happen."

"So who gets me?"

"Special Operations. We won the dice throw." Irliss smiled. He lifted the padd and read from it. "It's quite the bounty you've racked up. Piracy. Barratry. Misuse of senatorial privilege. Destruction of Romulan strategic assets. Unauthorized acts against neighboring powers."

The last shackle released, Bretorius slumped forward. The guards made no attempt to keep him from falling to the deck. It was spattered with long-dried blood, he saw.

"Collusion with hostile powers," Irliss continued. "Collusion with Romulan citizens, in the form of the fugitive Nerla. Conspiracy to unseat high officials."

Bretorius tried to force his muscles to work. "No treason?"

"It's *all* treason," the inquisitor said, aggravated. "I'm surprised that you haven't tried to deny any of it."

On his hands and knees, Bretorius looked weakly at the floor. He had needed sleep, food, and water after his experience. The Romulans aboard *D'varian* and here had done their best to deny him all three. That left little energy for denying what was plainly true. "It all happened. I have nothing to say."

"I expected you to plead innocence based on the Cytherians controlling you."

"Why would I do that?" Bretorius asked. He cast his weary eyes up at the inquisitor. "If you thought I was simply a puppet unable to resist, you would think me weak and a coward. But if you thought I had access to immense powers and didn't try to take personal and political advantage? Then you would think me a poor Romulan."

Irliss stared coolly down at him, a little surprised

at the comment. "Amusing," he finally said. He nodded to the guards, who yanked Bretorius back onto his feet.

Irliss walked back out into the brightly lit hall. The guards shoved Bretorius along after him. The Tal Shiar officer continued to read aloud from the padd as he walked. "It pleases me to say that you have become poorer still. You have lost your senate seat, of course. Your properties are stripped from you—and your record with the Imperial Fleet has been amended to read that you were discharged dishonorably in your first year as a cadet, never to serve."

This much was expected.

"We have parliamentary experts working on finding a way to expunge your name from the historical rolls of the Senate without changing the results of the votes you took part in. Fortunately, it appears that you never voted on anything where you would have made a difference."

"I was usually throwing up during the tough votes."

Ignoring him, Irliss stopped as they reached an intersection. "So much for your name; now for the man. You are to be confined for an indefinite period in our research laboratories." He turned back toward Bretorius and gestured down the hall to the right. "Our scientists would like to see what remnant effects the Cytherian powers had on your mind. Perhaps there is some small useful thing left in that mass of driftwood you call a brain." There was a glint in the officer's eye. "I suspect some of their techniques will be . . . *invasive.*"

That sounds about right, Bretorius thought. "And then?"

"If there is anything left of you, you will be removed to the Reman mines, where you will serve the Empire until death. Which I would expect would come relatively soon for one in your physical shape."

Bretorius sagged in the guards' clutches. Nothing at all he'd been told had surprised him. Maybe that was a remnant of the Cytherian experience. Instead of wondering about the horrible possibilities ahead until he made himself sick, he simply selected the worst possible future and figured on that one happening. It still ripped his stomach up, but he got through it a lot quicker.

The inquisitor snapped his fingers, and the guards turned Bretorius down the hall to the right. There was a darkened doorway up ahead, and he could see the flicker of lights beyond. The research lab. This was it—the beginning of the end for him.

"Oh, one more thing," the inquisitor said, trailing behind. The guards paused, and Bretorius looked wearily back. "Your wife has left you, too." Irliss smiled evilly. "We have put her out on the streets."

Bretorius's eyebrow raised slightly. "My in-laws, too?"

"All evicted and left with nothing. Absolutely nothing."

Bretorius considered the words for a moment. A smile crept onto his face. "Well, there's *that*."

He turned his head and walked deliberately toward the darkened room, each step lighter than his last.

THE ROMAINE CENTER
ABOVE BETAZED

After the captain disappeared into the aperture, Riker looked around for the promised escort. He had made several complete circuits of the fountain when someone emerged from the trees.

"They'll let just anyone in here," Deanna Troi said.

"Evidently." He smiled as his wife stepped out into the artificial sunlight.

Troi looked up and around. "You know, Will, I went for a walk in an arboretum with Reg Barclay after the Cytherians released him."

"You've found me out," Riker said, walking over to her. "This whole thing was my way of making sure I got the same walk."

"Mastermind."

"I thought this was a secret place. How'd you get in here?"

Troi straightened. "You've clearly forgotten the time when I was the pawn of the prisoners of Ux-Mal."

"I've tried to forget it," Riker said. "They made you talk funny." Troi, along with *Enterprise*-D crewmates Data and Miles O'Brien, had once briefly come under the mental control of evil entities. "You've been here before? You didn't tell me."

"I've stopped in on the way to Betazed. Simus likes having people check in now and again." She walked up and took his hand. "Our minds aren't built for multiple occupants. It's not always easy to get the house back in order after the guests leave."

"I think," Riker said, "I may be done with the metaphors."

She smiled warmly. "I'm just telling you you're not alone. Others have gone through this."

He released her hand and looked away. "Maybe we can start a parrises squares league. Those controlled by ancient spirits can be on one team, alien voyeurs on another."

Her eyes followed him as he turned to look across the parkland. "What's wrong?"

He looked back to her. "Nothing."

"Will, black humor usually means you're worried about something."

Riker walked over to a tree and leaned against it. He took a deep breath. "Simus and Jean-Luc said this whole thing was being forgiven. I'd love to believe that. But it sounds too good to be true."

A smile crossed Troi's face. "Oh, is *that* all," she said, her tone playful. "Worried about your career." He looked back at her, not amused—and she decided to let him off the hook. "Will, from what Captain Picard told me, Admiral Akaar has taken a great interest in your recovery—with an emphasis on getting you back as quickly as possible."

He weighed that. "Huh."

"'Huh' is right." Troi walked up to him. "Maybe Captain Picard didn't tell you, but Starfleet Command loved the fact that of all those the Cytherians touched, it was the Starfleet officer who broke free to help save the day."

"Squirmed free is more accurate."

She pulled his hand from the tree. "And having seen what you could do with three starships has made some people wonder what you could do with a wider bailiwick. They're curious to see how much was the Cytherians—and how much was you." Drawing him into an embrace, she kissed him. "So I hope you got some rest here, Admiral. Because I would say you have big things ahead of you."

Against Deanna Troi's optimism, resistance was futile. Riker grinned as they turned up the path. "Let's try some small things first. Like seeing Tasha."

Deanna smiled. "And that dinner we never got to have."

"No, that will be a big thing. I am *starving*."

ACKNOWLEDGMENTS

While I came to many readers' attention as a writer of stories set in a different galaxy, writing a *Star Trek* novel has been a longtime ambition for me. My first stab at writing licensed fiction, in fact, was for *Star Trek*, in the form of a submission to *Strange New Worlds*. I couldn't be more delighted now that the stars have finally aligned. I'm grateful to Margaret Clark and Ed Schlesinger at Pocket Books for not only giving me the opportunity but letting me chase the sort of story I've always wanted to write.

I'm greatly appreciative to John Van Citters at CBS for his input and feedback, and I am glad for the conversations I had with longtime *Trek* authors Kevin Dilmore, Christie Golden, David Mack, James Swallow, and Dayton Ward as I wrote my first full-length novel for the milieu. I really appreciate the warm welcome I've received from the *Trek* universe of fans and professionals.

Obviously, I also owe a major debt of gratitude to writer Joe Menosky and the team behind the production of the fourth season *Star Trek: The Next Generation* episode "The Nth Degree," which served as the inspiration for many of this story's events.

And finally, my thanks as ever to Meredith Miller, proofreader and Number One on my bridge.

ABOUT THE AUTHOR

John Jackson Miller is the *New York Times* bestselling author of *Star Wars: A New Dawn*; *Star Wars: Kenobi*; *Star Wars: Knight Errant*; *Star Wars: Lost Tribe of the Sith—The Collected Stories*; and fifteen *Star Wars* graphic novels, as well as *Overdraft: The Orion Offensive* and *Star Trek: Titan—Absent Enemies*. A comics industry historian and analyst, he has written for franchises including *Conan, Iron Man, Indiana Jones, Mass Effect,* and *The Simpsons*. He lives in Wisconsin with his wife, two children, and far too many comic books.